THE
BETRAYED

THE DAWNING OF MUIRWOOD

THE
BETRAYED

JEFF
WHEELER

Published by 47North, Seattle

www.apub.com

Amazon, the Amazon logo, and 47North are trademarks of Amazon.com, Inc., or its affiliates.

ISBN-13: 9781542035187 (paperback)
ISBN-13: 9781542035194 (digital)

Cover design by Kirk DouPonce / DogEared Design LLC

Cover image: ©EB Adventure Photography / Shutterstock;
© Africa Studio / Shutterstock; daizuoxin / Shutterstock

Printed in the United States of America

To BJ—my other "mom"

He came toward me with drawn blade, steel afire with magic he did not understand, drawn from the raven scabbard still bound to his waist, never to be loosed for fear an enemy's dagger might plunge into his back. His blood was as inflamed as the blade, albeit with unholy lust.

Teach me the word, *he commanded.* Teach me the word that can change my shape, to make me appear as my enemy.

To what purpose, *I inquired, not fearing the tip of steel he pressed to the skin of my neck. I already knew his thoughts, of course. He could not banish his lust for the other man's wife from his imagination.*

I tried to persuade him. I used reason, warnings, and even threats. I said our bodies are our gardens, to which our wills are gardeners. If he was determined to plant stinging nettles or soft lettuce, he would bear the harvest either way.

He could not endure the torment of thinking on her. And he said that I, not being a true man, should not preach idly against the matters of the flesh whereon I knew nothing about. I told him I did understand and suggested he might distract his thoughts. Did he wish for a garden left barren with idleness, a vineyard destroyed by war, or instead one manured with industry? It was all up to him! Power and corrigible authority lie not in the words engraved in tomes but in our wills. If our lives had not one scale of reason to counter that of sensuality, the blood and baseness of our mortal natures would conduct us to the most wasted conclusions. We have reason to cool our raging emotions, our carnal stings, the unbitten fruit of lust.

He'd not hear me. So in the end, I taught him the word that would lead to his downfall. One word felled a kingdom.

—Maderos, a Pig Keeper

PROLOGUE

Farfog Castle, Kingdom of Brythonica
ten years after the death of King Ulric of Leoneyis

The pig keeper had many sayings, but one was a favorite and often repeated—*Be as happy as a pig in filth.* On a certain day in spring, the boy sat watching the swine from a fence rail. The gate to the dark barn was open, allowing the animals to root in the muck for the kernels of corn that had been deposited there before winter started, buried under other decaying bits from the kitchen, the remains of the garden after fall harvest, clippings of leaves, and the drippings of cows and horses—the entire mound left to molt and rot during the cold season. The pigs rooted through the filth for those tiny bits of corn beneath the pile. Loving every moment of it—snorting, honking, squealing—they mixed the pile of manure in pursuit of the grain, so the laborers didn't have to do the work with shovels or rakes.

The boy, a lad of nearly twelve, looked up at the master pig keeper, enjoying the animals' noisy sounds of delight. "Who taught you this,

Master? How did you learn pigs would do all this work for a few kernels of corn?"

"By the pig keeper who taught me, of course," said the man, resting his arm on the knobbed end of a rake by the split-rail fence. The boy had always thought him a strange fellow. He was a little heavy in the middle, with dark hair that grew like a mane across his shoulders, streaked with white above his ears. He had a large nose, skinny legs, and the most serious eyes in the world.

The boy wiped his nose. The smell coming from the heap was overpowering, but it was a familiar scent. Everything about the farm was familiar, from the lopsided fence always in need of repairs to the row of fragrant eucalyptus that blocked the view of the sea. And, looming over it, the crooked castle of Sir Farfog with its belching chimneys, half-broken towers, and the ravens that squawked from atop it—all part of the daily scene for the poor serfs working the land.

"It's in a pig's nature to root like that, lad. Give 'em a little of what they want, they'll do it with joy. Men aren't much different from pigs, you know."

The boy smiled with affection for the master. The pig keeper was never unjust or cruel, unlike so many others who lived at Farfog Castle.

A shadow blotted the barn door, and the scullion Elle came in, straining with a bucket. The boy's smile faded when she entered and her nostrils flared at the stench.

"By Saint Cuthbert, how can you stand working in here?" she said with a revolted look as she wrestled with the heavy bucket. She stopped abruptly after stepping on a cake of manure and grimaced. "My shoe!"

The old pig keeper reached for and took the bucket from her and easily hefted it and brought it to the heap, where only a few piggy tails could be seen wriggling in the muck. He launched the contents of the bucket onto the pile, which earned a smart oink from the leader of the swine.

"This is disgusting," Elle complained, stepping back. For some reason, her wrinkled nose made her even prettier to the boy. She was fifteen but already so tall and mature it made the boy feel ashamed of himself. "Don't you smell it on yourself?"

The boy looked at his soiled shirt, sleeves rolled up to his elbows. He'd been working since before the sun rose, so of course he was filthy. She had a spot of soot on her cheekbone, but he wouldn't throw that back at her.

"'Tis the pigs' fault, not ours," said the master pig keeper. "You don't mind the smell so much when they're sizzling in a pan."

"Everyone likes the smell of bacon," she said to him with a hint of arrogance. "But my shoe! Cook will screech at me if I clean it off in the kitchen."

"There's a bucket of water," the boy suggested, pointing to one by the door. "I'll help you."

She took the empty bucket back from the master, looked at the spot the boy had pointed to, then nodded. As a scullion, she was always being ordered around herself, so having a little help was appreciated. The boy didn't mind it.

"Turn your bucket over. You can sit on it," he suggested.

"I hadn't thought of that," she said and quickly tried it out, lowering onto it next to the bucket of water. The hem of her kirtle was frayed and didn't even reach the floor. She'd outgrown it that year, but Sir Farfog was stingy about replacing anyone's clothes. They all had holes, patches, and torn seams. The boy knelt by her, and she removed her shoe and held it out to him. There was a large mash of manure there, but it wasn't awful to him—not worth such a look of loathing.

He found a sturdy twig of straw and used it to dig out the muck from the cracks in her shoe.

"Hurry," Elle pleaded, looking out the barn door. Chickens were rooting along the edges and clucking at one another.

Another voice could be heard, along with the jangle of spurs. "Oy! Where's Splotch? Who's seen him?"

"It's Sir Queux," said Elle tremulously, Sir Queux being Sir Farfog's only son. "Hasn't he gone to the tournament yet? I thought he'd already left."

Splotch was the pig boy's nickname. Ever since he was a young child, he'd had a little tuft of white hair over his left ear. Since his hair was thicker now, it wasn't as visible, although it'd been quite pronounced in his infancy.

The boy cupped some water from the bucket in his hand and splashed it on the bottom of Elle's shoe. Then he grabbed a fistful of straw and scrubbed it hard.

"Oy! Splotch!" The sound grew louder as the knight came closer.

The boy inspected the shoe, brushed some clinging straw from it, then was about to put it back on Elle's foot when he noticed how dirty her ankles were. He cupped some more water and quickly washed them.

She stared at him in surprise. Was that appreciation in her eyes? It made his cheeks sizzle with heat.

"There," he grunted, handing her shoe back to her. She quickly put it back on and then rose, her skirts twirling as she snatched up the bucket and sprinted out of the manure barn.

"Oy! Elle! You seen Splotch?"

"He's in there," came her rushed reply.

Splotch looked back at his master, who was staring at him intently, his eyes serious and probing. He had that unreadable look that he sometimes got when he stared at the boy.

Sir Queux barged in. "There you are. You deaf, lad? I've been calling for you!"

"The pigs are noisy."

Sir Queux wrinkled his nose, gave the master pig keeper a dismissive look, then kicked over the bucket of water. "Go water my horse.

Fresh from the well. Hurry! I'm going with Father to the tournament in Leoneyis! Come on!" He gave the boy a light smack to the side of his head, where the tuft of white hair was tucked away.

The boy, whose real name was Conn, picked up the bucket and rushed out of the barn. He caught sight of Elle, who was racing back to the kitchen, but she stopped and looked back at him. When their eyes met, she gave him a little wave.

His stomach churned with delight. Maybe this was how one of the pigs felt when it found a bit of spoiled corn. He reached the well, which was in the middle of the yard, and set his bucket on the ledge. As he turned to grab the rope and hook to lower it down, he bumped into the bucket and gasped in dismay when it toppled over the edge before he could grab it. There was a breath of silence, a moment of terror, and then a noisy splash as the bucket hit the waters.

"You daft, daft fool!" cried Sir Queux, who had seen it all.

The young knight, wearing his hauberk, tunic, and cape, strode up and boxed Conn solidly on the ear. "I asked you for a bucket of water, not to lose the whole thing!"

The boy's ear throbbed from the blow, and involuntary tears stung his eyes.

"I'm sorry, Sir Queux!" he gasped, holding his hand against his ear. He hoped that Elle was already gone. But no, with a little glance, he saw her standing by the door of the kitchen, holding her bucket as she watched his humiliation.

"Of course you're sorry! I don't have time for this! Get in an' fetch it!"

"Down the well? I'll . . . I'll . . . drown!"

"You won't drown, you fool!" Sir Queux grabbed Conn by the collar with one hand and then hoisted him under the armpits with the other. Panic made the boy's legs try to run, and he wriggled and shrieked, afraid he'd plunge into the well.

The knight thumped him on the head. "I'm not going to drop you. I'll lower you down. With the rope. Lad, you won't drown. Should be a simple enough task for one as small as you."

Sir Queux grabbed the rope and hook and dangled it for the boy to grab. His fears calming, he nodded and clenched the rope with both hands.

Sir Queux planted a boot against the rim, seized the rope firmly, and then nodded for Conn to start his descent. The boy squeezed the rope hard and began to sink down into the mouth of the well. He saw Elle's eyes widen as he dipped lower and lower. He held on tight, but his arms began to ache, and an itch tormented his nose. Conn tried to scratch it but fumbled his grip. He plummeted like the bucket.

Water exploded. It went up his nose, into his mouth. He thrashed and kicked and burst up to the surface like a bubble, gasping and dismayed. There was a circle of light high above. The smell of cold stone and wet mortar filled his nose. He sputtered, frantic, fearing he'd drown for sure.

A little shadow blotted the light. "You all right, lad?"

"It's dark!" Conn wailed.

"Here's the rope. I'm lowering it down. Grab the hook."

He felt something thump against his head. Not hard, but he grabbed the rope and pulled.

"Whoa, lad! Don't pull me down with you! Get the bucket!" yelled down Sir Queux.

The boy was frantic to leave, but he hadn't sunk as he'd feared he would. Still, being in a deep, dark well was an entirely different experience from splashing in the surf.

Everything was still dark to him, so he reached out with his free hand and groped around, trying to find the bucket.

It had sunk. It wasn't at the surface at all.

Of all the rotten luck!

"I can't . . . find it!" he called up.

"You can, Splotch! Reach down for it!"

"What if it's on the bottom?"

"Come on, lad! Just do it! I know you can!"

Conn bolstered his courage and then reached with his legs, trying to feel for the bucket. His foot caught the edge. He squinted, trying to hook his toe around the handle, but he couldn't. He'd need to dive.

"You can do it!" Elle added coaxingly. Had she come to the edge of the well?

Conn fought to keep up his courage, emboldened by the thought that Elle was counting on him too, and dived down. His first attempt failed, and he came up spluttering.

"D'you get it?" asked the knight.

"No! I'll try again."

"It's all right. Try again. You'll get it."

Conn didn't want to spend all day in the dark, musty interior of the well. He took another breath, plunged down a second time, and grabbed for the bucket. Only, his hand closed against something else. It felt long and . . . wooden? He popped back up to the surface. And, to his surprise, the bucket was floating next to his head.

"Did you get it?" Elle called down.

"Yes!" he shouted back. What was he holding in his hand? He lifted it from the water and saw the hilt of a sword enclosed by a roughed-up scabbard. A metal embellishment on the scabbard seemed to glimmer in the water, casting a cold blue light. A raven's-head sigil. The sting in his ear began to fade.

"Excellent! I'll pull you out!" said Sir Queux.

Holding the scabbard with one hand, he dipped the bucket to fill it and hooked its handle on the rope. "Got it! Pull me out!"

"The bucket first," said Sir Queux. "It'll be too heavy for both."

Conn frowned at that and watched as the bucket was pulled up to the top. "Ah, now my horse can have a drink!"

"Pull him out, Sir Queux," pleaded Elle.

9

"I was only teasing," said the knight with a laugh. He was young and capricious, though, and it wouldn't be unlike him to walk away and leave a difficult task to someone else, especially after getting what he wanted. Elle wasn't strong enough to lift him by herself, and his master . . . where was he?

"I found something else down here!" Conn cried. "A . . . a sword!"

Sir Queux sounded doubtful. "Are you jesting?"

"No! It was on the bottom. I have it."

"Show me."

Conn held it up.

The rope came down a second time, and Conn grabbed it with one hand and wrapped his legs around it. Both Sir Queux and Elle pulled on the rope, and he started rising up, higher and higher, the light growing brightly as he reached the top, relieved to be free of the well.

"What's this?" Sir Queux demanded, grabbing the scabbard and sword from him.

Conn wiped water from his face, noticing the sympathetic look Elle was giving him. But she also seemed interested in the sword.

"The raven mark," she said in wonder.

Sir Queux's eyes were wide with fascination. He held it in his hands, turning it over. "It's not even rusted."

Conn noticed his master, the pig keeper, standing in the doorway of the barn. A little smile was on his mouth. He gazed at Conn intently.

"That's the mark of Leoneyis, isn't it?" Elle whispered. She reached out to touch the sword, then withdrew her hand.

Sir Queux was still staring at the blade as if transfixed. "I must tell Father."

"I found it," Conn complained.

"It came from my father's *well*, boy. Everything on this land belongs to him and, by rights of inheritance, to *me*."

Conn thought it unwise to press the point.

Sir Queux was still transfixed by the sight of the sword. He began to walk back to the castle, leaving the bucket of water next to the well.

"Good luck, Sir Queux," said Conn. "I hope you win the tournament."

The knight didn't acknowledge him. His eyes were fixed on the blade and scabbard as he hurried back to the castle with the sword.

Elle touched Conn's wet hair. Then she gave him a smile, one that brightened her entire face, and went back to the kitchen door where she'd left her own bucket.

Conn stared across the yard at the master pig keeper. The man was laughing to himself, although the young man had no idea why.

But he recalled the order to water Sir Queux's horse. And an order from Sir Queux was as important to follow as if it had come from Sir Farfog himself. So the boy carried the bucket to the dappled destrier and gave the animal the long-awaited drink.

What he didn't know, not then, was that his life was about to change forever.

Nor that his real name wasn't Conn at all.

His real name was Andrew.

King Ulric of Leoneyis achieved his ends. Later, he confessed all to his pregnant wife, and she hated him with her whole heart. But with her eyes, her tongue, her silvery speech, she persuaded him that she would be reconciled to his overlordship of Leoneyis. Even so, I knew the hatred within her. She would kill their child, especially if it were a boy.

After the midwife helped with the delivery, the queen was too weak to nurse the babe. I watched and waited, knowing not even a mother's natural love could overcome such hate. So I took the child and fled to Legault. I found a nursemaid in the fishing village of Atha Kleah to suckle the boy, whose father had named him Andrew. We fled again when men came searching—soldiers from the king and kishion from the queen. From Legault we went to Blackpool in Ceredigion. From Blackpool to Glosstyr. The babe was able to walk eventually, which made traveling easier. For two years we were hunted.

Then Ulric died, betrayed by one of his own, and it plunged the realms into war again. I had taken the king's sword in exchange for the word of power I'd taught him. He'd accepted the price, however costly, but insisted he needed replacements to hide the fact that his Fountain-blessed weapon and sheath were gone. In their place, I fashioned him decoys to wear into battle to trick his enemies into believing in his invulnerability. The trick worked, but when a hunt commenced to find the missing heir, the king announced he was also missing his blade. Once it became known he was vulnerable, he perished with a knife in his back.

The boy and I found shelter at Farfog Castle, and I enlisted to keep the pigs as the wars raged around us. The queen was still wild with hate, wanting to destroy her son before he became a man. Another kishion was sent. Then another. When one was lucky or skilled enough to find us in Farfog—and cunning enough to realize the boy in the pig pens was a prince—I was there to intervene. Until the queen died from a fall off a horse.

That was when it was safe to finally reveal the sword to the boy. Farfog's son claimed it as his own and went to the tournament in Leoneyis. With such a remarkable sword, he won the contest, and some of the lords recognized the weapon and tried to hail him king. Others noted that he was too old to be the missing child. He was pressed for answers. Oh, how they pressed him! How did he come by the blade? Where did he get it? Was it not King Ulric's fabled blade Firebos? And something changed within the boy, who'd possessed all the pride of youth. He awakened to the truth that his claim to the throne was a false one. The sword didn't give him that right. So he told them about the boy in his father's castle.

And it was early in the spring that a muddy boy became a king.

—Maderos, a Pig Keeper

CHAPTER ONE

Mirror Gate

Eilean awoke to the gritty sensation of sand on her cheek, a cool salty breeze on her face, and a strange sound—almost a barking, although not from a dog. Disoriented, she opened her eyes as memories from the night before surfaced. She and Hoel had slept on a beach after crossing through the mirror gate at Dochte Abbey.

The magic of the mirror gate had transported them to another world.

They'd passed through in daytime, the feeling as wrenching as if they'd plummeted from a waterfall, and when the world stopped shaking, they were in a foreign sea *at night*. Hoel had battled the water with the oars, struggling to avoid rocks until a small cove had revealed itself in the starlight, and they'd washed up on a sandy beach at the base of a jagged wall of cliffs. Together, they'd hauled the boat higher up the shore before collapsing on the smooth, damp sand.

The beach, which had been empty before, was teeming with furry, whiskered creatures that barked in a cacophony down by the shore where the waves crashed. Some were wriggling in the sand. There was a mass of the plump, jellylike creatures, some with nubs of flippers at their sides. Eilean rubbed her eyes, staring down at the quivering mass of them, then brushed some tangled hair from her face.

She saw Hoel sitting near her, arms wrapped around his knees, whittling a shaft of deadwood with a dagger. Sand was captured in the creases of his clothes, some flecks of it sticking to his tanned skin. Tiny peels of shaved wood were scattered on the sand in front of him.

As she stared at his profile, taking in the handsome lines of his face, an unexpected sensation of longing tugged at her heart. They'd kissed for the first time before plummeting through the mirror gate, and the memory was still fresh. He'd chased and hunted her since she'd fled Muirwood Abbey, but everything had changed when she'd saved him from a dungeon cell in Dochte Abbey. Together, they had fought off a poisoner and a kishion. Now they were not only allies, they were . . .

She wasn't quite sure yet. The only thing she knew was that the safety they'd enjoyed on the beach wouldn't last long.

When he noticed her sitting up, Hoel continued to nick and smooth the deadwood staff but gave her a smile.

"Good morning," he said softly.

The way he looked at her made her heart ache again. The new feelings were very delicate. It was all so strange and wonderful. "Good morning," she answered, turning back to gaze at the mob of barking sea creatures. "Noisy brutes, aren't they?"

"Sea lions," he said. "They're common at Avinion and Mon, but I've never seen so many in one place before. Their arrival woke me up."

"You should have awakened me too."

He tilted his head. "I liked watching you sleep."

"Oh? Was I snoring?"

"A little," he answered, and she wasn't sure he was joking. He wasn't the kind of man who typically joked.

It made her immediately self-conscious. "Don't do that, I beg you. Wake me when you do. We don't have long in this foreign world. Only a fortnight to make it back to the mirror gate with Maderos's tome." She stopped, blinking in surprise.

His brows knit together. "You just said his true name." Then he tried it. "Maderos."

In their world, the High Seer had put a binding sigil on his name, preventing anyone from uttering it. Instead of Maderos, he was called the druid Mordaunt. Preventing others from knowing his true name had allowed her to further conceal the corruption within the maston order.

"The binding sigil does not work in this world," Eilean said. "It has no power here."

"So it seems."

She noticed some white-breasted sandpipers scuttling along the shore, going after little insects with their long beaks. They were tiny, yet deliberate in their movements, unafraid of the water sliding up the shore. It was a beautiful scene, the undulating mass of sea lions, the gentle tide, the fiery streaks of orange in the sky revealing the coming sunrise, the softness of the sand beneath her. Yet there was urgency as well, a nagging feeling that they had to travel quickly.

Hoel slid his dagger into its sheath and then rose, bending slightly to offer his hand. She gripped it and let him help pull her up. She brushed sand from her dress while he tapped the deadwood against his palm.

"What's that for?" she asked him.

"It's your weapon," he said with a wry smile, handing it to her.

She took it, her brows knitting in confusion.

"I thought we might spend a little time this morning with some rudimentary training. You have the words Mordaunt—I mean *Maderos*—taught you. But sometimes things move too quickly for them to be used, and our enemies know enough to silence you. This is your sword."

"I don't see a stick for you?" she said, enjoying the idea of sparring with him.

"I'll use the real one," he said, nodding to the raven scabbard and the blade.

"Shouldn't I get the real one since I need the practice?"

"I don't want you hurting yourself, Eilean. Sticks are best at this stage. Trust me. I've trained a lot of men."

"And women?"

"Some," he said.

He then proceeded to explain the proper grip and stance, all without grabbing his own weapon. Sometimes he directed the movements of her body with his hands—adjusting her hips, bending her elbow slightly to reveal the ideal arc for the weapon. Mostly he taught her to parry, how to retreat and swivel off the line of battle. Then he unsheathed his blade and began to demonstrate the attack motions, going slowly enough so that she could practice the blocks. As he pressed forward, she retreated.

Some of the sea lions took interest in them after the clacking sounds of their weapons were noticed, and the noise of barking decreased. A few even shuffled closer.

"Are they dangerous?" Eilean asked, glancing at the spotted pelt of one of them.

"Keep your eyes on mine," he said. "They are harmless. I am not. Watch my eyes, not my weapon. Learn to judge my intentions. You are already Gifted with knowing thoughts, but I can use my blade to distract you." He swung his weapon around to the side, and she easily blocked it, then he brought his foot behind hers, their ankles crossed. "If I straightened my hips, I'd be able to trip you." He didn't follow through on it, though.

"Do it," she said. "Don't go easy on me."

She stiffened her leg muscles, determined to prevent herself from falling, but he easily toppled her. Down she went, onto the soft sand, and her wooden stick went flying.

He reached down to help her up. She took his hand and then tried to plant her boot into his stomach and hoist him off his feet.

With reflexes so fast they surprised her, Hoel stepped away, but he still gripped her hand. She used that grip to pull herself into a sitting position and tried to get her legs up.

She felt a thought radiate from him—if their situations had been reversed, he would have hooked an arm around her knees and quickly stood up. So she did. That forced him to hop. He would have fallen backward, but he let go of her hand and wrapped his other arm around her neck. If she lifted him any higher, they'd both go down. So she let his leg go.

"Good instincts," he complimented, releasing her as well.

She smiled at the praise. "I can't really claim to have the instincts of a warrior," she said. "It's more that we're . . . connected. Our thoughts get a little tangled."

"Does that just happen with me or others too?"

"Some more than others, but it happens frequently."

He rubbed his chin, looking bemused. "I've spent months trying to *think* like you. To determine why you choose the way you do, to understand your motives. The better a hunter understands the prey, the more opportunities present themselves. In the dungeon, we could speak mind to mind through the Medium. I've never had that happen to me before. Have you?"

She nodded, brushing sand from her hands. "Yes. I've been able to catch glimpses of others' thoughts for a long time now."

"Truly? So you could do a Gifting?"

"I think so. Maderos has the same Gift, only his is clearer and more attuned. That's how he knew Aldermaston Gilifil was concealing his lack of power in the Medium. He knew all of our thoughts."

Hoel glanced at her with a little wariness. "It's a powerful Gift."

"It is. And a helpful one. But it doesn't tell me everything I need to know. I only get glimpses. There's so much I still don't know." Feeling a prick of disquiet, she took a moment to work through her conflicting thoughts—she wanted to trust Hoel because she *liked* him, yet she shouldn't forget who he was, or to whom he'd promised his loyalty. "I want to trust you. We need to be united in purpose if we're going to succeed here. But I can't help worrying. You've sworn your allegiance to the High Seer. Yes, our interests align right now. We both want to get the tome back. But if you're only working with me so you can take it to the High Seer . . ." She sighed and stopped.

He was still studying her, although his eyes seemed warmer now. "You're wise to be cautious, Eilean. By Cheshu, I've given you every reason to be. All I can give you is my word. You *can* trust me. If not for you, I'd be languishing in that cell still, my mind and my heart slowly being twisted until I was no longer myself. While I have a duty to the High Seer, which I intend to repudiate when we return, I want you to know"—he reached out and took her hand—"that my loyalty is to the Medium. My stubbornness blinded me to its subtle whispers, but no longer. I'm supposed to help you." He squeezed her hand. "We do this together or not at all."

Relief cascaded through her, for she felt in her soul that he was trustworthy. She nodded.

He grazed his thumb across her knuckles, sending a prickle of something different through her. "More fighting. This time, no weapons. Remember when Kariss twisted your arm back? There's more than one way to escape that sort of hold. Let me show you."

And he did. He taught her how to escape different kinds of grips and holds—and how to use leverage to compensate for his additional bulk. By the end of the training, she'd managed to flip him on his back once. His patience had yielded high returns. She admired him for that, and for his strength and prowess. And, if she were being truthful, this new intimacy, this wrestling and twisting and knocking down, made the bond between them more visceral. Being this close to him stirred something inside her.

Afterward, she was tired and thirsty and more than a little aroused by the experience. They couldn't drink the seawater, but he pointed to a trickle of water that fed into the sea from the cliffs. From that source, they were able to fill their water flasks, drink plentifully, and fill them up again. As she watched him drink, she felt the urge to kiss him again. She didn't act on it. But she secretly hoped he would instigate it. He did not, although the looks he gave her, like she was a gooseberry fool, suggested he wasn't unaffected by the experience.

After securing their water supply, they went back to their little makeshift encampment and brought out some of the food they'd taken from Dochte Abbey. She'd also taken a coin purse with the raven markings on it, knowing they'd need food and shelter during their journey and presuming the coins were from this new land. None of the coinage from their world had that symbol, after all, and they'd found it in Dochte Abbey amidst Kariss's things, who they knew was from this other world and had traveled through the mirror gate.

While they sat to eat a little breakfast, she posed a question. "Do you remember when we traveled together from Tintern by wagon?"

"Yes."

"You gave me a little tub of ointment to protect me from the bugs. Do you remember?"

He nodded, tilting his head.

"Did you offer that to anyone else? Or just me?"

The quirk of a smile lifted his lips, and he looked down. "Ah. What did I mean by that gesture?"

"Did you already fancy me?" she asked.

"It's best if we're honest with each other," he said, lifting his gaze to meet her eyes. "You are a pretty lass, Eilean. I've always thought so, from the moment we met. But I confess my attentions back then weren't of an amorous nature. I knew that Aldermaston Gilifil had chosen you to serve the druid. I hoped, at the time, to gain your trust. I had a sinking feeling you were being used, and I feared you'd get in trouble for it. Many had the potential of getting ill during the journey. I didn't want it to happen to you."

It was a kindness, then. "Thank you. I still have that little tub, you know. I packed it when we left Muirwood."

"Any other probing questions?" There was something in his voice. Something he wanted her to ask him.

He knew about her parentage, a mystery she'd never thought she would have the chance to solve. The truth had been conferred to him by the Cruciger orb, which did not lie. But the thought of learning about her background made her queasy.

What would the answer mean for her? Would it make her feel more worthy of Hoel's affection? Or less? Although his uncle was the King of Pry-Ree, he didn't seem all that troubled by her background. Maybe that meant she was more important than she knew.

Or maybe not.

Either way, her parents had left her, and she wasn't eager to find out why.

She nibbled on the crust of bread and watched as the sea lions suddenly began to flee back into the surf. The wriggling mass of creatures were all pointed back toward the sea, their loud *arf*s growing more frenzied as they fled.

"Something is scaring them away," she said.

He turned and looked. "There's a boat coming." She looked in that direction and saw it—a vessel twice as large as the one they'd come in. A little square sail was fixed to a middling-size mast. Her heart began to quicken with fear.

The two of them quickly stowed their meal and grabbed their packs. Hoel strapped Maderos's sword across his back, his eyes on the approaching vessel. It was close enough now for them to see the armed men who stood inside. She counted eight.

One of them lifted a horn and blew a long, heavy blat from it.

Hoel brushed off his hands. "They're telling others they've found us," he said coolly.

Grabbing his bow, he secured the quiver to his belt, then withdrew one feathered shaft and fixed it on the strand.

The kingdom of Leoneyis is an island realm, similar in size and features to Hyksos of old. As one of the Twelve, I witnessed the rising of Safehome. I knew the emperor-maston who went off in search of other worlds to spread the mysteries of the Knowing. Ulric had had the potential to unite the warring factions on his troubled island. He was a strong and capable warrior, not bloodthirsty and savage like the Naestors. He listened to wisdom and created laws that provided a modicum of justice and fairness. But his capacity for honor was thwarted by what sprouted in his heart when he met his enemy's wife. Their son was just a tender sapling of a tree birthed from powerful roots, but I sensed he could do what his father could not.

The boy's sudden rise changed how everyone treated him. Sir Farfog immediately treated him with honor and respect. So did the lord's son. Prestige has that effect on most people. So when Andrew left Farfog Castle, he brought Sir Farfog, Sir Queux, and all the servants, milkmaids, and scullions to the seat of his father's domain—the fortress of Tintagel— which is situated on a cleft of rock on the southern tip of the island. It cannot be assailed by ship. By land it is equally difficult to reach, save by a bridge that is guarded day and night and fashioned so it can be folded up midspan to make the approach impossible for all except birds.

As I advised Ulric under the name of Myrddin, I continued to use that name with his son, who began to grow in stature, wisdom, and discernment. It was his idea to create a table made from the slice of a trunk of a sui-sha tree, which grow plentifully in that land, and he asked me to fashion it and bring it to Tintagel to be kept in the great hall. This table possessed no head or tail, no hierarchy at all. To gain a seat at it, a knight must display the traits favored by the maston order, traits demonstrated in thought, word, and deed. It was called the Order of Virtus—including faith, knowledge, temperance, patience, brotherhood, kindness, benevolence to the poor, humility, and—perhaps the greatest virtue of all—diligence.

The first knight to claim a seat at the table was Sir Queux. Responsibility changed the man—it helped him grow—and his devotion to the young king was unparalleled. The sword Firebos was too heavy for the lad, so Sir Queux wielded it on his behalf and took personal responsibility to ensure Andrew achieved knighthood by the age of fourteen.

The fame of the Ring Table drew knights from other realms to Tintagel.

I was proud of the boy. I respected the young man. But he was not the only one I tutored. The scullion girl, Elle, brought the king and I our food. She asked me to tell her stories from the past. She wanted to be more than a scullion girl. Her mind was strong. Her will impressive.

If only I had possessed the Gift of Seering as the Harbinger did. I would have done so many things differently if only I had known what she would set her mind to.

—Myrddin, Wizr of Tintagel

CHAPTER TWO

Firebos

Before we attack them, let's see what they want," Eilean said in a low voice.

Hoel grunted. "I'm not going to be a prisoner again," he replied, his eyes fixed on the approaching boat.

"Nor am I. But the only way out of this cove is by sea." She'd noticed the cliffs blocking each way. The stone arch in the cliffs to their left marked the mirror gate. There weren't any hiding places to stow their boat, so they'd have to take it with them to leave the cove.

The echo of the horn continued to sound in her mind. She closed her eyes and sought the Medium's will.

Patience. You will be directed.

"I can kill three or four of them before they reach the shore," Hoel murmured to her. But that action felt wrong.

"No. The Medium bids us wait," she said, glancing at him.

His mouth tightened into a frown of displeasure. She could see him gauging the enemy, trying to find an advantage against their superior numbers. It was unnecessary. She knew a word of power that could explode the coming boat. But everyone within it would be killed, and she was loath to take life without the Medium commanding it. The barrier command would prevent the intruders from physically seizing them . . . and also hinder the two of them from leaving. Still, there had to be another way . . .

She put a calming hand on Hoel's arm. "I'm not defenseless. Neither are you. Let them approach. We don't even know where we are."

"This is another world, Eilean. Are you expecting them to speak Pry-rian?"

"It won't be a problem for either of us. I know a word of power that will allow us to communicate with them. Let's wait."

The crashing of the waves got louder. Was the tide coming in? That thought sparked another in her mind. In Maderos's tome, the Sefer Yetzirah, she'd learned the words to control the waves of the sea.

"I don't like this," Hoel muttered. His hand was squeezing the shaft of the bow so hard his tendons were bulging and white, but he heeded her.

Draw the sword.

She heard the whisper cut through the noise of the waves. Hoel started, then shot her an inquisitive look. "Was that you?"

So they'd both heard it. "It was the Medium," she said. "Do it."

Hoel still looked wary, but he put the arrow back in the quiver and slung the bow around his shoulder. As the boat of soldiers rode a wave to the patch of shore just ahead of them, some of the men leaped out and began to haul the ship higher up the sand embankment. A soldier in a chain hauberk remained on the boat, his cloak fastened about his neck with a large brooch that caught Eilean's eye. It was a two-faced woman, half-black, half-white, the profiles facing in opposite directions. She stiffened, remembering the symbol from the maston test.

The symbol of the dark empresses.

The cloaked man stepped out of the boat, his boots sinking into the slush of sand and surf. He had a longsword belted to his waist, which he gripped with one hand. The tunic was very fine, and the boots were well made.

"Xenoglossia," Eilean touched Hoel's arm and whispered, invoking the power so that Hoel would also be under its influence. The throb of the Medium came immediately.

Hoel drew the blade. As soon as it cleared the raven scabbard, it shimmered with an aura of blue flame, but Hoel's eyes were fixed on the other man, the obvious leader. Still, it was clear the others were soldiers, not sailors—all were equipped with longswords or daggers, or both. One even had a battle-axe strapped across his back.

The leader stared at the flame dancing up the naked blade in Hoel's hand, his eyes widening with recognition. "That is the sword Firebos," he said. There was no difficulty understanding him—the magic revealed both his words and their meaning. His eyebrows lowered menacingly. "Where did you get it?"

Eilean had found it alongside Mordaunt's tome, hidden in the gorge by the Dryad tree. But she certainly wasn't about to reveal any of that to these men.

"What is your name?" Eilean asked the leader. "Whom do you serve?"

"I am Sir Moriaen, son of Aglovale. I serve Her Highness, the Queen of Brythonica, on whose lands you trespass." He drew his sword. "Many have searched in vain for that weapon. The reward offered is worth a king's ransom. Set it down, lad."

The knight before them was probably twenty years older than Hoel, but the reference to his younger age was clearly meant as an insult and a threat.

Hoel did not tense or show offense. "I think not," he answered calmly.

"Where is Queen Essylt?" Eilean asked. That was the name Kariss had given her mistress, to whom she had sent the tome.

"You'll be meeting her shortly, in chains and on your knees," said Moriaen spitefully. He motioned for his men. "Surround them."

The one with the battle-axe had a cruel look in his eyes as he brought out the weapon. The soldiers began to approach them from either side, circling in on them.

Hoel ignored the others as he stared at Moriaen.

What now? he thought to her.

"*Gheb-ool,*" she whispered, invoking another word of power. The hairs on her arms tingled and stood on end, and she felt a little shiver run across them. The shield now surrounded them. If the men attempted to touch her or Hoel, the magic would fling them back.

Hoel glanced both ways. "Nothing happened," he whispered.

Words came to Eilean's mind. Words she felt compelled by the Medium to say. "Tell your mistress that she has stolen what is not rightfully hers. Warn her that the end is coming. Tintagel will fall. Leoneyis will be drowned in the sea, and Brythonica with it if she does not relent and obey the Fountain. I give you this warning. It is not too late to turn back."

Eilean didn't fully understand the message she'd delivered. She knew a little of King Andrew's history from reading Maderos's tome and had always supposed the king to be a righteous follower of the Knowing, a possible ally. But she didn't know what had transpired since Maderos was banished from this world and trapped on the other side of a mirror gate. The warning she'd uttered was grim.

Sir Moriaen gave her a distrusting look. "The Fountain? Are you a seeress or a witch instead, I wonder? No matter. You threatened my queen. Kill him. Bind her. We return to Ploemeur. Now!"

Eilean felt the Medium's command pulse through her mind. *Now.*

"*Hayam ubeqaehu,*" she said, uttering the words of power that controlled the sea.

The soldiers rushed at them from all sides, all except Sir Moriaen, who stood still, watching his men attempt to fulfill his command. Hoel and Eilean simply stood there as the men were shocked and sent flying backward, unable to cross the boundary she'd set in the sand.

Sir Moriaen glared at them. "'Tis magic! Who taught you, lass?"

Eilean felt the magic tingle in her blood and watched in wonder as a coming wave doubled and then tripled in size. She swallowed in fear as its roar filled the air.

"Look!" one of the soldiers shrieked, pointing at the massive maw of water bearing down on them.

Another began to flee toward the cliff wall. But none of them were fast enough.

Sir Moriaen looked confused and then turned just as the wave slammed into him, sweeping him off his feet. Hoel gripped Eilean's arm with one hand, bracing himself for the deluge, but the waters went around them, unable to pass the magical barrier she'd imposed. The sand roiled around them as the wave knocked over the soldiers, sending some tumbling head over heels. The sailboat the soldiers had come in was heaved up the shore like a battering ram. Even over the din of the surf, Eilean heard the cracking wood as their boat was smashed into a nest of boulders. That would make it unfit to use.

The wave struck the cliff wall with a froth of white and then began to rush back down the beach. The soldiers were flailing in the water, some choking, all of them drenched. Most had lost their weapons.

Eilean turned and looked up to where she and Hoel had stowed their small fishing boat. The waves had lifted it up from the rocks, and it was gliding toward the sea with the retreating tide.

She and Hoel looked at each other, and they knew what to do without speaking. Eilean released the shield spell, the water already down to their knees. Still gripping Firebos, Hoel rushed toward the boat to catch it before it went past them. He grabbed one side, straining against the pull of the sea, and Eilean rushed over and grabbed the other. They ran with the boat as it met the next coming wave and pushed it over the hump of water.

"Get in!" Hoel said with a grin.

Eilean clambered on board, then grabbed for the oars while Hoel continued to push. Some of the soldiers ran toward them, shouting. She grabbed Hoel by the arm as he flung himself into the boat.

Wiping water from his face, Hoel turned back and began to laugh. "By Cheshu, the look on their faces." He took the oars from her and slid them into the locks, then began to row hard to get them away from the cove.

Eilean glanced back at Sir Moriaen, who appeared to have lost his longsword. He stood on the beach, hands on hips in frustration and helplessness, dripping wet.

"What was that . . . warning about?" Hoel asked, his breath coming fast from the exertion.

"I don't know," she said. "It just came into my mind."

She was reminded of another warning she'd delivered on the Medium's behalf—this one to the High Seer. After delivering the message, she'd collapsed, and while she was unconscious, she'd had a vision of the Dryad in the Bearden Muir.

"You have a stewardship to protect that tome. It is your burden. Visions of the future are written into it. Maderos wrote them down, but I was the Harbinger who spoke them."

Queen Essylt could not be allowed to translate that tome. Again Eilean felt the urgency to reclaim it. They were in Brythonica, where the tome had been taken, and Sir Moriaen had said his queen was in a place called Ploemeur.

"The Cruciger orb," Eilean said. "Can we see if the tome is where that knight said it was? It told us Brythonica last time. Maybe it will be more specific now."

"Did you see the brooch that knight was wearing?" Hoel asked, pulling on the oars in a disciplined rhythm.

"Yes," she answered. "It bore the symbol of the dark empresses."

Hoel nodded. "No surprise since Kariss is a hetaera. But they wear it openly here. That's not a good sign."

"Indeed, no," she agreed, sitting back. Although she hadn't lost consciousness this time, she felt a little light-headed from using so much magic.

Her mind returned to the warning she'd delivered. What could it mean? She had come hoping to meet the high king. Had hoped a faithful man such as the king she had read about in Maderos's tome might be able to help the maston order avoid a schism. And yet, her warning had implied that both Leoneyis and Brythonica would be drowned.

Worry began to trouble her. What if she'd gotten everything wrong, and the Medium had another purpose for her—one she'd never even suspected?

As the reputation of the Ring Table grew, knights started arriving from other lands, all seeking a place at the table. They coveted the favored chair, the Siege Perilous, which King Andrew had reserved for his greatest knight, a position that had not yet been earned by anyone. Nor had a timetable been established for bestowing that honor. A boy of fifteen named Peredur followed a group of knights to the castle, hoping to earn his own place at the table. They sent him back with hardly a thought, but before he left he insisted that he would one day earn his place—and the right to sit in the Siege Perilous. He was a naïve young man, but very determined. The other knights scoffed at him, especially Sir Queux, who wanted the chair for himself.

Mockery induces most men to step down, lest they be accused of presumption. It is a tool that is used to dominate others. Young Peredur heard their insults calmly, however, and set forth to prove them all wrong. Before leaving for home, he ate one last meal in the kitchen and shared his ambition with the scullion girl Elle. She shared with him some of the counsel and knowledge that I had been sharing with her.

When he returned a few years later, Peredur was the greatest knight to come to Tintagel. He defeated all the others in single combat. Even Sir Queux.

—Myrddin, Wizr of Tintagel

CHAPTER THREE

Peredur

The harbor of Ploemeur was situated on a promontory south of the mirror gate that had brought them to this world. There were ships of differing sizes in the slips, and many disgorged cargo brought from other lands. Hoel and Eilean entered the town. Their destination, the castle of the Queen of Brythonica, stood on a jutting cliff overlooking the harbor. A series of switchbacks went up the steep slope of rough granite. It reminded Eilean a little of Prince Derik's palace above the town of Isen, although the castle at Ploemeur was taller, more elegant.

Banners showing the double-face symbol flew throughout town, and carts and wagons crowded the busy streets. Eilean had never seen so many berries for sale. There were small round purple ones, baskets of strawberries, and others that looked like the shrewberries she'd seen in the Bearden Muir except pinker. Other berries were black, with thick juicy buds. Another vendor was selling fresh gooseberries, which she knew from experience were tart except in cream.

Hoel paused to admire the variety, then gestured to her to ask if she wanted him to try buying some with the money they'd found at Dochte Abbey. She agreed—it was a good time to test the coins. She handed him the purse, and he bought a small basket with an assortment of berries. Hoel held the basket in one hand, nodded to the seller, and they both continued down the street.

Eilean felt confident she could get them into the castle. It would be possible to pass the guards invisibly, or she could transform them with another word of power to match the clothing and style of these people. She did not feel out of place because so many were wearing different fashions. Ploemeur's status as a major trading kingdom would make their infiltration easier.

Hoel offered her some berries. "The town is friendly enough," he said in a hushed voice. "There are tax collectors going from stall to stall. Did you see them?"

"I didn't," she confessed.

"Common for a port city. Did you notice the way he looked at us when we paid with those coins?"

"No."

"He accepted it, but most people were paying with a different kind of coin," Hoel said. "The kind we were given as change. One type of coin means there is a royal mint, a foundry that makes all the coins of the realms. One authority to oversee it."

"The Queen of Brythonica? Or do you mean the high king, Andrew?"

"I think the latter more likely. Whoever controls trade dominates the politics. You saw what happened with the kingdom of Moros in our world. When the king converted, they began exchanging their currency for the one approved in Avinion. War isn't the only way that power conquers."

"Should we try to approach the castle before nightfall?"

Hoel pursed his lips. "It might be better to see what we can learn first before going up there."

"I need to get that tome back."

"The orb showed us it's there, but let's be prudent. If we spend the night in one of these inns, we can go up to the castle at first light. That way we'll have time to circulate and see what else we can learn. Still, I don't know how soon the men we stranded on that beach will make it back. They will be looking for us. Can you disguise us?"

"I can." Eilean nodded in agreement and tasted the small handful of berries, one by one. "These are very good."

Hoel popped a few in his mouth, chewed quickly, then nodded in appreciation. "They taste the same as the ones from our world."

That wasn't a surprise to Eilean, though. Through the maston test, she had learned how the Essaios populated new worlds with the animals and plant life available in others. She wondered which of the two worlds had come first or if one had helped form the other.

As they stood there, a loud horn was blown from back at the dock. Hoel immediately turned and looked, and they both noticed the sudden activity coming from the piers. Those who had been purchasing sweetmeats, berries, and other delights were suddenly craning their necks to see what the news was about. Hoel motioned for her to follow him, and they both joined the crowds that had begun to gather around.

Their sense of confusion only grew as the people began to exchange murmurs in low, urgent tones. A ship was coming into the harbor, they said, far larger than the others that had already docked. The crowds thronged to see it. Eilean felt the press of bodies around her—one in particular. Hoel gripped her arm and stood very close to her, so close she could smell his leathers. He gazed above the heads of many in the crowd. They were higher up the street than many onlookers, which allowed them a better view of the harbor.

The enormous ship docked, its single mast taller than a tree, with a sail so wide it could have covered several huts. A horse emerged from the crowd and approached the plank. On the deck of the ship, Eilean saw a knight in gleaming armor beside a veiled lady. He led the way down the plank, guiding the lady with him, hand in hand.

More murmurs rose up from the crowd as the knight mounted the horse and then pulled the woman up behind him. The crowd parted, creating a chasm for the riders to travel.

Eilean didn't think it was the Queen of Brythonica, for the Cruciger orb had already revealed Essylt was at Ploemeur along with the tome. No, these were visitors from another realm.

"Could it be Andrew?" Eilean whispered to Hoel.

"If I pull out the orb, it'll draw unwanted attention," he said, eyes fixed on the newcomers. "Let's wait."

The question was answered as a name began to be murmured through the crowd. *Peredur. Peredur.*

Eilean recognized it from Mordaunt's tome. "He's King Andrew's champion," she said to Hoel. "I read about him in the tome. He came to Andrew's court at Tintagel as a young man, and he was scoffed at for wanting to sit on the Siege Perilous."

Hoel's brow wrinkled. "Siege Perilous? You can't *sit* on a siege."

"'Siege' is the Glagolitic word for *seat*. So it literally means *to sit*."

"Oh," Hoel said, nodding. "When one party holds a defensive position. So you could also say it's a Perilous Seat."

"True. It was created by Maderos, who is called Myrddin in this land, for a knight worthy of being the king's champion. One capable of claiming the lost artifacts of the Essaios, which were given to this world before they departed."

Hoel's brow furrowed. "Are these like the artifacts left in our world? The Cruciger orb and the glowing stones?"

"Yes, I think so. Perhaps the gifts are different in every world. There were many listed in the tome. One is a sword called the Sword of Fire. Another is a spear, which when wounded from it, the wound cannot heal. The third gift was the Lia Fáil, or the swearing stone, also called a speaking stone. If a false king stood on it, the stone would roar. If a true king stood on it, the stone would sing. There are many stories of the artifacts and the knights who tried to find them for their kings."

"That sword sounds a lot like the one you got from Maderos," Hoel said.

"It must be. Another gift was the Gradalis, a dish made of silver. It could open a rift back to Idumea, the world of the Essaios. Only a person of unblemished purity could find the Gradalis. Peredur was chosen to sit on that chair, so maybe he found it. I guess it was the most difficult to find, but he's the best of the knights."

"And he's coming this way," Hoel said.

The gap in the crowd closed behind the riders as they made their way up the high street of Ploemeur. Watching them, Eilean felt a familiar sensation coming from the person on the horse. The power of the Medium, though she could not tell whether it originated with the man or the lady. Whoever it was, their ability was as strong as that of Aldermastons Utheros and Kalbraeth.

The rider had black hair, cropped above the neck, which was curly and tangled. He had a scar on his brow, a firm jaw, and eyes the color of steel. His expression was determined and stiffly controlled. His nicked and battered armor suggested that he was well accustomed to battle. There were two flanges on the shoulders, welded into the shoulder guards. Murmurs from the crowd revealed the deep respect they had for the knight.

The woman, astride behind him, wore a noblewoman's gown the color of wine. Her dark tresses escaped part of the veil that obscured her face. If she had a name, it was unknown, and Eilean heard gasps and whispers at her beauty. No one appeared to recognize her.

As the knight reached where Eilean and Hoel were standing in the crowd, his stony expression suddenly altered into one of confusion. He turned his head abruptly and looked directly at the two of them. His sudden scrutiny brought a spasm of worry in her heart. She had sensed his approach. Did he sense their presence as well?

She normally had glimpses of the thoughts of others, but his mind was blocked to hers, as if protected by a wall of stone. Nothing but cold silence came from him.

The horse continued on without stopping. The knight looked forward again, then twisted in his saddle to get another look at them. Again she felt the void of thought.

"He picked us out of a crowd," Hoel murmured in warning. "We should go."

Peredur. Maderos knew him. Maderos had spoken to him. Was there a deeper reason for this chance meeting?

"Wait," Eilean said, resisting the gentle pressure on her arm as Hoel tried to guide her away.

The tide of onlookers were now converging around them, following the knight and lady as they continued up the street. There was no doubt they were headed to the castle. Eilean felt a premonition that the moment was important, although she couldn't have said why.

As the crowd surged against them, making standing still more and more untenable, she let Hoel guide her to a gap between buildings, and soon they were alone.

"That was strange," Hoel said, looking back at the flow of people they'd left.

"Strange that he came here when he did?"

"No. He looked unhappy."

Eilean turned her head. "Why do you say that? He was very stern." She was still wrestling with her own impressions of the encounter.

"It was more than sternness. I've seen that look before, in men who have known too many wars. How old do you think he was?"

"Not yet forty, I should think," Eilean answered.

"I think you're close. And he's been a knight since he was a young man?"

"Fairly young, yes. He proved the others wrong. He was exceptionally gifted."

"We've been followed," Hoel said.

Eilean turned back to the crowd and saw a man watching them with wary eyes. He wore a cape secured with the same pinned brooch they'd seen Sir Moriaen wear earlier. He also had a longsword at his belt, and he was already gripping it in one hand as he stared at them.

"Let's go," Hoel insisted. They were already near the next crossing of buildings, the alleys between them empty except for a few chickens.

She went with him and rounded the next corner when he did.

Three more men stood blocking the way. Gazing at them.

"Let's go back the other way," Eilean suggested, preparing to draw on the words of power to escape. She felt a warning not to from the Medium.

Hoel sized up the three men. "If the man in the cape thought this far ahead, the other ways will be guarded too, possibly with even more men. These are supposed to make us bolt. We should fight through them. Use your spell. Knock them down."

"I can't. The Medium warned me not to."

The three men started walking toward them.

Hoel glanced back, but the man in the cape hadn't arrived yet. "It won't let you?" he asked worriedly.

He is your protector.

Eilean licked her lips. "I'm not supposed to use magic. They're yours," she said.

A smile quirked on his mouth. He advanced on the three men, holding his hands up defensively. But that was just a deception. As soon as he drew near, he launched into a blur of action, stomping on one man's boot so hard Eilean could hear the crack of bone. Then Hoel swiveled around and rocked the second in the jaw with his elbow. A howl of pain came from the broken-footed man. The second was already sprawled on the street. The third managed to draw a dagger before Hoel attacked him. The two pummeled each other, but Hoel quickly seized the man's wrist and flipped him onto his back. He coughed in pain as he tried to rise again, only to be punched in the nose by Hoel's fist. A spume of blood came up from his broken nose, and then he fell slack to the ground.

Hoel motioned for her to come to him.

She heard the sound of boots behind her and hastened away. The sound of a blade clearing a scabbard followed her.

Hoel drew the gladius instead of Firebos.

Finally turning around, Eilean saw the caped man holding his weapon protectively as he studied the three injured and writhing men in the street.

"What are you doing, Kishion?" he asked Hoel with a distrusting look. "Aren't we on the same side?"

"They were in my way," Hoel answered grimly.

The other man lowered his blade, then sheathed it. He looked worried that Hoel was going to kill him.

"Does the queen know you're here?" the man asked.

"I don't serve the queen," Hoel said.

A ripple from the Medium came. Eilean thought to Hoel, *Tell him you serve me.*

Hoel pointed the gladius at him, even though they were too far apart for him to use it.

"I serve the lady," Hoel said, nodding to her. "On your way."

The man looked troubled, but he backed off. And when more soldiers hurried toward them from down the alley, the man with the brooch waved them off too.

"Let them go," he said.

He looked at Eilean, and she could sense his troubled thoughts. He was worried. Very worried. He believed that Hoel was a trained murderer. One who had been conquered by an even stronger magic than a kystrel.

Thoughts become things. And there is one thought, above all, that comes to every man or woman at one time or another. I've seen the thought come to the very young, as young as six. I've seen it strike the aged, lying crippled in their beds, for the first time in their lives. The thought is this. Will anything I say or do endure after I am gone? Even the wisest of the ancient kings realized that all is vanity. Time erodes everything—wars, songs, speeches, even prayers. We leave no mark that truly lasts.

Still, every person wants to endure, to be remembered for something. The boy-king Andrew was no different. He had the throne of Tintagel. When he was nearly eighteen, he asked the question many have uttered before him. He wanted to leave a legacy that would prevail, and so he asked for my counsel on whom he should marry to achieve such ends.

I told him what I have told others before him. There are many wealthy, prosperous lasses he could marry who would bring him certain advantages. But to address his fear of eventual extinction, I said this: It will be no greater miracle that brings us into another world to live forever with our dearest friends than that which has brought us into this one to live a lifetime with them.

I asked the young king if there was a girl who was already his dearest friend. The king looked confused and said yes, it was the scullion girl Elle from Farfog Castle who was apprenticing to be a Wizr. But surely I did not mean her. Surely a scullion could never become a queen.

I looked at him, knowing his conflicted feelings, and answered with a shrug, "It seems to me that you've already made up your mind on what will or won't do."

That was the first time I sensed his pride, quivering and throbbing, disguised by layers of self-deception. A scullion become a queen? But did not an assistant pig keeper become a king?

—Myrddin, Wizr of Tintagel

CHAPTER FOUR

Tintagel Castle, Kingdom of Leoneyis
Sixth Year of the Reign of King Andrew Ursus

The view of Tintagel Castle was a sight of which Andrew never tired. The castle occupied a spit of land battered relentlessly by the waves crashing down below. Having spent his childhood at Farfog Castle, he'd always loved the smell of the sea and been soothed by the noise of the surf. A long narrow bridge connected his castle to the cliff shores of Leoneyis. He rode his hunting horse, Pygmalion, over that bridge while listening to the bantering of the knights who followed him.

When they arrived, the dead boar they'd killed and trussed up would be carried from the back of Andrew's horse. He still felt a little pain where a tusk had pierced his side when the beast had turned and charged him. But the raven scabbard was healing the wound. None of the knights knew the secret of the scabbard. To them, it was a miraculous sign of Andrew's blessed kingship that he healed so quickly from any wound, wounds which would have crippled or destroyed lesser men.

The early sunlight shone from a thousand reflections on the enormous stained-glass windows decorating the facade of the castle. After the years of unrest following Andrew's birth and disappearance, the castle had come to ruin, but Andrew had restored it to the glory it had enjoyed during the early reign of his father, Ulric, the first high king of Leoneyis. A castle his father had taken from its previous owner, the late husband of its queen. It shone like a beacon, drawing men of Virtus from every kingdom to come and claim fellowship at the Ring Table. The sordid past had been forgotten at last.

As they crossed the bridge, the trumpets blasted from the castle parapets to announce their return. He could imagine the welcome they were about to receive. They'd been due back the day before, but his injury had forced them to camp in the woods that night, so he was expecting some relieved and worried looks. Andrew didn't feel like he'd been in any real danger, though. Not with Firebos to wield and its scabbard to protect him, not to mention an armed escort of knights who were all better swordsmen than him. He didn't begrudge them their valor or their skill. As Myrddin was fond of saying, Andrew's success didn't come from being the best. Instead, it could be attributed to, as the Wizr put it, his ability to recognize and choose others whose understanding and experience exceeded his own.

A young man of nearly eighteen could hardly be expected to know better than a Wizr who had lived for generations due to some arcane magic in a piece of fruit that no one else knew where to find.

"A hearty breakfast will do us well," said Sir Moriaen. "I think I can smell it cooking from here."

"That's last night's dinner," quipped Sir Owain. "It's old and stale by now."

Andrew smiled at the jest. Sir Peredur, who rode in sync with the king, didn't break a smile at all. He was a serious young man, the nearest to the king in age, whereas the other knights of the Ring Table were more seasoned in war. But although many men had attempted to win the Siege Perilous, none had bested the young upstart. Even King Modredus of Occitania had ridden to Leoneyis to join the Ring Table, demanding the coveted seat in exchange for his obedience and fealty. Although the man had the skill to warrant it, he lacked any of the other qualities Andrew sought in his knights, and Myrddin had advised against it, saying Modredus's ambition eclipsed that of any of the knights who served Andrew, and his heart's desire—unspoken but heard by Myrddin nonetheless—was to claim Andrew's throne for himself.

So Andrew had sent him away without the seat and then given it to Peredur, who'd proven himself worthy of it. The young knight had also become a good friend and trusted confidant, someone Andrew felt he could rely on.

The gate of the castle was wrenched open, and cheers of welcome greeted the party. The grooms immediately rushed up to take the knights' horses as they dismounted. Andrew caught sight of Elle by the palace door, arms folded crossly. He waved at her, pleased to see that she'd been worried about him.

"Come, Peredur, let's brave her wrath together."

"As you will, my lord."

Having dismounted, Andrew instructed that he wanted the boar cooked and carved up for dinner in the great hall, where their successful hunt would be celebrated with wine and music. Then he clapped Peredur on the back, and the two walked up to the door where Elle waited with a scolding frown.

"Could you not have sent one of the knights to tell us of the delay?" she said with barely controlled anger. "We had guards stationed all night to keep watch for you." Her brow furrowed. "I was *worried*, Andrew. That was thoughtless of you."

"He was injured by the boar we hunted," Peredur said.

Elle's eyes widened with surprise. "Was it grievous? I see you're not limping."

"I'm well; it was just a scratch." Andrew waved off her concern, but secretly he relished it. No one had mothered him as a child, so he'd always craved female attention.

"My lord is being modest," Peredur corrected. He was never one to conceal or embellish. "The boar gored him, flung him apace, then came at him again before any of us could intervene. It was a worry to us all."

Elle touched Andrew's arm worriedly. "But you look hale!"

"I'm fine!" he protested. "The night was miserable, but I felt as hale as a hare this morning. Sorry we were delayed, but it wasn't out of thoughtlessness."

She closed her eyes in relief and then gripped him by the tunic and gave him a little shove, her mouth quirking into a frown. "You are too reckless!"

The door opened, and Sir Queux came rushing out. "I heard the trumpets, but I was at the far side of the castle. Forgive me!" he said, panting. "You're home! All is well. We were very worried about you."

"A boar nearly ripped his innards out," Elle said.

Sir Queux's eyes widened with shock. "That's terrible! I'll call for a—"

"I'm well, nothing to fear," Andrew said and started ahead into the castle, Peredur on one side, Elle on the other. Sir Queux came quickly after them.

"Shall I fetch the castle midwife? That wound should be examined," Sir Queux insisted.

"'Tis a wound, not a babe," Andrew laughed. "And it troubles me not."

"Still, my lord, we should be cautious. I know a knight who suffered naught but a graze in a tournament and ended up losing his arm to rot."

"That's horrible," Elle said worriedly.

Andrew continued walking. The palace servants were bowing and greeting him as he passed. Instead of going to the great hall, which he knew would be full of well-wishers, he took the nearest stairs up to the second level and proceeded to the solar. After all these years at Tintagel, he still felt like a stranger there at times. Sometimes, in the darkest hours of night, he worried that his mother had somehow survived her accident and was still alive and well, creeping around the castle with a cup of poison she'd compel him to drink. Myrddin had said that the scabbard would prevent him from bleeding to death. But it could not save him from all forms of peril.

When they arrived at the solar, his friend and mentor Myrddin was already inside, enjoying a dish of vegetables and onions in a trencher bowl. The man glanced his way, then went back to eating.

"Did I worry you too, Myrddin? I've returned."

"Were you gone, lad? I hardly noticed." The Wizr gave him a teasing smile.

Andrew threw himself down onto a cushioned bench. Elle sidled up next to him, her hand touching his chest.

"Let me see the wound," she asked in a low, coaxing voice.

Sir Queux huffed with impatience. "My lord, I beg you, do not encourage her being so *familiar* with you."

Elle flashed him an angry look. "I'm surprised you're not more worried about him, Sir Queux."

"I offered to send for the midwife, if you'll remember!"

Andrew held up his hand. "There's no need, truly." He placed his hand on Elle's and gave her an encouraging pat. "I'm well, truly. And the day is young still. What business is in order this morning, Master Seneschal?"

"So you don't want to see the midwife?" Sir Queux pressed.

"No! None of that. What business?"

"The business of yesternight, for starters," he said. As master seneschal, he controlled the household, which included deciding which visitors could have an audience with the king. He acted for Andrew when he was gone and handled a multitude of details.

Andrew sighed. "I expected such. And what were we supposed to do last night that I missed?"

Elle picked a few bits of dried grass from his dirty tunic and flicked them away. She was wearing that perfume again. The one that smelled of honeysuckle. He'd told her once that he fancied it, and she'd used it ever since. She was sitting very close to him, and the smell was distracting.

"Did you hear me, my lord?" asked Sir Queux impatiently.

Indeed, he had not. "I'm sorry. Once more?"

Andrew noticed a little smile on Elle's mouth. He started staring at her lips again, then realized that doing so would not aid his concentration. He sat up more, breaking the connection of closeness.

"I said that you need to make a decision about who to begin courting, my lord. You need to marry. Especially if you continue to risk your life galivanting—"

"It was a *hunt*, Sir Queux," Andrew interrupted. "You were the one who taught me how to do it!"

"What I'm trying to say, my lord, is that you need to begin *hunting* for a queen."

He felt Elle brush something from the hair above his ear. It tickled just a little. "There are limited options at present, Sir Queux. Remind me again?"

Sir Queux sighed. "We've been over this how many times?"

"Humor me. If you would."

"King Lamorcan of Legault has an older daughter—"

"The shrew?"

Sir Queux breathed out slowly. "Who is *eligible* but has been known to terrorize suitors. Her name is Kathryn."

"I think not," Andrew replied. "And the Legaultans believe in some rubbish about the Aos Sí, do they not, Myrddin?"

"I've traveled among their people," Myrddin answered. "It is a corruption of the tales of the Essaios. They are stubborn in their beliefs, but I think they may be persuaded over time. Your influence in their court would aid that understanding."

"It's a kingdom always full of infighting, and they're always raiding our western shores. I think I'll send Sir Owain to tame them. He can marry her."

Sir Queux coughed into his fist. "Moving on. King Modredus of Occitania has a sister, Morwenna, who is of age. Their kingdom is very powerful, and if you make a marriage alliance with them, it might convince him to overlook your refusal to grant him the Siege Perilous."

Andrew rubbed his forehead, impatient for the conversation to be over. "Morwenna is a beauty, I've heard, but they say she has the same nasty temperament as her brother. She'd probably kill me in my sleep. No, that won't do at all. What of Brythonica?"

"King Greu is getting old and has no heir. It's quite likely Modredus will seize power over Brythonica when he dies. He would be a powerful ally . . . or a powerful enemy."

"He's fifty, not a hundred," Andrew reminded him. "He could live another twenty years."

Sir Queux shrugged. "Possibly. Next is Ceredigion. Sir Owain is from there and has a cousin he wishes you to meet."

"He's mentioned her many times. I'm not interested. Ceredigion is another land that needs taming. I'm happy to let Owain do it. He is clever enough to outsmart those feuding warlords."

Owain's prowess in war and strategy had made him a trusted member of Andrew's court. But the Ceredigic people were troublesome and defiant, and wedding one of their noble daughters might prove to be more bother than it was worth. While he trusted Owain's judgment in war, matters of the heart were entirely different.

Elle started grazing her fingers along the edge of his neck. It sent a shiver through him.

"The last is Atabyrion. King Llewellyn Fawr has two daughters, no sons."

Andrew remembered that. The daughters were several years apart in age.

"King Fawr was my father's ally," Andrew said.

"Yes, and Atabyrion was the first to bend the knee in fealty when you were proclaimed Ulric's heir. It would be wise, my lord, to consider that loyalty."

"What were their names? The daughters."

"Genoivre is the elder. Genevieve the younger."

"How old are they? If I recall, both are very young."

Sir Queux frowned and began pacing. "Sixteen and thirteen."

Andrew grimaced. "The younger is prettier, you said once. But that's very young."

Sir Queux stepped closer. "It is not unheard of, my lord, for matches to be made very young. An alliance with Atabyrion has many advantages. Think on *that*."

Andrew rubbed his lips. He was only twelve when he'd begun to fancy Elle. She and Sir Queux—and Myrddin of course—had known him during his humble days when he smelled like pig filth all day long. He valued their long years together. It helped keep him humble.

"Sir Peredur?" Andrew asked. He was always silent as a stone during such exchanges.

"Yes, my lord?"

"Haven't you been to Atabyrion?"

"Once, my lord."

"Have you met King Fawr?"

"I have, my lord. Briefly."

Andrew considered it. "I would like you to go there on my behalf. Make no promises. Tell me about the daughters, both of them, when you return."

"My lord, I thought perhaps that *I* might go as your envoy," Sir Queux said, his eyes suddenly intense. "I am your master seneschal."

"I need you here, Queux. I trust Peredur. We're practically brothers." He looked at the knight. "See what you can learn about them both. I'm in no mood to be hasty in this."

"As you command, my lord," Peredur said. Something stirred in his gray eyes, there and then gone before Andrew could identify it. But he trusted Sir Peredur implicitly. He was as faithful as they came. Solid, dependable. Or, as Myrddin liked to say, *diligent.*

"I'm hungry, Queux." He put his hand on Elle's and found it surprisingly cold. Looking at her, he said, "Have something brought up for us to eat from the kitchen?"

He knew his words had upset her, and truly, they upset him too. He esteemed her. He found her beautiful. He wished things were different. But there was nothing for it—he was a king, and she was a scullion. They both knew there could be nothing between them now.

"I'll return shortly," Sir Queux said.

Elle nodded and rose from the couch and proceeded to walk away so quickly she beat Sir Queux through the door. Sir Peredur bowed and then exited as well.

That left Andrew alone with Myrddin.

"Can I ask your advice?" he said to his old mentor.

He chose to marry the younger daughter of the King of Atabyrion. To the world it was a sensible choice. A perfect match of interest and compatibility. Genevieve was genial, wise, and totally devoted to the King of Leoneyis. But his heart was divided. After four years of courtly wooing, the Princess of Atabyrion came to Tintagel, escorted by the redoubtable Sir Peredur, who'd often visited the court at Edonburick to press his master's cause.

It was the eve before the wedding when King Andrew's friend, confidante, and true love left Tintagel. The girl, my protégé, refused entreaties and forsook his side to return to the kingdom of her birth, Brythonica. She visited the elderly king and quickly won a place as the Wizr of his court.

Not long after, she won another place—and a crown of her own.

—Myrddin, Wizr of Tintagel

CHAPTER FIVE

Privus Inn

The inn Hoel had chosen for them in Ploemeur was less rowdy than the others on the road leading south to the neighboring kingdom of Occitania. They'd passed several farmsteads to get there, each with row after row of berry bushes tended by the local farmers. They'd discussed bedding down in one of the fields shortly, but then they'd passed some brush and come upon the Privus Inn. Prior to entering, Eilean had transformed them to look like Celyn and Stright to make it more difficult for anyone attempting to find them.

The inn was quiet, the dinner an amazing roast venison with herbs and golden-crusted potatoes, along with an assortment of fresh berries picked from the fields. They ate together at a small table, where Hoel could keep an eye on the door, and they spoke in low voices so that their conversation could not be overheard. There were only three other patrons in the place, all of whom were frequent travelers accustomed to staying there on their journeys. Eilean could sense as much from their idle thoughts. She and Hoel were the only strangers.

"Tell me what you know about the knight who arrived today," Hoel asked, his tone urgent. "You mentioned during our walk here that you recognized his name from Maderos's tome."

"Sir Peredur espoused all the attributes of Virtus, the order which the knights of the Ring Table had to follow."

"And this table is significant somehow?"

"Yes, it's a symbol of King Andrew's authority. A knight who has a seat at that table can represent the king. All positions are equal, save one."

"The Siege Perilous. I remember." He tilted his head, studying her. "How long has Maderos been gone? Much could have changed since he left."

"True. We had many conversations when I served in the castle, but he never mentioned how long he'd been in our world, only who'd banished him. And the tome was stolen from me before I got to that point in the story."

"Tell me what you know of her. The woman who betrayed him."

"It was a girl who started as a scullion somewhere here in Brythonica. She was present when the sword was found. When Andrew became high king, he brought her with him to Tintagel. Although they loved each other, he felt it would be unsuitable to marry her because of her low birth. He chose one of the daughters of the King of Atabyrion instead, and the scullion girl married the ruler of Brythonica. She is Queen Essylt. She was not married for very long, as I understand it, before her husband died and she became the ruler in his stead."

"Was he murdered?"

"No. I don't think so. His health had already been a challenge."

"He could have been poisoned."

Eilean thought longer. "That's true. I didn't think of that."

He held up his hands. "I'm not saying he was. It's just how I think. Especially after learning that Kariss has been poisoning my father. It makes sense."

"You're right. We should consider all possibilities." She bit her lower lip.

"So the high king, Andrew, rules Leoneyis, if I understand things," Hoel says, "but other kings pay tribute to him? Like the holy emperor and the maston order?"

"Correct. It is similar to the tithes paid to Avinion."

"But there is no maston order here," Hoel pointed out. "Nothing but the knights. And the hetaera have a distinct presence. Kariss is one, and she serves the Queen of Brythonica. Perhaps they used the mirror gate to flee persecution and established the order in secret here. We've seen the symbol throughout Brythonica." He tapped his finger on the table. "That means Ereshkigal may be here. She could be hiding in the guise of the Queen of Brythonica. And if that is true, we should be *very* cautious in how we approach her." He leaned back in his chair. "I'm glad we didn't go straight there."

Eilean's stomach wriggled with doubt and concern. "We both wear the chaen. We're protected from her, surely."

"It only serves as protection if we have it on. Mine was stripped away from me, remember." His look darkened with the memory, and she put a comforting hand on his wrist.

"You're right. We should be careful," Eilean said, then paused. "Kariss implied that she's serving another interest."

"Maybe the hetaera are preparing to come back to power in our world?"

"That makes sense, Hoel. When I visited your father, we talked about seeking help from King Andrew."

"So you said. But I still don't agree with it."

"I know. Maybe I was thinking about it the wrong way. Maybe this world is already sending help to overthrow the maston order in our world."

He leaned back in his chair and rubbed his mouth. "The Queen of Brythonica seems the most likely."

"Indeed. She has the tome, but she'll need help translating it."

"She needs *you*. Or Maderos."

That made the wriggling feelings in Eilean's stomach even worse. "I don't know why she betrayed him after she became a queen."

"It seems ungrateful, by Cheshu. He helped her rise far above her station."

Another thought came to her. It made her shake her head.

"What?" Hoel asked.

"Before the tome was stolen, I stayed up all night reading it. I couldn't sleep. Reading about the rise of King Andrew's power in Leoneyis fascinated me. But there are also references in the tome to certain trees. Ones that can give and strip someone of immortality."

Hoel leaned forward again, his eyes showing his sudden interest. She sensed the question in his mind. *Could Maderos be made mortal again?*

"Yes, and I'm convinced the Queen of Brythonica wants the tome to find where those trees are. So she can become immortal herself."

The innkeeper approached their table with a plaintive look. "The others are heading off to bed now, my friends. I'll be locking the door soon. Is there anything else you require? Some wine for your room?"

Hoel looked at Eilean, who shook her head.

"No. That won't be necessary. Can we stay in the common room longer?"

"Of course! It's not usual for other travelers to arrive this late." He stifled a yawn. "Pardon me. We're not used to late company here. You can stay here as long as you like, but I'll be heading to bed myself shortly."

Eilean could see it was well after dark outside. Other than the fire in the hearth, there weren't any candles, which might have been considered a luxurious expense.

"Thank you," she told him.

He smiled, and she sensed from his thought a pleasant weariness. He was trying to be hospitable. There were no ulterior motives.

As he walked away, Hoel rubbed his arm. "He said there's a tub in the kitchen behind a screen for patrons in need of one. The sand we slept in last night has been chafing me all day. Would you like a bath as well?"

As a wretched, she was used to bathing in kitchens. Only the nobility could afford private baths. Still, the thought of seeing Hoel in the tub made her cheeks flush. It brought back memories of him stripping off his shirt after they'd found his chaen.

"It's been a while since either of us have bathed," she said slowly.

"You go first," he said. "I'll keep watch so no one disturbs you."

"Thank you," she said. She was exhausted. They'd left the mirror gate in day and arrived in darkness, and her body still felt strange because of the sudden shift from day to night.

They waited until the innkeeper locked the door and the rest of the patrons had left.

***

Eilean brushed her fingers through her damp hair. She wore the wretched kirtle that she kept in her travel pack. She'd scrubbed away dirt stains from her gown and hung it from a peg on the wall to dry out during the night. The room had no hearth or brazier. It certainly had no Leerings. There was a single bed with a lumpy straw mat, which she sat on while untangling her hair. After the tangles were out, she quickly braided it.

There were no candles in the room, but moonlight came in from the small, square window. She could summon light with magic, of course, but that would attract unnecessary attention. Hoel had already checked the latch to make sure the window was secure. It was big enough, he said, for them to escape from if needed. That had made her smile. He was always searching for ways to escape.

A light knock sounded on the door.

She rose, padding barefoot to it.

"It's me," Hoel whispered.

She hadn't heard his steps down the hall, but that didn't surprise her—he was very light of foot. She drew the latch and opened it. He entered, carrying his pack. The longsword and bow had already been stowed in their room for her to watch over, but he had kept a dagger and gladius with him. His hair was damp, and she could smell the soap he'd used.

He closed the door and then slid the latch in place.

They were alone together, in a dark room, far, far away from their own world. It was different from sleeping together on a beach with the surf crashing nearby. The idea of being alone with him, in such an intimate way, both troubled and thrilled her.

He set his things down by the door, then went to the window to gaze through the glass. Staring at his profile, she felt as if the starlings from Muirwood were swarming inside her chest. Although she'd had feelings for Aisic, or thought she did, it had never been like this. It had never been such a sweet yearning.

"Get some rest," he whispered from the window. "I'll keep watch until midnight."

She sat down at the edge of the bed. "We could share it," she suggested, hoping that she could fall asleep cushing with him.

After she made the suggestion, she sensed a struggle in his thoughts. He looked in her direction, taking in the sight of her in her kirtle in the moonlight. His feelings were roiling within him. He wanted to kiss her again. The thought was one he was failing to suppress.

"We'd better not," he said, turning away to the window again.

"Why not?" she said, desiring it even more. "I trust you, Hoel."

He let out a desperate sigh, then laughed. "Perhaps you shouldn't. As lovely as it sounds to cush with you, it would be too much of a temptation for any man to bear."

"We did it in the dungeon at the abbey," she said, her longing intensifying.

"A slightly different circumstance," he said. "You'd been injured. I know myself . . . and my feelings. I respect you too much to risk a transgression."

The feelings of excitement shriveled with disappointment, but his steadfastness only made her admire him more.

She lay on the bed, the straw crunching beneath her. It wasn't very comfortable. She'd already removed her travel blanket and pulled it over her, facing the room and him.

Hoel retreated from the window and then sat down, his back against the door, an arm draped over one of his knees.

"Have you cushed with anyone else?" she whispered in the stillness. There were no other sounds coming from the inn. She could see the angles of his face in the dim light as he stared down at the floor.

"Do you really want me to answer that?"

That made her worry but even more determined to know. "Did you?"

"Yes," he whispered.

"Did you love her?"

"At sixteen, I did believe it was love."

"Who was she?"

He chuckled. "Why do you ask that, Eilean?"

"I know your thoughts, Hoel. I want to know your heart."

He sighed. "Her name was Rhiannon."

Eilean sat up. "The laundry girl at Muirwood?"

"No! Not her. It's a popular name in Pry-Ree."

"Was she a wretched?"

"A nobleman's daughter. We were learners together in the same year."

"Was this at Tintern?" she asked, feeling more than a little jealous.

"Aye," he said. "You were just a little waif in the kitchen back then, I should think. I don't even remember you being there."

"And you cushed with her?"

"Aye," he said, his voice thoughtful. "And kissed her. Like that man you were with, in the Bearden Muir."

Eilean felt her cheeks tingle. "I remember that day. How you found us."

"I was a little jealous, Eilean. I didn't think he would be satisfied with just a little cushing."

"No . . . he wasn't," Eilean confessed. "And from what you said earlier, you wouldn't be either."

Hoel chuckled in the dark. "It isn't easy knowing where to draw the line once your heart and your brains get muddled. Back then, I knew I had a choice to make. If I remained in Pry-Ree, I would end up serving my uncle, the king. And it was possible that someday I might be called upon to rule." He paused, and the stillness thickened. "I gave up that life willingly. And I confessed to Rhiannon that I was going away to study at other abbeys. I knew if I stayed at Tintern, I'd lose my conviction to walk away from the royal life. It hurt us both." He sighed again. She could sense the regret in his mind, but she wasn't sure what had inspired it—leaving the girl or walking away from his future role in the kingdom. "But my visions started after I chose the Medium. I knew she'd marry another and I would join the Apocrisarius."

Eilean felt her heart throb for him. "Did she marry?"

"My best friend."

That must have hurt him a great deal. She could hear the pain in his voice and discern it in his thoughts. "You lost two people with that decision."

"It was worth it, though." He turned and looked at her. "I have someone better now."

She wanted to cush with him even more for saying that kindness. She wanted to make him forget Rhiannon altogether.

Instead, she said softly, "Good night, Hoel."

"Good night, fair one," he whispered. "I'll wake you when it's your turn." He kissed his fingers and held them out to her, as if the kiss would flutter over and land on her cheek.

If a gelding is brought into a fold of three mares, they will bite and mar the newcomer to make him feel his rank is below that of the pigs in the sty. People are the same way. Names and titles are important in the ranks of man, but a force even more powerful than these is reputation. Reputation forges and supports the standing between individuals. Especially kings. Modredus of Occitania is the type who takes every advantage to bite another.

Queen Genevieve is a different sort, and she soon became known for her compassion, wisdom, and complete devotion. But the king and queen's marriage produced no heir. After four years, the whispers began at court. The king honored his vow, but his desire to create a legacy began to torment his soul. Had he made the wrong decision in his choice of wife? There is no whisper so insidious as that of self-doubt.

Some in Occitania began to whisper that the queen was barren because she, too, loved another. That her heart had been won by the king's champion, Sir Peredur. Gossip is an evil thing. It is the destroyer of reputations. It is a tool men use to cut one another. Words may not have wings, but they can fly a thousand leagues. Especially on horses paid with Occitanian gold.

—Myrddin, Wizr of Tintagel

CHAPTER SIX

The Grove

Eilean didn't remember falling asleep, but she was awakened by Hoel gently shaking her shoulder. The inn was dark and quiet as ashes, the window open slightly, letting in a refreshing breeze. The moon was no longer shining brightly. She rubbed her eyes with the backs of her hands and sat up.

"Is it my turn?" she whispered.

"Yes. I could use a little sleep."

"Of course." She sat up on the crinkly mattress, stretched, and then stood and stretched again. A yawn came, but she stifled it as she rose and walked away from the bed.

Hoel lay down on the mattress, turning so his back was to her, and unsheathed the gladius and set it down next to him. She walked in a few circles, trying to clear the fog from her mind, and then stood by the window to feel the breeze on her face.

Within moments, Hoel's breathing turned slow and steady in a way that suggested sleep. It was a comforting sound, one that reassured her she wasn't alone. She ran her hand along the windowsill, feeling the smooth wood against her fingertips, and her thoughts drifted to Celyn. Had her friend and the learners she'd traveled with reached Aldermaston Utheros and Prince Derik yet? Had the different Aldermastons begun to gather for the conclave that would hopefully strip the corrupt High Seer of her position? Those events seemed so far away from them now. But still she worried about her friends. Had Celyn been reunited with Stright yet? She hoped all was well.

She turned her head and looked at Hoel asleep on the bed. He'd turned over, facing her, eyes shut and breathing shallow. The High Seer had made him the head of the Apocrisarius. Would she strip Hoel of his title if the Aldermastons didn't succeed in having her removed? He'd sacrificed his chance of being a prince of Pry-Ree in order to follow his father into serving the maston order. She hated the thought that he might lose that too.

She moved away from the window and then followed Hoel's example by sitting with her back against the door. Her hair was still in a braid, and she toyed with it, gazing periodically over at Hoel. His expression was peaceful, not troubled by dreams. She noticed some hair falling over his face and longed to smooth it away. His eyelashes, even in the moonlight, were distinguishable and cast little shadows against his cheeks. Everything about him had become so dear to her, so very dear. She was grateful that he had finally chosen to help her, but that wasn't all her heart felt. Her feelings ran as deep as a river. As much as she'd wanted to cush with him before falling asleep, she realized that such intimacy would have caused great temptation between them.

She wrapped her arms around her knees and lay her head on her forearm, listening to the sound of his breathing. Thinking of this honorable man she was falling in love with—and how very different he was from the boy she'd once doted on.

An owl flew by the window, its wings rustling. It must have landed on the roof. Then, to her surprise, she heard a familiar snickering sound.

She jumped up from the floor and then walked to the window. Was it the púca? Could it have followed them into the mirror gate? She hadn't seen it since it had counterfeited as a seagull.

Looking out the window, she saw it hanging upside down from the roofline, suspended by its big claws. It snickered again.

"Púca, what are you doing here?" she whispered. "Is it really you?"

It snickered again and fanned its bat-like wings. The púca had a fox-like face and snout, with little sharp teeth that gave it the appearance of grinning. They were mischievous spirit creatures, known for assisting druids in their aims. This one had been Maderos's companion, and he'd sent it to assist her.

It scrabbled down the wall, and Eilean pulled open the window so it could land on the sill. She glanced over at Hoel, who was still in a deep sleep.

The creature wagged its head at her in a familiar manner, presenting its furry pelt for her to touch. She knew if she touched its fur, its magic would seize her and she'd be swept away into the darkness.

"Are we in danger, Púca?" she asked it.

Its wings rustled, and it scurried to one side, picking up a dead bug from the windowsill and popping it into its mouth. That wasn't a sign of urgency.

Go.

She felt the whisper of the Medium more than heard it. Without hesitation, she reached out to pet the creature. Magic fused her hand to the púca's pelt, and suddenly it grew in size—or she shrank—and the creature leaped from the window into the sky, hurtling up toward the stars with Eilean on its back. She worried that Hoel would awaken and worry about her, or that he might be attacked while asleep, but surely the Medium wouldn't have asked her to leave if that were so. She still felt she'd done the right thing in listening.

The spirit creature swerved and banked sharply, and Eilean gasped, having forgotten how much the fox-bat loved to torment those who were trapped on its back. They were quickly outside the boundaries of Ploemeur, soaring over fields of berry bushes and then a deep woodland. Wind rushed against her face, making her shiver since she wore little else than her kirtle, but the fur was warm enough, and it wasn't the same as flying in the snow-capped mountains near Cruix Abbey.

The moon had already set, so the night was especially dark, and the whorl of stars overhead held an unfamiliar pattern.

With a burst of speed, the púca launched down into the trees, where the smell of cedar and another kind of bark she didn't recognize filled her nose and a swarm of branches tried to claw at them. She cried out in worry, but the púca was sure and never collided with a single branch. Then it pitched sharply, and they were on the ground, the spell on her removed. They'd ended in a small grove of trees near a stand of massive boulders. A trickle of water from a brook could be heard, but there wasn't enough light to see by.

The púca scrabbled up onto the boulders and snickered at her.

"Why did you bring me here?" she asked, walking around slowly, trying to understand the strange woods. She felt the presence of the Medium, though, much as she had when she'd ventured into the wilds of the Bearden Muir to seek a connection with it—and its guidance about Maderos.

It was then she noticed it. The trees were mostly pine and cedar, but she saw the silhouette of an oak tree near the mass of boulders. Her instincts responded to the shape of the branches, which were more crooked and splayed than the straight limbs of the pine trees. And there, in the shadows, she thought she saw lumps of mistletoe.

Eilean approached the tree and then knelt before it, closing her eyes. "Did you summon me here?"

The trickling sound of the brook was nearby. And then, in the quiet, she heard the faint crack of a twig. Then another.

"I come with a message from the Lady of the Fountain," said a woman's voice. "Welcome, wayfarer. Welcome, blessed. Welcome to the grove."

"Thank you," Eilean answered. "Do you know the Dryads from the Bearden Muir?"

"They are sisters to us," came the answer. "Although we cannot depart this world, we can meet one another in Mirrowen. I have a message for you."

"I am grateful," Eilean said.

"You will not be glad once you've heard it, mortal. A Blight is coming to this world. The King of Leoneyis has turned from the Knowing. He persecutes light and truth."

Eilean's heart clenched with fear. "That is dreadful news." It confirmed what the Medium had bidden her to say earlier. Disappointment put a bitter taste in her mouth. She'd still hoped she might have gotten it wrong—that the high king could be the answer to their problems.

"The Blight will destroy his kingdom. Leoneyis will be drowned in a flood."

Her fear quickly turned to dread. She had but a fortnight to retrieve the tome and fulfill whatever other purposes the Medium had for her here. "When will this happen?"

"Upon the king's death. He accepted a challenge from the King of Occitania, entering a magical game with deadly consequences. The fate of his kingdom is now controlled by that magic. If he dies without a true heir in this world, not only does he forfeit his kingdom, but he forfeits the lives of multitudes."

"And does he not have an heir?" Eilean pressed.

"He is blinded to the truth of things. You must warn him. The fate of many hangs on it."

"Must *I*?" she asked with confusion. She had the sudden urge to open her eyes, to look at the Dryad full in the face, but she knew her memories would be torn away from her if she did so. She would remember neither the warning nor the task that had been given to her. There was a part of her that wanted to flee from such a duty.

"That is the message from the Fountain. Warn Andrew of the price he and his people will pay if he does not alter his course."

"Will he heed me?" Eilean asked worriedly.

"His choice is his own to make. Pride and stubbornness are twin brothers. When he accepted the game and its deadly consequences, he believed he would prevail. Now he has convinced himself the covenant he made with the magic will not be binding. Warn him. That is all you can do. This is his final chance before destruction comes."

Eilean's heart clenched painfully. "I am . . ." She struggled to breathe, to speak the words.

I am a wretched. I am no one.

The thoughts surprised her. She'd come so far in so many ways, yet in her heart she still doubted that the insignificant girl she'd been would be called upon for such an important role.

"You are precious," said the Dryad tenderly. "And this burden will also fall on others in your posterity. You are the first of *many*."

Eilean swallowed, trying to master her emotions. "I will go because I promised to obey the Knowing. But I dread this task."

"So it must be. Farewell, wayfarer. Farewell, sister. Touch not the bowl."

Eilean waited, eyes clenched closed, for several moments, listening to the snick of breaking twigs and then silence. After a while, she heard the chirp of birds. When she opened her eyes, it was nearly dawn. A little mist coiled above the waters of the brook, which came from beneath the boulders lurched together in a heap. The oak tree looked radiant. The sun hadn't risen yet, but the sky was brightening, and she could see herself, the matted twigs, and a dense carpet of desiccated leaves. And then she saw a flat slab of rock nearby and a silver bowl with ancient carvings on it chained to the rock. Instantly, she understood that it was the Gradalis, one of the lost treasures from the Essaios.

Touch not the bowl.

She had no idea what would happen if she did. But she rose, brushed the debris from her skirts, and walked around in the circle, feeling the power of the Medium grow stronger and stronger.

A warning in her heart told her it was time to go. The púca snickered and clambered down from the rocks toward her.

"Who are you?" said a man's deep voice. She saw a man in armor appear from behind the oak tree. He marched toward her menacingly.

"Kozkah gheb-ool," she said, invoking her magic to ward him away.

She felt the ripple of power, but the knight was not blown back. He was still coming.

Eilean's heart spasmed in terror. The púca flew from the rocks and flapped its wings in front of the knight. She touched its back, and the two of them soared up through the trees, the sound of a blade clearing its scabbard ringing through the still air below them.

It is possible for a scullion to become a queen. I have seen it. It did not hurt that she was fair of face. An eager learner, she sought me out to instill in her the wisdom of the Sefer Yetzirah. Her heart was in the right place at first. But when she left Tintagel, her pride bruised by King Andrew's, she harnessed the power of her thoughts to make herself his equal.

The King of Brythonica gladly accepted her service. He gladly accepted her praise. Then he gladly accepted her counsel, which included, in the end, marrying her. Since he was a far older man, she knew that she would outlive him. But even she was surprised by how soon he died. Some whispered that a poisoner of Pisan had been hired to that end. She could not deceive me, for I knew her thoughts. I knew, beyond doubt, that she had not arranged his death. With a word, she could have stopped her husband from breathing, so what need had she of poison?

—Myrddin, Wizr of Tintagel

CHAPTER SEVEN

False Knight

As the Privus Inn came into view, Eilean wondered if Hoel had awakened while she was gone and was worried about her absence. The púca brought her back to the window, and she climbed over the sill and came into the room. Her heart was still racing from the encounter with the knight. Some magic had shielded him from her ability. She didn't understand it.

Dawn had come much faster than she'd imagined possible, yet she saw Hoel still asleep on the bed, her pack where she'd left it on the floor. She'd noticed a lazy plume of smoke drifting from the kitchen chimney, which meant the innkeeper's cook had already begun the morning meal.

Once in the room, she padded up to the bed and sat down at the edge, gazing down at Hoel's peaceful profile. His tousled hair made her want to comb her fingers through it. As she stared at him, she sensed the lingering effects of a word of power on him. Her brow wrinkled in concern, but then the thought from the Medium came that Hoel had been subdued by a sleeping spell so as not to awaken while she was gone. It had been done to keep him resting.

Gratitude swelled in her heart.

Can I tell him about the Dryad trees? she thought. She wanted to share with him some of what she'd learned, but she knew those secrets would be dangerous if the Apocrisarius discovered them. She wanted to fully trust Hoel, to let him know everything she knew. Nonetheless, she didn't want to go against the Medium's will.

No answer came. At the same time, she had not been warned against telling him, and the Medium had sent them here together, had it not?

With the tips of her fingers, she stroked his cheekbone down to his chin, where his beard and stubble tickled her skin.

Hoel started awake instantly, eyes blinking, his hand grasping for his gladius.

"You won't need that; I'm not going to stab you," she said.

He turned toward her, looking up, and a smile came, interrupted by a yawn. He pressed his fist against his mouth, and she tousled his hair like she'd wanted to.

Sitting up on his elbow, he looked at her face, then over her shoulder. "It's dawn?"

She nodded. "I just returned."

Immediately, his brow crinkled.

"I've been gone," she confirmed. "I wanted to tell you where."

He sat up and turned, reaching for her hand. "Why didn't you wake me?"

"The Medium had a message for me. I needed to go into the woods to receive it." She bit her lip. "I want to tell you, but you need to promise to keep what I say a secret."

She could sense the churn of worry in his thoughts. He was wondering how he'd slept through her departure and return. He chided himself for a lack of vigilance.

She stroked his hair again. "You were supposed to sleep, Hoel. You didn't do anything wrong."

"You were unprotected," he said sternly.

"No. Not really. Well, except at the end when the knight came."

His eyes bulged, and she laughed nervously.

"I made it away safely. Trust me, as I trust you." She rested her hand on his. "Do you promise?"

"I give you my word," he said simply.

That satisfied her. "What I'm going to tell you is druid lore. In another world, the druids fulfill the same role the maston order does in ours. Theirs is a different tradition, but it has the same roots. Does that make sense?"

"What you're saying isn't what I've been taught."

"Yes. After Celyn and I left Muirwood Abbey, we met Stright, who had been living in the Bearden Muir. He explained that the druids came from their world to ours seeking two druids—a man and woman—who'd come to our world. They may have been the First Parents we read about in the tomes. But there is knowledge the tomes *don't* contain." A flash of wariness came from Hoel's thoughts, and she squeezed his hand. "Please, try not to dismiss what I'm saying."

He gave her an awkward smile. "I'm *trying*, Eilean. I've been trained to doubt everyone and everything that doesn't match what I've learned in the order."

"I know it's difficult. Just . . . listen. Don't judge what I say yet. Just hear it."

He sighed and nodded for her to continue.

"There is a race of beings throughout the worlds. They are the protectors of the woods. The Dryads. I know what most Aldermastons say, but they're real. When we went to the gorge to find the tome, we were there to visit a Dryad tree." She shot him an earnest look. "That's how I knew you were there. She told me. She said you'd arrived before us. Hoel, she was the one who healed you after the Fear Liath attacked you. At my request."

For a moment, she felt no thoughts at all coming from him. He just gazed at her intently, listening. Then he nodded. "Go on."

"Maderos had hidden the tome, the sword, a money pouch, and a set of greyfriar robes beneath a stone under the tree. Anyone who looks at a Dryad risks losing their memories. I know I lost some of mine after visiting her. Last night, another spirit creature—a púca—came and took me to a nearby Dryad tree. There was no reason for you to come since it can only carry one person at a time. And the Dryad might not have shown herself if you were there." She stopped talking, watching for his reaction.

She sensed he was confused but not doubtful.

"What did she tell you?" he asked.

Eilean then explained the message she'd been given and the charge to go to Leoneyis to warn King Andrew. As she spoke, she sensed reluctance begin to boil within him. His look became stern and hard-edged. He wasn't convinced.

"Hoel, I know it's hard to believe."

"It's not just that," he said, holding up his palm. "It's incredibly *dangerous*. If what you say is true, and Leoneyis is going to be drowned, we should get the tome from Queen Essylt and flee back to our world."

She sensed his urge to protect her, to keep her safe. Traveling to Tintagel, the seat of King Andrew's court, would be inviting many difficulties.

"But we must go," she insisted. "The Medium warns before destruction happens."

"They don't believe in the Medium here," he reminded her.

"They do believe in it, but they have another name for its inexplicable powers. I learned from Maderos's tome that Ilyas, the great maston from the past, used to visit this world. He named the power *the*

Fountain." She took a deep breath. "Hoel, the Harbinger was a Dryad too."

Hoel gaped when she said that. Again she felt the resistance in his mind, his unwillingness to believe it.

"Please . . . don't reject it out of hand."

"What you're saying is *impossible.*"

She shook her head. "No. It's not. It's just different from what you were taught to believe."

"And Maderos taught you all this? While you were serving in the castle." Disbelief was surging through his mind, and the look on his face was close to outrage.

"Not all of it. I've learned much since I left—quite a bit of it from the tome. Please be patient a little longer." She knew it wouldn't do any good to reveal more until he'd settled down.

He took a few slow breaths, calming himself, but his mind was like a beehive that had just been bludgeoned with a stick. Angry thoughts zipped between them, but he was self-disciplined enough to not vocalize them. The smell of cooking bacon filtered under the door, along with the mumble of voices and noise of footfalls in the corridor.

She cupped his cheek with her palm. "Thank you for listening," she said. Up close, his eyes were more green than brown. The play of colors fascinated her.

"You can imagine how it comes across," he said defensively.

"Yes. I can. I've wondered at it myself. Aldermaston Utheros had his eyes opened to the world of spirit creatures after he was trapped in a thunderstorm. Lightning almost destroyed him, and after the storm, he began to see things that troubled him. Spirit creatures. I've seen them too, Hoel. The evidence is all around us. But the maston order is blind to them."

He rubbed his forehead. "So we're going to Tintagel?"

She nodded. "Yes."

"You'd better change back into your gown. I'm not sure you'd be allowed to visit court dressed as a wretched."

She wrapped her arms around his neck and hugged him. "Thank you. I'm so grateful you're here with me."

The heat from him felt so much stronger now. His hands slowly crept up and embraced her. He was still unsure of himself around her. She sensed his hesitation before he touched her, his arms wrapping around her back.

"I see why you need a protector, Eilean. You always seem to put yourself in dangerous situations."

She laughed, feeling the scratchiness of his cheek against her temple. As she pulled back, she kissed his cheek and then his lips. Being this close to him, she only wanted to be closer, to greedily drink in more of him, so she pulled away, thinking it best to not let things escalate. She stood again.

"Wasn't it *you* who wanted me to become a hunter?"

"I'll go check with the kitchen to see when food will be ready. You can change while I'm gone."

"I won't be long," she promised.

Hoel sheathed his blade, scooted off the bed, and then unbolted the door and left. She bolted it after he was gone, leaning her forehead against the wood, trying hard to hear his footsteps.

She heard nothing.

✳✳✳

For months, Eilean had enjoyed Celyn's help changing into and out of the fancier gowns a lady was supposed to wear. After stowing her kirtle, she checked and made sure her gown was dry and started to put it on, only to realize that the lacings in back, while easy to untie, were difficult to cinch. In fact, she couldn't do it. She'd put on her travel boots, untangled the braid in her hair, secured her travel bag, and then freshened up the bed when she heard a soft tap at the door.

She opened it to Hoel, who had an urgent look on his face.

"There's news this morning," he said.

She waved him in. "Tell me. But first, I can't get the lacings tight. Can you help me?"

He entered, bolted the door, and stepped behind her to examine her frock. With dexterous hands, he pulled the lacings tighter and then quickly knotted them. She sensed the desire in his thoughts as he looked at the expanse of her neck.

"Thank you," she murmured, turning around to face him, and tugged at her hair, which still had kinks in it from the braid.

"Sometimes it's inconvenient that our thoughts are so entwined," he confessed. "I find it hard to hide my feelings from you."

"I don't want you to hide them," she said. "But you have news. So soon?" She reached up to cup his cheek, then shyly pulled her hand away.

"We're facing the back of the inn. The road is full of carts and wagons. People are fleeing Ploemeur."

"What?" Eilean said in surprise.

"Remember what we saw yesterday, when that knight showed up with the veiled lady?"

"Yes. Sir Peredur."

"The lady he brought was King Andrew's wife. Queen Genevieve."

Eilean felt a jolt of surprise at the information.

"Tongues are wagging right now," Hoel said. "They say the knight and the lady are lovers. Some of the travelers called Sir Peredur a 'false knight.' Apparently the two of them have run away together, and King Andrew is doubly wroth. The people are fleeing because they're afraid of what will happen when King Andrew arrives to punish them."

Eilean was still amazed. She remembered, from reading the tome, that King Andrew had married Genevieve even though his true love was the scullion girl, now Queen of Brythonica. There was something oddly similar about Eilean's own story. She, a wretched, had been trusted and trained by the same man who'd elevated Elle. She rubbed her mouth, her mind whirring with thoughts, her stomach twisting with dark emotions.

Was this why the Medium was sending her to Tintagel? To warn the king against invading Brythonica?

Would this be why Leoneyis drowned?

"What do you make of it?" Hoel asked her.

"I'm shocked," Eilean said. "Sir Peredur is the knight who sits at the Siege Perilous. He's supposed to espouse all the traits of Virtus."

"Maybe it's not what we think. Rumors aren't always true," Hoel said thoughtfully.

"Indeed not. But there's no denying he was traveling with a veiled lady."

"Your visit to the woods is even more interesting in light of this news," Hoel said. "I was anticipating that we were supposed to come and go, with few people knowing we'd been here, but maybe there is more that you're to do while you're here. A role you are supposed to play in the events that are unfolding."

Eilean felt a shiver go down her back at his words.

"Please don't say that," she whispered.

He approached her, smoothing away strands of hair from her brow. "Whatever it is, I'll be at your side the whole time."

That gave her some comfort.

"Andrew must be devastated," she said. "Such a betrayal. But Maderos was betrayed too. He didn't speak of it often, but he was banished from this world because the Queen of Brythonica turned on him."

"Do you know why she did?"

Eilean shook her head. "But he knew her thoughts, Hoel. He *knew* it was going to happen before it did. I think that is worse than what they say happened to King Andrew."

Hoel sighed. "The king might have known about Genevieve and Peredur. It's hard to keep secrets in a court."

"That's awful," she said, shaking her head. Feeling the weight of it. Then she gripped the front of his tunic and looked up into his eyes. "Don't do that to me, Hoel. I couldn't bear it."

He pulled her close and rested his head on her brow. "I won't," he promised.

But deep inside her, a little seed of doubt was planted.

What if he did?

Trust was truly a fragile thing.

Ambition can creep as well as soar. Elle's desires were not sated by winning a kingdom. She desired more than a crown and a throne. So she asked me how to become an Unwearying One. She coveted immortality, the ability to endure past the tenure of mortal life. Even though she couched it in words of her desire to serve humanity, to use the immaculate gift solely to benefit others, I sensed the intent behind her words.

Every ruler who has achieved the pinnacle of their power does not wish to relinquish it. Ilyas told me of a conqueror on another world so powerful that he ruled a kingdom beyond the grave. A gift of immortality to such a being becomes a curse to all. Sensing this, I refused to impart the lore from the Sefer Yetzirah. My refusal to impart that knowledge only made her more determined to have it.

—Myrddin, Wizr of Tintagel

CHAPTER EIGHT

Flotsam

E ilean and Hoel had eaten half of their breakfast when six soldiers entered the inn. Hoel set down the knife he was using
to slice the bread, his eyes fixed intently on the armored men
who'd arrived. One of them wore the badge of the two-faced woman.

"Greetings, kind sirs," said the innkeeper. "Are you in need of
refreshment?"

"We have orders from her ladyship. We're in search of two fugitives,
a man and a woman."

Eilean's stomach soured. She laid her hand on top of Hoel's, feeling the pleasing warmth of his skin. She had already disguised them
as Stright and Celyn, but this request for a man and woman traveling
together would make them conspicuous regardless of whether they met
the physical descriptions of the couple who was sought.

"Sahn-veh-reem," she whispered, invoking the word of power that
would render them invisible.

The innkeeper rubbed his beard. "We do have two travelers who came yesterday. Over at that . . ." He turned toward them and started in surprise. "They were just eating breakfast at that table a moment ago."

The captain with the badge turned to his men. "They must have fled through the kitchen. After them! Barncroft and Lux, guard this door!"

In a rush, the soldiers obeyed the orders and hurried to the kitchen, only a couple of them staying behind to stand guard. Hoel and Eilean sat at the table, unmoving. Shouts could be heard. Then, after a few moments of commotion, one of the soldiers returned.

"Any sign of them?" he asked breathlessly to the ones on guard duty.

"None."

"Has anyone tried to leave?"

"Look at them, they're all frightened," replied the other guard, gesturing to the nervous-looking merchants. "Where's Horrock?"

"He thinks they may have escaped into a farm. Come on! Join the hunt."

The guards followed in a hurry. Eilean smiled. She reached in her pouch and left coins for the breakfast on the table with one hand, keeping hold of Hoel with the other. He took the bread, and then the two of them rose from the table while the few patrons left began murmuring, wondering what the fuss was about.

Eilean guided him back to the kitchen. It would have been noticed if the front door had suddenly opened and closed. An alarm would have been raised.

Once they were safely down the road, heading back toward Ploemeur, she released the spell of invisibility and felt the drain in her strength from using it so long.

Hoel tore the rest of the bread in half and offered the larger piece to her.

"I'll take the smaller one," she insisted, reaching for the other half.

"So we're going back the way we came," he said. "As for reaching Tintagel, we may encounter some trouble. I don't think that little rowboat will be helpful crossing the sea, and if the people fear war is coming, it won't be easy finding someone willing to take us."

"The Medium will provide a way," Eilean said. Then she thought of the púca. "Even if I have to *fly* across the sea."

"Oh? You know a spell that makes us fly?"

"Spells aren't the only way to accomplish things, Captain Hoel," she said, giving him a smile. "You've much to learn still."

They shared stories along the road, Eilean telling him of her adventures since leaving Muirwood Abbey, and Hoel sharing more of what he'd learned as a hunter. As they walked, they saw many wagons still coming from Ploemeur, some with belongings strapped haphazardly on board. Children and pets walked alongside many of the overstuffed conveyances as the parents sought refuge far away.

"Why aren't they going to the castle we saw?" she asked Hoel. "Do you think the queen turned them away?"

Hoel shook his head. "No one wants to be in a castle during a siege. And with the size of the town—not everyone would fit. The queen will gather her forces there. Only a portion of the population are fleeing now. Others will wait to see what happens. It will come in waves."

In fulfillment of his words, before noon a band of knights passed them on the road, parting the crowds as they fought against the current of bodies and carts toward Ploemeur. There were enough people on the road that Hoel and Eilean did not stand out. The knights wore armor that showed the dents and scratches of fighting—not a recent battle but the scars of regular use. She studied their faces to see if she recognized any of them, but they were all unfamiliar. She did not sense the power of the Medium with any of them as she had with Sir Peredur.

When they finally reached Ploemeur, they entered the town and found the streets were more empty than before. Some vendors were still out, but most hadn't bothered to open their carts that day. They bought some food and drink and then decided what to do next.

"We should try another fishing boat," Hoel suggested. "That work won't stop until the enemy comes. People need to eat, and I have no doubt the queen is buying all of the catches to help increase provisions at the castle."

"We're not going to steal the boat, are we?" Eilean asked.

"We'll try persuasion first. There are a lot of coins in that pouch you took."

"So we make for the docks?"

"Agreed."

They finished eating, bought more food supplies for the journey and stowed the provisions in their gear, then started back toward the shipping yard. There were decidedly fewer vessels that day. Word traveled fast.

As they approached the harbormaster's station, Eilean felt Hoel squeeze her hand suddenly.

"Kariss," he whispered.

A jolt of surprise fluttered in her stomach. "Where?"

"To our left. She's with several knights, watching the people approaching the docks. Look closely."

They didn't break their stride, but Eilean averted her gaze enough to see the poisoner whom she'd fought in the dungeon below Dochte Abbey.

"Mareh," Eilean uttered, transforming their likenesses again. She didn't turn herself into Celyn, however, because she knew Kariss was familiar with that guise. Instead, she transformed the two of them into Ardys and Loren, the cooks at Muirwood.

"You had to make us *old?*" Hoel whispered.

"Hush. They're the first people I thought of. She wouldn't know them."

Eilean saw that there were knights guarding both sides of the harbor entrance, their eyes going from face to face. They didn't stop anyone, but they were being very vigilant. Despite their impenetrable disguise, Eilean didn't want to meet Kariss's eyes for fear of betraying something with her expression, so she kept her gaze fixed on the path ahead, wondering which of the fishing boats they might barter passage on.

As soon as they reached the line of knights, Eilean's spell melted away.

She felt their disguise vanish as surely as if she'd suddenly walked beneath a thin sheet of water from a waterfall. Something had stripped it away from them.

"*Sahn-veh-reem,*" she tried again, but nothing happened. She felt a lump in her throat, the sudden stirrings of panic. Something was blocking her power.

"There!" Kariss shouted, pointing at them. "Over there!"

Hoel turned and looked in Eilean's eyes. He must have seen the panic written there, her dumbstruck look of helplessness.

The sound of ringing metal announced the knights drawing their weapons.

"I can't—" Eilean started to say, but Hoel was already springing into action. He drew the blade from the scabbard on his back, and it instantly burst into a white-hot flame, sending tendrils of smoky mist from its surface. Why were the blade's enchantments working when her magic wasn't?

They were still sorely outnumbered, but Hoel charged at the oncoming knights, parrying the first attack with the edge of the blade. The opponent's blade shattered, surprising the knight. Hoel kicked him in the stomach, then dashed to the other side, swinging the blade around and battering another attacker on the helmet with the pommel.

Eilean watched in fascination, sensing the power of the Medium exploding within Hoel. He performed feats of swordsmanship that astonished her, quickly disarming and defeating the knights who attacked from that side.

She backed away from the other knights, wondering if she should run down the dock and into the gathering crowd who were congregating to watch the fight. But she couldn't bring herself to leave him, even though she was useless at combat without her magic.

Kariss brought out a dagger and raised her arm.

"Hoel!" Eilean screamed.

The poisoner flung the dagger at him. He twisted, swung the blade, and the dagger shattered when he struck it midair. He whipped the blade in a circle and then went after Kariss. Her eyes suddenly turned silver as she invoked the power of the kystrel. A blast of fear shot at Hoel, so powerful that Eilean could feel it from her position ten paces away.

He charged through it relentlessly.

Strong arms wrapped around Eilean from behind, and she was hoisted off her feet.

"Take her to the queen!" shouted one of the knights.

Eilean snapped her head back, just as Hoel had trained her. She felt the man's chin rock with the blow, but she didn't rest or relent—she thrust out her arms, wriggling until she managed to free herself.

"Kozkah gheb-ool!" she said, then immediately realized it wouldn't work. It didn't. Then she realized why. The queen must have engraved the null sigil somewhere nearby, which would block any spells from working in its vicinity.

Hoel rushed the knights who had attacked her. Three against one, but he couldn't be beaten. One of the knights sliced Hoel in the ribs with his sword. She saw the rip in his tunic and the gash in his skin, but no blood gushed from the wound. She knew Hoel would sense the raven symbol on the scabbard glowing. Hoel struck down the knight who had slashed him just as another rushed him with a dagger and plunged it into his shoulder.

Eilean grimaced to see the hilt poking from his back, but Hoel didn't even seem to notice it. He reverse-thrust and impaled the man with his sword, then pulled the dagger out of his own shoulder and tossed it down. His look was full of wrath, and the knight Eilean had injured scrabbled away in terror.

As Eilean looked at Hoel's face, she saw he was swept up in the magic of the blade. He was breathing fast, his nostrils flaring as he turned, looking for any other enemies intent on stopping them.

She knew that going into the docks was foolhardy. Eventually, they'd be overwhelmed. Not even the magic of the blade could last forever.

"The blade! It's King Andrew!"

Someone screamed it. Then the crowd scattered in terror.

Eilean knew that even the null sigil had boundary limits. It had been placed where people coming in or out from the docks would be unmasked and revealed. As soon as they walked out of its radius, she could use her powers again.

"Hoel, this way," Eilean said.

He looked at her, his eyes blazing still, and she sensed in his thoughts he didn't want to leave. He wanted to stay and fight them all. He felt invulnerable.

"Trust me, come!" she beckoned. It was mayhem now as people fled from them, as if Hoel were a lion seeking prey. He still gripped the sword, but he nodded in acceptance, and they held hands and started back toward the city.

When she tried casting the invisibility spell again, it worked. She cast her gaze for Kariss, trying to see where the poisoner had run off to. But it was impossible to spot anyone amidst the madness in the streets. People feared King Andrew.

***

They made their way farther north along the cove before stopping to rest. Hoel sheathed the sword, and Eilean dropped the invisibility. He leaned back against the wall of a shack, panting.

"You're injured," she said, touching his shoulder but avoiding the wound.

"It . . . it doesn't hurt. Not a bit," he said. "That was . . . incredible."

"It's powerful magic, Hoel."

"Yes, you were right. We had to leave." He took a deeper, steadying breath.

"And your side?" Although she saw the red mark from the cut, no blood oozed from it.

"I don't feel it," he said. He patted the wound with his hand. "The blade, Eilean. It . . . I've never . . . how to explain it?"

"What do you mean?" she asked, feeling nervous about the intense look she'd seen in his eyes. It hadn't been rage, just a burning determination. She sensed his thoughts, but they were jumbled and confused. Through them, she could sense an urge forming in him—an attachment to the weapon.

"I wasn't myself anymore." He looked up at the sky. "I had memories from others. It was as if every man who had held that blade left his mark in it. His experiences in battle. The wars he'd fought. I felt . . . I felt like a *king*."

As he said the word, she sensed the thoughts behind it. He'd enjoyed it, and a part of him regretted abandoning the life he might have had.

"Hoel," she said warningly. "That blade is altering your thoughts."

"Clearly," he said, chuckling. "I thought I'd given all of that up. But this sword has awakened something in me. Something I thought was dead."

"What? Ambition?"

He looked at her for a moment before nodding. "It would be better, I think . . . if I didn't use it again." He sniffed and swallowed. But she could tell he'd have difficultly holding himself to that conviction now that he'd had a taste of it. Is that why Maderos had hidden the weapon all these years?

Hoel sighed. "The docks are overrun. There has to be another way to Leoneyis."

"Use the Cruciger orb! Ask it to show us another way."

He jerked his head in agreement and opened the pouch that held the orb. He held it in his hand, still panting, his thoughts tangled from the experience he'd had.

With the orb in his palm, he stared at it. Nothing happened. His brow furrowed.

She sensed a kind of resistance within him—a straining. He was too spent to use the Medium on his own, and Eilean felt a prompting to put her hand beneath his. "You can do it," she coaxed.

He tried again. The Cruciger orb whirred slowly, ponderously, but at least it was working again. There were no words, just the pointers aiming in a certain direction.

Since there was no one around them, they kept it out and followed its guidance. Their path took them to a beach west of town. Waves continued to crash on the shore, and she could see cliffs to the north and west, higher up on the sandy beach. In the distance, an old man and a little girl walked along the shore between driftwood logs. By the cliffs, pulled up on the shore, sat a small boat with a single mast.

"The orb is pointing right at them," Hoel said.

"And they have a boat," Eilean said. She flashed him a smile. "Well done."

"It took both of us," he said. "I'm feeling tired again. Like I've been hiking to the peaks of the Myniths." She had noticed his labored breathing.

"Let's see who they are," she said.

After putting away the Cruciger orb, they climbed down the rocks to the sandy beach. The smell of salty brine and washed-up seaweed was pleasant to her nose, and the sand beneath their feet was a fine powder stippled with broken shells. The harbor could be seen far off to the south.

The old man and the girl were wandering to and fro. Eilean felt a prickle of the Medium's power coming from him, similar but not identical to what she'd felt from Sir Peredur.

As they approached the pair, Eilean could overhear the man talking.

"There's something I'm supposed to find here, Tabitha. So many rocks and shells. Rocks and shells everywhere. But where is it? Why did you lead me here?"

"Grand-Père, look!" said the little girl, holding up a conch shell.

"Oh, that's beautiful! Put it in your shell bag." The old man was short and walked with a slight limp. He had thick hair that was more gray than black and a prominent nose. He hadn't shaved in several days, and his whiskers extended down his neck.

The girl, maybe eight years old, continued to wander along the beach, stopping and picking up broken shells and then discarding them.

"Where is it, Tabitha? I know the feeling that brought you here. Where? What was left here?"

Hoel gave Eilean a quizzical look. The old man didn't appear to be talking to the little girl. It seemed like he was muttering to himself. But Tabitha was a woman's name.

As they approached him, the old man looked up. "Not much flotsam to pick through," he told them, waving his arms around. "Lots of shells. My granddaughter found a pretty conch. You might find one too." He kept scanning the sandy beach. Then he lifted one end of a piece of bleached driftwood before setting it down. "Where is it? Hmmm?"

"Did you lose something?" Eilean asked him.

"Yes. My *mind*." He waved his hand at her. "Many years ago. Very sad."

"What are you doing here?" she pressed.

"What does it look like I'm doing? I collect things. I go from beach to beach. Some of it is very valuable." He looked at Hoel's weapons, his eyebrows lifting. "I don't want any trouble. Sometimes I find little things now and then. Nothing of value today, though. I don't have anything worth robbing."

Hoel smirked. "I'm not going to rob you, friend."

"Good. Because you look like the kind of man who gets into fights a lot." He turned away from them, taking a few more steps. "Where is it, Tabitha? I feel it's so close. I can taste it. Where? Where?"

"What is your name?" Eilean asked. She felt the prickle of the Medium again, coming from the old man, who kept muttering while he searched.

The little girl was walking farther away. A sliding wave came up to her feet and Eilean watched as the water parted around her before slithering back down the shore.

Eilean swallowed, amazed at what she'd seen.

"What is your name?" she asked again.

The old man scratched his neck. "I'm normally very lucky. I find things that no one else can. In the water. Washed up on shore. But I can't find *anything* today. It's very frustrating."

Words came to her mind.

"But you have found it," she said to him. "You found *us*."

He stopped dead in his tracks. He turned and looked at her.

"I was led to this beach," he stammered. "For . . . for you?"

Eilean nodded. And then she saw his thoughts as if they were a tome that had been opened to her. His dead wife's name was Tabitha. He was so lonely without her that he spoke to her as if she were still with him.

The little girl walked up and held his hand. "We're supposed to take them somewhere, Grand-Père," she said gently. "The Fountain wants us to."

Eilean could feel the strength of the Medium coming from both the child and the old man. Emotion stung her eyes, and she blinked quickly to avert tears. A man like this was oft overlooked, much like a girl born a wretched, yet the Medium had found roles for them both.

"What is your name?" Eilean asked the man for the third time.

He didn't like saying his name. Now that his wife was gone, he didn't like anyone saying it. She could feel the pain in his heart. He wanted to be dead. But if he died, he feared no one would be left to remember his sweet Tabitha. And the thought of her memory fading tortured him.

"Tell them, Grand-Père," said the little girl.

The old man sighed. "My name is Penryn."

When he divulged the name, his eyes suddenly widened as if he'd been struck. He blinked at her and Hoel and then he dropped down on his knees in the sand.

"You *do* serve the Fountain," he gasped, head bowed.

There is a special bond between learners and teachers—a union of minds, a stitching together of thoughts. Indeed, one of the most beautiful qualities of true friendship is to understand and to be understood. I had such a relationship with the Harbinger. I was loyal to that friendship, obedient to her cause. And so was the scullion girl at first. But when I would not reveal the knowledge she craved, it began to twist our friendship. She believed that I would help her achieve her aim should I come to love and desire her. She used words at first to try and tempt me. Then actions. I rebuffed her, gently at first. Then more forcefully. But that only made her more decided. In the end, I think she persuaded herself that her feelings were real. We can believe a lie to be true if we feed it to ourselves often enough.

—Myrddin, Wizr of Tintagel

CHAPTER NINE

Duchy of Lionn, Kingdom of Occitania
Twelfth Year of the Reign of King Andrew Ursus

An eagle shrieked overhead. That was the only warning he got within the maelstrom of battle before the bird's claws ripped into his gauntlet, piercing the hauberk protecting his forearm, as the great beast tried to snatch the sword Firebos from his outstretched arm. Through the visor of his helmet, he saw the golden plumes of its feathers and its wild eyes. And then the eagle had its claws wrapped around the sword, and it began to lift skyward, dragging the blade with it.

After landing in the duchy of Vexin, Andrew and his knights had bypassed the fortress of Auxaunce and invaded Lionn, advancing quickly toward the outskirts of Pree, where he'd join with that phalanx of knights who had sailed around the continent and landed at Castillon, led by Sir Queux. It was a bold attack, dividing up their force like that, but Andrew believed that news of the Castillon landing would draw the Occitanian king's gaze southward, which would lead to victory. In order to reach Pree, Andrew's knights had crossed a valley between the Oyonnax Mountains and the foothills of Cluny. That was the most direct route. And exactly where Modredus had ambushed them.

Now his heart spasmed with a rush of fear. He didn't care about the wounds the claws had punctured in his arm. The raven scabbard would heal them quickly enough, but if he lost his blade, he felt certain he would fail in this war. He would be slain like his father before him.

"Myrddin!" Andrew screamed, ripping his visor up despite the hail of arrows raining down on them. He pointed at the eagle, which was flapping its powerful wings furiously, rising.

Myrddin was nearby, swinging his staff into an oncoming knight with such ferocity and power that the man was thrown back a dozen feet, the dent in his helmet unsurvivable. The Wizr whirled, gripping the staff in both hands, responding to the call for aid. Andrew already felt the loss of the blade, the sinking desperation of weakness, the sickly sensation that he was about to die in King Modredus's lands, amidst enemies who would gloat over his failure and snatch his kingdom as their prize.

Myrddin stretched out his hand and uttered a command—a word of power that could not be heard over the commotion of violence, the clash of arms through the deadly valley where they'd been ambushed. The eagle was struck by invisible blades. A spray of crimson, then both bird and blade plummeted to the earth.

Andrew watched where they landed and scrabbled forward. He felt no pain in his pierced arm, the scabbard already doing its work. But he saw another knight heading for the sword—Sir Owain—and a desperate frenzy filled him. He had to reach it before Owain, or he knew in his bones that the knight he trusted would never return it. It was Owain who had come up with their strategy for the attack, which would have worked brilliantly if it had gone according to plan. In fact, if Andrew were honest with himself, Owain would have made a strong king had he been so favored by the Fountain. With the sword, he'd be invincible.

It made him . . . cautious around Owain. Eager to get to him before temptation struck.

An Occitanian knight jumped in his path, swinging a bastard sword at Andrew's head. He ducked and then grabbed the dagger from his enemy's belt and plunged it between the creases of his armor, a fatal blow. The enemy knight barked with pain, sinking to his knees, and Andrew rushed past him just as Owain lifted the bloodstained sword from the carcass of the dead eagle.

Seeing the treasured weapon in another man's hand made Andrew half-mad with jealousy.

"Give it here!" he shouted, rushing up to Owain.

His trusted knight, his *cunning* knight, gazed at the weapon in his hands with something like wonder. The power of the weapon was invoked, causing a swirl of blue flame to emanate from the blade.

Suddenly Myrddin was in front of him, appearing out of nothingness to stand beside the knight. Words were spoken, indiscernible in the melee, and the Wizr's hand clamped on the knight's shoulder. Myrddin's humble tunic belied his awesome powers. Even after all these years, he still looked like the pig keeper of Farfog Castle. Andrew was grateful for the friendship, wisdom, and counsel of this man who wasn't truly a man. With Myrddin near, he knew he could escape. But he wouldn't leave his men to perish.

Owain lifted his visor, then he turned and saw Andrew hobble forward, hand outstretched, grasping for the blade.

"Give it here, old friend," Andrew implored, seeing the war of emotions in his friend's vulnerable eyes. One of the traits of the blade was that it imbued the holder with the ambition to lead. It had become a compulsion now for Andrew. He could not have given up his kingdom for any price.

Owain hesitated, glanced at the Wizr, then returned the blade to its rightful master.

"Take it," he said. "I never wish to touch it again."

As soon as it was in Andrew's grip, he felt the soothing influence of the magic sweep over him.

"We're vastly outnumbered, my lord," Owain said, "but our men will stand by you to the last."

"We must fight our way back to our ships in the Vexin," he said, still savoring the feeling of the sword in his grip. It was a desperate hour—the most desperate of his kingship so far. He had no idea how Modredus had figured out that they would be there, but he had. And now, nearly all was lost.

"They're killing all our horses," Owain said gruffly as he looked over the battlefield. "We must move now. To the king!" he bellowed. Knights were already rushing to join them.

"May the Fountain grant us victory," Andrew said. "Not by our strength alone, but through its power."

"Modredus comes," Myrddin warned, swiveling around and clenching the gnarled staff in his hands.

The Occitanian knights began to cheer and scream, their lines parting to reveal a row of pale white stallions, glittering with armor and the badge of the Fleur-de-Lis. The knights of the Ring Table and their squires quickly gathered around Andrew, forming a wall of steel and blades to defend him.

The man at the forefront of the riders was dressed in black armor and a forest-green cape. He blended into the wood-veiled crags of the Oyonnax. Modredus had a warrior's body, even more heavily muscled than when they'd last met.

Today, in the valley of the duchy of Lionn, Modredus approached them with his own Wizr, a stern-looking man with pale skin, hair the color of butter, and eyes that shone like gemstones. Andrew had heard that the pale-skinned man came from the East Kingdoms of Chandigarl. It was said his magic was truly impressive. The Wizr wore embroidered designs that must have been the work of countless hours of labor and held a straight staff made of silver bark with a carved end showing a sigil of power.

"Steady," Andrew ordered. "Let them come."

The two companies met, the battle ebbing in response to the new arrival. Men moaned in pain across the battlefield. Owain was right. They were vastly outnumbered.

"Well met, King Modredus," Andrew said with disdain in his voice. "Have you come to surrender?"

The handsome king gave him a mocking look. "Already the vultures begin to circle above. The ending is foreordained. Do you regret spurning my offer of service now?"

"Was that your pet eagle you sent after me?" Andrew snorted. "You feared to face me in battle yourself?"

"That eagle belongs to my Wizr and was worth more than the hundred of your feeble knights who lie dying. Set down your arms, King of Leoneyis. Submit to being our slaves, and I will spare your life."

Andrew saw Modredus's Wizr smirk. But the Wizr's eyes were focused on Myrddin, watching him intently.

"As tempting as that sounds," Andrew replied, "we will fight now or another day of your choosing. You attacked the smaller of our forces, I'm afraid. Soon Pree will be burning."

He was hoping for a reaction. A surge of fear in Modredus's eyes. The city of Pree was the jewel he prized the most.

It had been a gamble, of course, and like the other one they'd taken, it had failed.

"Pree is safe from Sir Queux's army," Modredus said. "They are being besieged at Gison at the moment. There is no way for them to escape. Kneel or perish. The choice is yours."

Was it true? Andrew looked to Myrddin, who could know the thoughts of other men.

Is he lying? he asked, joining thought to thought.

He speaks the truth. Sir Queux's men were ambushed as well.

"Your failure is inevitable," said the other Wizr, eyes still locked on Myrddin's. "My king has won the day."

There was a greedy look of hunger in the man's eyes. He wanted something. He wanted it desperately.

"Rucrius speaks truly," said Modredus. "Bend the knee."

Andrew felt the precariousness of the moment keenly. At least Genevieve was safe at Tintagel and his best knight, Sir Peredur, had been left behind to defend Leoneyis. If Queux was dead, Andrew would never forgive Modredus.

He looked from Myrddin to the Wizr Rucrius, and then back to the enemy king who had somehow known the attack was coming. Had someone betrayed them? Andrew couldn't imagine who. All of his knights were trustworthy and loyal. If they hadn't been, Myrddin would have known, for he could sense deception with a single errant thought. No, he couldn't believe he'd been betrayed. There had to be another reason.

No matter now. There was no way out except by blood, and he would rather sacrifice his own than risk the lives of his men. Wizrs were powerful, but they could not transport entire armies.

"I will only bend my knee," Andrew declared, "to the man who can defeat me in battle. Vanquish me, and I will submit and command my loyal knights to submit to you. If I win, you let all of my knights go, without ransom or cost. A truce between our people for a season . . . or two."

"*Are* all your knights loyal?" Modredus quipped. Andrew understood his meaning. A traitor.

"Every last one," he said confidently.

Rucrius sneered. "Are you so sure of that, my lord?"

They were trying to make him doubt. Who did they besmirch? Peredur? Owain? He would not yield to their insinuations.

"I would bet my life on it," he said simply. "I challenge you, Modredus. By the order of knighthood."

Rucrius looked alarmed by this turn of events. "We have them *beaten*, my lord. Kill them."

Modredus stared into Andrew's eyes for a long moment. Then he nodded.

"My lord, no!" the Wizr hissed in concern.

The enemy king held up his hand. "*I* am the king, Rucrius." He turned and shot a baleful look at him. "Never forget that."

A snarl came to Rucrius's mouth, but he said nothing. Andrew noticed that Myrddin's gaze was fixed on the other Wizr.

Modredus swung off his pale steed, his armor jangling as he landed, and withdrew a massive bastard sword. Andrew looked at the faces of his knights, those who had been so loyal to him over so many years. Many were older than him. He saw in Owain's look a plea to let him fight on Andrew's behalf. Peredur would have done the same. Both men were better warriors than Andrew. But with Firebos, he could have defeated any of them. It was the sword of kings, bestowing the knowledge of battle from one generation to the next.

But the scabbard was even more powerful. Andrew knew that he couldn't be slain in battle as long as he wore it—something Modredus didn't know.

It was an uneven contest from the beginning.

Andrew stood tall and allowed Modredus to strike him without defending himself. He was cut in the arms, the side. He'd even taken off his helmet so Modredus could try to shear off his head. Then he began walking forward relentlessly, not defending, although he could have, watching as the enemy grew worried, then fearful, then humiliated. Andrew went on the attack, sweeping Firebos around and knocking past Modredus's attempts to defend himself. The battle was over quickly, with Modredus panting on his knees, his bastard sword knocked into the scrub.

Andrew stood over him, gripping the blade tightly. He could decapitate this ruler of the Occitanians. And he saw the same realization in Rucrius's eyes.

"I . . . yield . . ." Modredus gasped.

A cheer rose up from the knights of Tintagel.

Rucrius snarled with the infamy of the defeat, glaring at Andrew. Then he gripped his staff, swung it overhead, and slammed the end into the sand.

As soon as the staff struck, there was a shivering in the ground.

An earthquake rocked the valley floor, and a great chasm rent the valley, causing rockslides. Boulders larger than horses began tumbling down, smashing through trees. The violence would destroy everyone, including the Occitanian knights.

Myrddin stood implacable through it all. He uttered a word of power, and the valley cleaved together, whole again. The shaking ended. The boulders slammed still.

Rucrius's eyes glittered with hatred. He uttered another word of power and then disappeared into a mist of vapor. Once the mist vanished, the Wizr was gone.

Modredus looked up at where the Wizr had been standing, watching for a moment as if he might reappear, then turned and bowed before Andrew.

"You may go free," Modredus said, his voice strangled with humiliation.

***

The celebration at the fortress of Folkestone was just getting started, even though the moon had begun to set. Andrew clashed goblets with Sir Owain, and the two shared a laugh. Andrew was more than a little drunk, but he deserved it after cheating certain death. They had been escorted by Modredus's knights to Gison. The siege had been lifted, and they'd been allowed to retreat back to the docks where Queux's ships were berthed. Their change of fortunes was still dizzying.

"My lord," Sir Owain said. "When can we return to Tintagel?"

"Will you be returning with us?" Andrew said in confusion. "I've made you King of Ceredigion . . . why not begin its conquest now?"

"So soon after what happened here?"

"Why wait for Modredus to try and carve any more of the pie for himself? No, I think you should start straightaway."

"It will take a month to cross it all. I'm grateful you made me over-lord. Truly, I am. But they have five squabbling rulers who argue about everything. It'll take time to knock their heads together."

"Not . . . with . . . a Wizr!" Andrew said, feeling a little unsteady on his feet. He saw Sir Queux approaching through the crowd of revelers and felt another surge of gratitude that his friend had survived the ambush. Andrew's return had been timely, for the men in Gison had not been prepared for a siege. They'd already run out of food.

"I will visit my tower in Ceredigion before heading back," said Owain with a sigh. "Now, I'd not trade that blessed place for three of Modredus's duchies."

"You are mad," Andrew teased. "That lonely little tower?" Then he unhooked his arm from around Owain's neck. "What ho, Sir Queux! You're not drinking?"

"I've had my share already, my lord," said Sir Queux. "And I'd be remiss as your seneschal if I could only vomit on the morrow and moan of a headache."

"As you know I will do," said Andrew with a laugh.

"Queen Essylt just arrived from Ploemeur," said Sir Queux meaningfully.

That sobered Andrew. What was she doing so far from her own lands? Brythonica was on the opposite coast. Of course, she was now a Wizr herself and could travel great distances in an instant with naught but a word of power. That was the way Andrew would return to Tintagel, with Myrddin's help, while Sir Queux took the knights and ships the long way home.

Andrew hadn't seen Elle in a long while. Since his marriage—and hers—their interactions had become painful. She still resented him for choosing Genevieve as his queen.

"My lord? Will you see her?"

Andrew realized he'd been standing there for several moments, lost in thought. She was here in person. Why would she have come all this way?

"Of course!" he said distractedly. "The news must be urgent."

"I'm afraid so. She wouldn't tell me what it was about."

"Where is she?"

"In the solar upstairs. I'll bring you."

Andrew nodded. He left his goblet with Sir Owain and followed Queux. He wished that wine didn't make him feel so befuddled. He'd never had a strong stomach for it, although he enjoyed the feeling of bliss it brought. One of the squires saluted his health, and a band of knights and squires all drank to him. He waved at them, his stomach queasy from the drink and the anticipation of seeing Elle again.

As they approached the solar, Andrew clapped Queux on the back. "We did it, old friend. We survived an ambush that should have killed both of us. I don't know how they knew we were coming. We must find that out. You hear me?"

Queux smiled and nodded.

"You're my seneschal. You know people better than most. Avoid sending knights. We must be more discreet. Choose men who speak Occitanian like a native." He pointed at Sir Queux. "We have treasure enough to pay them, and you will be their master. You are wise, my friend. It is your greatest strength. Play to it."

Queux loved to be praised, but no more so than other men, and his help really had been invaluable all these years. The details of preparing the knights for war, from arranging for the supply ships to accommodating for the horses, had been a terrible burden, and Sir Queux had borne it dutifully.

"My liege, I am devoted to you and your success. I feared I'd failed you."

"I must learn how they surprised us," Andrew said. "Occitania is the only kingdom that refuses to kneel to me. I want Modredus to kneel before me and my heir. That is my aim."

"But her ladyship still isn't with child," warned Sir Queux.

"Tosh," said Andrew. "We have time still. We're young."

They reached the door of the solar, and Sir Queux opened it. As Andrew entered, he saw Elle touching Myrddin's arm in a familiar way. The two of them were conversing in low voices, and Elle looked so beautiful it made his heart burn with pain. She was dressed in all the royal splendor of her rank. Seeing her like that clashed with his memories of her as a scullion. How he'd scraped pig dung from her shoe with a bit of straw.

She wore a teal silk gown with an intricately embroidered brocade overskirt. It was form-fitting and open at the bodice in a way that made him thirsty again. A braided gold necklace at her throat revealed a mesh of jewels. Her long, supple hair, the color of a golden sunset, shone in the light of the torches bracketed to the four walls.

Myrddin looked at her intently, then turned to regard them as they entered.

Elle dropped into a deep curtsy. "Your Majesty," she said, greeting him in that mocking tone of hers.

"You know I don't care for that sort of greeting," Andrew said, coming to her to take her hand and kissing her ring. "Not from *you.* What news from Brythonica?"

She pulled her hand away. "King Gowter of Bayree has invaded my lands," she said, her look intense with displeasure.

Andrew wrinkled his brow. "Is the Fisher King really such a fool?" Bayree had an alliance with Occitania. It was only a matter of time before Modredus prevailed and annexed those lands. The Occitanians were everywhere—an infestation—but at least he had dealt them a powerful blow.

"Men are known to be foolish when it suits them," she said, her green eyes flashing at him.

He grimaced at her words. Yes, even after so many years she was still bitter about his choice.

"What did Sir Peredur have to say? Surely you went to Tintagel first? Or were my plans not a secret to anyone?"

Her lips pursed, and she gave him a haughty look. "Of course I went to Tintagel first. He was gone. With your *queen*."

A feeling of heartburn surged in Andrew's chest. He coughed into his hand, trying to quell the sudden pain. "Gone?"

"To Atabyrion, so I was told at court. I don't have time to traipse around your massive kingdom looking for them, but heard about your little invasion. So I went to Pree, in disguise, expecting to find you there. That's when I learned about Modredus's defeat. They said you were with your fleet at Folkestone, and here I am. I cannot abide such insolence from the Fisher King. I'm one of your vassals, am I not? I'm entitled to your protection?"

What were Peredur and Genevieve doing in Atabyrion? Thoughts sloshed back and forth in his mind. The pain in his heart intensified, but he quelled it for a moment, long enough to ask, "Do you *need* my protection?"

She sighed and gave him a disparaging look. "You've had too much wine. Permit me to bring Sir Queux or one of your knights to return and provide defenders for Brythonica."

He turned to Myrddin and Sir Queux. "Grant me a moment alone with Her Ladyship."

Sir Queux's eyebrows rose in concern. Myrddin, without expression, walked out. The knight followed.

Andrew walked over to the nearest couch and sat down, holding his head in his hands.

"You're drunk," Elle accused.

"Only a little," he answered, feeling a wave of nausea. He needed to burp but held it down. She would have laughed at him if he did. They'd known each other for so long. In truth, he'd considered breaking royal protocol to marry her. The part of him that had been the pig keeper's apprentice had desired it. He wondered what would have happened if he had dared to make that choice. His wife, a Wizr. Wasn't Elle the one whom Myrddin had suggested he marry? No, that wasn't true. Myrddin had suggested his "dearest friend," and it had been many years since that was true.

"You look weary," she said, her tone gentler this time.

"I *am* weary. A king has no peace. There is always one problem after the other. And we all nearly died."

She approached him and put a hand on his shoulder. "You chose to invade Occitania. You sought out trouble, not the other way around."

"He insults my knights by seizing them and holding them for ransom. His ships attack ours unprovoked. He refuses to allow passage between our lands. You can hardly blame me, Elle."

Her hand on his shoulder flinched. "Don't call me that."

When he looked up at her, there was sadness in her eyes. Regret. He felt it too. He'd missed her presence, sorely, when she left Tintagel.

"But that's your name," he said. "Your *real* name."

He shouldn't be alone with her. Why had he dismissed Queux and Myrddin?

Because he'd *wanted* to be alone with her. Just as his father had wanted to be with his mother, the Lady of Tintagel, even though she was wed to his enemy. He clenched his eyes shut, trying to ignore the pounding in his heart.

"Andrew," she said, raising her hand and stroking his hair. She used to do that. Casually, as if it were nothing. She never touched him now, and he craved it more than wine.

If she offered, he would accept. They both wanted it. They'd always struggled against their feelings for each other.

He looked at her hopefully.

But she wasn't overcome with desire. No, she was regarding him with *pity*. That was an awful realization. "I love another," she said. "You had your chance to claim me. You chose another. And now, so have I."

There was an earnest look in her eyes, which made her all the more beautiful to him. The pangs in his chest dug in deeper. Stunned, he realized she was talking about Myrddin. That what he'd witnessed upon arriving had more significance than he'd realized.

"Elle, I . . ." His throat choked closed. He didn't know what to say.

"My name is Essylt," she replied. "May I bring Sir Owain back with me? King Gowter will back off if Owain is there to face him."

"Of—of course," Andrew mumbled, still stinging from her words. From feeling thwarted.

It was better this way. Surely it was better.

His hand dropped to the hilt of the sword. He always checked to make sure it was at his side.

"Go to sleep," she said kindly. "You need your wits back. *Tenumowet*."

Her spell caused a heavy lethargy to fall over him, and he slumped down on the couch.

Though he has eyes, he cannot see. Though he has ears, he cannot hear. Though he breathes, he does not live. It is happening again. Why must it always happen again? I feel the foreboding from the Medium. I will not be allowed to stay here for much longer, which is in some way a boon. It would be torture to stay and watch it happen. I cannot be killed or starved or drowned. But I can suffer for the choices of others.

—Myrddin, Wizr of Tintagel

CHAPTER TEN

Tintagel

The desperation in the old man's tone wrung Eilean's heart. She did not know why he searched through the debris washing up on shore, or who the little girl was who couldn't be touched by water, but she felt an immediate connection to the man. She didn't want him to perish in the flood.

"Yes, I serve the Fountain," Eilean said. "And I've come with a warning."

Hoel looked from her to the old man, his expression wary.

"Of course you have!" the old man declared. "What is the message, my lady?"

She saw in his thoughts that he didn't believe she was an emissary. He was convinced that Eilean was of the Fountain.

"We must go to Tintagel to see King Andrew." She paused, not sure what else to say. But the Medium sent her a distinct impression that Penryn needed to hear the warning. *He* would heed it. And help others to.

"I will take you there in my boat," he said at once.

"We are going to warn his people," Eilean continued. "Leoneyis will be drowned if the king dies."

"The king will die? That is a terrible omen."

"Indeed, Penryn. And we must warn his people and save as many as we can who will heed our message."

"I have family in Leoneyis," Penryn said worriedly. "Can I tell them to flee?"

"Yes. You must. Spread the word to everyone you can."

"My boat is over there," he said, wagging his arm in the direction they'd seen it. "I'll get it ready." He sprang to his feet, scattering sand, and then started ambling toward the boat. She could hear him talking under his breath. "Did you hear that, Tabitha? The Fountain has sent a lady to help us. You led me right to her!"

Eilean glanced at Hoel, taking in his wary look, but he said nothing. The little girl was still nearby.

Eilean approached her. "What's your name?"

"I cannot give you my true name," said the child. Eilean felt the Medium emanate from the girl in strong, comforting waves. "He calls me Evie."

"And you are not his granddaughter."

"I am not," the girl said simply. "I'm from the Deep Fathoms. I was sent to comfort him after Tabitha drowned. I'm a water sprite." Another sliding wave came up, parting around her, and doused Hoel's and Eilean's boots.

"You're a spirit creature," Eilean said in wonder.

Hoel raised his brow, his eyes a mix of curiosity and confusion. He'd doubted the existence of creatures such as her, yet here was the evidence before his eyes.

"I am. He knows it too, but we do not talk of it. We should go to the boat. I will help him spread the message."

Eilean reached for Hoel's hand, and they walked that way, hand in hand, after the girl as she made her way toward Penryn. She covered the last bit of distance at a run, and the old man hoisted her up and into the boat he was pushing toward the surf.

"This is where the Medium led us?" Hoel said under his breath. "His mind is a little addled."

"He's still grieving," Eilean answered.

"He thinks you're a manifestation of the Fountain."

"I can't help what he thinks. I was truthful."

He nodded. When they reached the boat, Hoel scooped Eilean up into his arms and lifted her inside. She rather liked him doing that. Then he joined Penryn in pushing the boat into the water.

"It's easier to push with two people," said the old man. "You're a big help! A little farther!"

The two men continued to shove and slide the boat. When the front end struck the waters, the old man gave a cry of excitement, and water sluiced against the hull. Eilean sat down on one of the worn wooden benches. The girl, Evie, stood at the prow, staring at the waves. Eilean felt a jolt of magic come from her, and then waves caught the bottom of the boat, making the old man's work easier. Penryn and Hoel splashed in the water a bit before climbing aboard.

Evie looked back at Eilean and gave her a knowing smile.

"It's so heavy, but we did it," Penryn gasped. He went to the main mast and began untying the ropes. Hoel moved to assist him, demonstrating his seafaring skills in the way he helped unfurl the sail. Penryn lashed the crossbar in place and then took up the captain's position at the tiller in the back of the boat. The sail gathered in the wind, and the craft began to glide smoothly away from the cove.

Eilean turned back and gazed at the beach they'd just left. The caves in the cliff wall had been carved out by the comings and goings of the tide. There was something about the beach that felt significant, although she wasn't sure what.

"Oh, Tabitha. This is important. This is *really* important," Penryn said under his breath. "I'm sailing with an emissary of the Fountain. In *my* boat. I never thought. This is so special, isn't it? I'm glad you could see this too."

Hoel joined her on the bench, and the two leaned against each other. Although she still felt rattled by the way he'd acted with the sword, she felt safe with him. Safe and cherished. She examined the wound at his side and saw that the cut was closed over, the skin more pink than red. She could sense through Hoel's thoughts that the raven symbol on the scabbard was glowing, although the effect wasn't as easy to discern in daylight.

She took one of his hands in both of hers and stroked the edge of his thumb, and he put an arm around her. Leaning her cheek against his chest, she stared at the gray waves rippling in the distance and soaked in the moment.

They had not sailed for long before the outline of land appeared in the distance.

Leoneyis.

***

Eilean roused from sleep when she heard the crashing of waves against rock. Blinking quickly, she started in surprise at the sudden change of scenery. Hoel stroked the curve of her cheek and then nodded at the cliffs their boat was approaching.

Leoneyis was a gorgeous land, all green jagged hills and choppy gray cliffs. The waves roared as they smashed against the lower cliffs. She saw a harbor to the left, along with a series of wooden steps and rails that crisscrossed up to the verdant hills atop the cliffs. She saw seabirds soaring overhead but then realized they were ravens, not gulls.

What drew her eye most, though, was Tintagel Castle.

It was the largest castle she'd ever seen, dwarfing Prince Derik's castle in the mountains of Hautland. It stood on a cleft of land, separated from the rest of the island kingdom except for a narrow bridge that spanned between them. The waves crashed through the gulf between the castle's rocky perch and the mainland as the waters relentlessly hammered against the cliffs. There were boulders in the waters, revealed in between the bursts of violent waves, and Eilean realized there had once been a land bridge connecting the spits of land. And that meant there had probably been a mirror gate below Tintagel long, long ago.

"Impressive," Hoel said to her, nodding to the castle. "More impressive than Avinion."

The castle was not a uniform shape but a series of square and round towers crowded together on the promontory. It reminded her vaguely of Dochte Abbey, although it was clearly much larger. Another castle had been built on the other side of the bridge, creating a double fortification, though the smaller edifice didn't have moss on the walls like the larger one, which meant it was newer. Flags whipped from pennants attached to the high spires. As their boat drifted closer, she saw dozens of trickling waterfalls twining down the cliffs to join with the rushing gallop of seawater.

"This is the castle King Ulric could not take by force," Eilean said in a low voice, her eyes feasting on the scene. It would be impossible to attack it by sea. Even if all his enemies combined against him, King Andrew could hold this fortress until the end of time.

Or until it was swallowed by the sea.

"And Ulric is Andrew's father? The one who eventually married his enemy's wife?"

"Yes. The castle was nearly impossible to siege. He only managed to win it by shifting the fight to a more favorable battleground."

And yet, the castle did have vulnerabilities. The cleft between the parts of land suggested that the land could be further rent apart. An earthquake would do it. She'd learned the word of power for "earth-quake" in the Sefer Yetzirah.

"There have been earthquakes here," said Evie in a low voice.

At the words, Eilean felt a shiver go down her back. She looked at the girl, wondering if the water sprite could read her thoughts. Whether the girl could or could not, she did not say.

"One of 'em knocked down one of the towers," said Penryn. "Things washed ashore from it for weeks afterward. That was . . . nigh on twelve years ago."

"More harm than that will happen this time," said Evie gravely.

Cold shivered through Eilean's body. Could the Medium have sent her to Leoneyis to destroy it?

Hoel noticed her shiver. "Cold?" he asked, hugging her closer to him.

She shook her head. Sunlight flashed in her eyes as it reflected off the enormous stained-glass windows on the east and south facades of the castle. So many windows. She could only imagine how brightly lit the castle was on the inside.

It struck her viscerally that her mission was to enter that stronghold and inform the high king that his empire was about to be destroyed because he'd turned against the will of the Knowing. How would he react? A feeling of dread welled up in her stomach.

"I'm worried," she confessed.

"I'll be by your side," Hoel promised. He stroked her hand with his thumb. "We do this together."

Penryn waved to them. "We're making for the harbor on the west!" he cried out against the noise of the thunderous surf. "We'll spread the message, my lady. We'll do our part. But if we get any closer to the rocks here, we'll be thrown against 'em!"

She nodded to him and wrapped her arms around Hoel's waist as the boat began to rock with the turbulent current. The waters calmed as they approached the western harbor. There were several massive ships already in dock, but Penryn's small boat easily found a slip.

Hoel rose from the bench to help the old man, but Penryn was quick to secure the boat with a rope and then assisted the passengers in disembarking.

"It's quite a climb to the castle," he warned them. "Lots of steps. A maze of 'em. I'm going to send word to my friends here, but I'll stay near the boat to take you anywhere you need to go. There's an inn on the wharf, the Chalice. Evie and I will stay there. You need to go somewhere, you just send word, and I'll take you."

"Thank you," Eilean said, grateful the Medium had led them to the strange pair.

Penryn took Eilean's hand and kissed it. "Thank you, my lady. It's an honor, truly."

After parting with the two, Eilean and Hoel followed the main road in the harbor. They could see the first batch of wooden ramparts rising overhead, and as they continued walking, they found that the road itself led directly to the castle. And they began to climb the ramp, which was scuffed and marred by hooves and feet.

The wooden slats of the road continued to follow the path of the hills, winding up and down, with new ramps to help them rise to the next height.

Her stomach continued to twist with dread as they walked, the sun rising before them. Would they even reach the smaller castle by noon? During the journey, they were overtaken by companies of knights that passed them, requiring them to step off the wooden road into the grass on either side. Each knight had a banner with a different standard on it.

After the third group of knights passed, Hoel said, "Seems like they're answering a summons."

That made sense. King Andrew intended to invade Brythonica. And in doing so, he would bring the calamity to his people that the Medium had warned about.

In addition to the ramps, there were interconnected staircases, and Eilean and Hoel used those to shorten the distance whenever they were available. The air was crisp and cool, but after a few hours of climbing, her legs were sore from the constant effort. Ravens were everywhere, leaping from rock to rock, soaring overhead, and their symbol was carved into the wooden rail markers.

The repeated emblem reminded her of something Mordaunt had once told her. *To have a raven's knowledge means to have the most powerful Gift of all—the Gift of Seering, to see the future.*

She did not have the Gift of Seering—that was Hoel's talent—but she knew what was coming nonetheless. Could she hope to prevent it? Or was the destruction absolutely going to happen?

"Have you had any visions since we came here?" she asked him, trying not to gasp as she spoke.

"None," he said. "They may only happen in our world."

"Or they happen when the Medium needs to tell you something."

"True."

They were much closer to the castle now, enough so that they could see the bridge spanning the gap. She imagined King Ulric, desperate to have another man's wife, walking alone down this road, a word of power cloaking his appearance. A deception to satisfy his desire. And how, when the Queen of Leoneyis discovered the truth, she'd sought to murder the child.

How had that affected Andrew as a boy? As a man?

"It's a beautiful land," Hoel said, gazing at the various hamlets in the distance.

"I don't see any farms," she said.

"Nor I. It doesn't seem habitable for that. No sheep either, which you'd think would thrive in this kind of area. Maybe they mine ore? These cliffs might have an abundance."

They reached the small castle on the near side of the bridge before dusk. There were guards wearing the Raven badge posted at the gatehouse. Other than the knights who had overtaken them, there had been no other travelers heading to or away from Tintagel.

"You look weary, travelers," said one of the guards as they approached. "Welcome to Tintagel."

"Thank you," Eilean said. "We seek audience with the king."

The guard gave her a shrewd look. "Anyone who wishes to speak to the king must first get past his seneschal, Sir Queux. Do you bring news worthy of that noble lord's attention?"

"Indeed, sir," said Eilean. "We've traveled from a great distance."

"So you say," answered the guard. "Are you prepared to *pay* for an audience with the king?"

Eilean frowned at this. It didn't seem right that one should have to pay for an audience with a king.

"My lady, it's very simple. Multitudes seek an audience with the King of Leoneyis. Few are granted one. If you did not bring sufficient coin to pay Sir Queux, then it will not bode well for you."

Hoel lifted the bag of coins they'd taken from the coffer, and he jiggled it so that the coins clinked.

The guard smiled broadly. "Ah. At least you won't be wasting his time."

After escaping the clutches of King Modredus of Occitania, Andrew was determined to discover how his enemy had foreseen our attack. He asked me to interrogate the servants to see whether I could unmask an enemy in our midst. There was such a man, one who had been discreet enough to never come near me. After he was confined in the dungeon, I interviewed him and then learned of a special relic in the possession of King Modredus—a game called Wizr that had been invented by the Wizrs of the East Kingdoms. Played on a special board made of precious stone with figurines representing the rulers and vassals of two warring kingdoms. This was no ordinary trivial pastime, however. It was a contest of wills, to see which ruler could establish a dynasty capable of enduring for centuries. At risk were the very lives of the people under the dueling leaders' rule. Many of the East Kingdoms had been destroyed by playing Rucrius's game.

I told Andrew of this artifact and promptly went to Pree myself in disguise. King Modredus kept it in a locked chest in his palace chamber. I retrieved and studied it, and the king himself discovered me in the act. Thoughts are the betrayers of men. When he saw me holding the chest and the Wizr set, the truth was revealed to me. Rucrius had insinuated himself with Modredus's father, who had challenged Ulric to play the game years before, after I'd fled with Andrew to safeguard him. The covenant of the game had been enacted, pitting Leoneyis against Occitania, and the game would go on until one ruler failed to create a dynasty.

From what I discerned, I believe that Ulric's queen may have plotted his demise and that of her child to ensure the permanent failure of his line.

I brought the Wizr set back to Tintagel and warned Andrew of the consequences he was bound to. Although he had not chosen to participate, he was fascinated by the idea of seeing the strength of his kingdom arrayed on a board made of alabaster and marble. Thus we learned how our movements had been detected by the other side. The two kingdoms were evenly matched. Any defection from one side to the other changed the color of the pieces in play.

He thought himself invincible. With the sword and the scabbard, he believed it was his destiny to rule the entire world. Upon our return from Occitania he complained that his injuries had not fully healed. He believed the raven scabbard was losing its efficacy.

I examined it. And saw that it was, in fact, a subtle counterfeit. The blade flamed when drawn, and the raven mark glowed as it should. But those effects were only for show, a magic that went skin deep. The true blade and scabbard had been taken from the king without his knowledge. Only a Wizr could have accomplished such a feat. But which one?

—Myrddin, Wizr of Tintagel

CHAPTER ELEVEN

The Seneschal

T he smaller castle guarding the bridge to Tintagel was called the Citadel of the Seneschal. It was the gate that controlled access to the King of Leoneyis, and Sir Queux was the man guarding it.

Eilean had read about Sir Queux in Maderos's tome. His honesty at the tournament he'd entered with the sword Firebos had earned him a valuable position in Andrew's court . . . so why was he accepting bribes for access to the king?

She whispered these qualms to Hoel as they were escorted to an opulent waiting area for news to travel across the bridge to Tintagel and back. The room had several decorative couches, a view of the sea from a massive stained-glass window, and fruit held in decorative basins.

"Why are you surprised?" Hoel answered. "The same happens in our world."

"Truly? I didn't think greed was a virtue espoused by the order."

"Mícheál Nostradamus sounds much like Sir Queux. He controlled access to the High Seer. Rather, he controlled which messages were delivered to Lady Dagenais and which were not."

Eilean frowned. "Why would she want her information so limited? How would she know if something untoward was happening?"

"No ruler has the time to absorb every piece of information that comes through the Apse Veils. Most of the letters that come through are complaints anyway. People don't want to solve their own problems. They want someone in power to solve their problems for them. I heard Nostradamus once say, with the sarcasm only he could pull off with such aplomb, that mortals are born crying, live complaining, and die disappointed."

It was an amusing sentiment, if an overly cynical one.

"That's not true for everyone," she countered.

"I've seen it enough times in my own experience, by Cheshu. I used to tell my men not to just bring me problems. I wanted to know how they proposed to solve them."

"Not everyone is as diligent as an Apocrisarius hunter. Mordaunt used to say that most men are driven by the need to feel important. That they'll do almost every task because it satisfies that need."

Hoel lifted a fruit from one of the bowls. It had a rough peel and was the color of carrots.

"What kind of fruit is that?" Eilean asked when she saw him observing it.

He withdrew his dagger and began to peel it. She noticed the scars on his hands again as he dug into the peel with his blade. He had so many scars. The sudden memory of watching him being ravaged by the Fear Liath made her wince. It had been her doing, that, although saving him had been her doing too.

The flesh inside the fruit was pink and red, covered in a yellowish pith. He sliced a round from it and then tasted it, his eyebrows shooting up in surprise. "It's very sweet." He cut another round and offered it to her.

Eilean took the slice, which had little sacks of juice clumped together within fibrous sections. She took a bite, and the explosion of flavor on her tongue startled her.

"It's delicious. It tastes a little like cherries."

"I thought blackberries," he replied. "Not tart, though."

He wiped his blade clean and sheathed it, then used his thumbs and fingers to tug away the peel, which came off easily. The spherical shape was divided into segments, which easily pulled apart. He offered half to her, which she gladly accepted.

"In truth, a king—or even an Aldermaston—cannot function without able people to assist them," he continued, after enjoying a few more slices. "Leading anyone requires trusting those beneath you to do the right thing."

"And such trust must be earned."

"Of course. Maderos didn't trust you at first, did he? He tested you to see if you were truly loyal to Aldermaston Gilifil."

She nodded. "He was the one who pointed out the inconsistencies in the Aldermaston's reputation. But it was when he brought Celyn back to life that he won me over. He didn't *have* to do that. People die of illnesses every day. He did it because he knew *I* cared for her."

Even all this time later, her heart throbbed with gratitude for the selfless act.

Hoel studied her. "I remember that day. Everyone assumed the Aldermaston had raised her using the Medium. But I recall the stunned look on his face. I knew he hadn't done it, so I worried it was druid magic."

Eilean wondered where Maderos was at that moment. Was he languishing in a dungeon in Avinion? She'd come to this world because the Medium had commanded her to retrieve his tome. Every day she hadn't reclaimed it made her worry about getting back to the mirror gate in time. But she was also worried about her other friends, new and old. Celyn, Stright, Aldermaston Utheros, as well as Hoel's father and Lady Anya. She had no idea what dangers they were facing, and they had no way of helping so long as they were here.

"My father had a saying," Hoel continued seriously. "The true measure of a man is how he treats someone who can do him absolutely no good."

"A noble sentiment," said a man's voice, startling Eilean.

She'd been facing Hoel and hadn't seen the door open, but Hoel had. Had he said the words to make a point?

Eilean rose from the couch, setting down the uneaten wedges of pink fruit, and made a graceful curtsy to the man she assumed was Sir Queux.

He was closer to forty than to fifty. His hair was shorn to little nubs across his head, but he had a handsome face and the firm musculature of a man bred for war. His eyebrows were very dark, and his look was probing and alert. There was a half smile on his mouth, not quite welcoming.

"I am Sir Queux, the high king's seneschal," he introduced himself, inclining his head just a little. He gripped the pommel of a longsword in his left hand. His tunic was elegantly cut and embroidered with the insignia of the Raven, which he also wore on a chain around his neck. The glint of a hauberk beneath the tunic suggested he was on the defensive with them, and perhaps always. His black leather gloves gave a little stretching sound as he squeezed the pommel.

Hoel said nothing in reply. He ate another segment of fruit.

"Thank you for coming so soon," Eilean said in greeting. "My name is Eilean."

"I see you are enjoying a bit of fruit from the East Kingdoms," he said. "The cara fruit is rare in these parts."

"Is that what it is called?" Eilean asked.

"Anyone can get berries from Brythonica," he said with a proud smile. "Some peasants may go their entire life without tasting what you have." She sensed Queux's thoughts. He had judged them already by their different style of clothing and their lack of knowledge about the fruit. A worldly man, he felt he was wasting his time with people below him.

He was disinclined to grant their request.

Eilean knew these things instantly, the Medium providing the information to her. She would not have long to persuade him.

"I have information to communicate to King Andrew," she said.

"The king is a very busy man," replied Queux evasively. "If you share it with me first, I can deem the value of it."

"I must speak with him," she said, pushing her thought at him.

Queux's eyes narrowed. "That's . . . impossible. I'm afraid you've wasted your time coming here."

"We do not understand the word 'impossible' the same way," Eilean replied. "Please take us to him now."

A frown wavered on his mouth before it lifted into a gracious smile. But she sensed his resentment. He was the king's seneschal, and he was used to being treated with fawning and compliments. He expected a little groveling. Maybe more than a little.

Eilean was treating him as if she were his equal, if not his superior.

"Your message? You must say something about it for me to even consider this."

"I come with a message from the Fountain."

That startled him. His brows wrinkled in confusion. "That is unlikely," he said.

"But it is true."

"It is not ordinary for people with important messages to arrive unexpected," he said, tilting both hands in a subtle appeal for a bribe. Perhaps the guards had assured him he'd get some coin out of it. She could see in his thoughts that he was inherently greedy and easily rankled. He was going to walk away and order them banished from the castle if no offer of coin was given. That brazen thought took predominance in his mind.

Eilean stepped toward him, assisted by a whisper from the Medium.

"I have information the king seeks," she said.

Queux sighed. "If it is concerning the whereabouts of Sir Peredur and Queen Genevieve, I assure you that such knowledge has already passed this way, and the king wouldn't—"

"No," she interrupted, offending him in the act.

His patience was at an end. She watched the flicker of animosity in his eyes. Her unwillingness to play by his rules had fanned his hostility.

He was seething still, trying to master his emotions before responding.

A thought impressed itself in her mind, and she gave voice to it. "I have information about Myrddin."

That stunned him. And *terrified* him. She immediately saw sweat bead on his brow. Guilt, worry, and fear mingled in his mind, although his expression was carefully guarded, save the sweat trickling down his face.

"You know where Myrddin is?" he whispered. His tone implied that he was surprised and delighted, but his thoughts were black. He was going to order their deaths as soon as he left the room.

That surprised her. This man was *afraid* of Myrddin. He was deathly afraid of the king knowing anything about the Wizr at all. And he would *kill* to prevent Andrew from hearing what they'd come to say.

Her stomach shriveled with dread, but she kept her own expression as calm as the seneschal's.

"I must speak with the king," she said succinctly, forcefully, pushing her thought into his mind once more.

"Of course," Sir Queux answered. "He will be anxious to hear any news of his old friend, I'm sure. Enjoy another cara fruit. Let me prepare horses for you both to join me back to the castle."

It was a bald-faced lie, and she knew it. But he didn't know that she could discern his thoughts.

Sir Queux bowed, this time at the waist in an attempt to show he was humbled by their visit. Then he walked quietly to the door and stepped outside.

As soon as he was gone, Eilean turned to Hoel.

"Don't trust him," he whispered, reaching into the bowl for another fruit.

"I won't. He's going to execute us," she said in reply, holding her hand out to him. "Or at least he thinks he will."

Stuffing the cara fruit into his pocket, Hoel closed the gap and took her hand.

"*Sahn-veh-reem,*" she uttered, invoking the words of power for invisibility.

Moments later, the door opened again, and six soldiers burst inside. She could sense their murderous intent as they came in, but they quickly looked around in astonishment.

"They're gone!" one of them growled.

Eilean tightened her grip on Hoel's hand. She had no doubt that he could have defeated them all. But it was not the Medium's will. One of the guards hurried out, and shortly after, Sir Queux came in with a look of panic.

"Who was guarding the door?" he demanded.

"We both were, my lord. No one came out! I swear it!"

Sir Queux rubbed his mouth with his gloved hand, his mind whirling. She could sense an image in his mind of a beautiful, courtly woman with rose-gold hair and a glittering crown.

It may have been Essylt in disguise, thought the seneschal. The possibility of being deceived infuriated him.

"The king's in danger," Sir Queux shouted. "Back to Tintagel! It was a trick!"

The seneschal and his henchmen rushed from the room, leaving the door open in their wake.

At least one good thing had come from the visit.

Sir Queux would lead her directly to King Andrew.

A loose thread unravels quickly. Before I confronted Elle about whether she had taken the sword, I crossed the mirror gate and returned to my own world to seek counsel from the Harbinger's daughter. She warned of the queen's plans for me. The wheels of destiny were already turning. In but a single day, I would be captured, my tome confiscated, and I would be banished from the world of Leoneyis. I hid my tome in the vaults of the maston citadel of Avinion and then returned to the other world, taking the fake sword and scabbard with me to Brythonica to confront Elle with the evidence of her treachery. The Harbinger had given me knowledge of where the true one was hidden, so I switched the original for the false and pretended to arrive by the ley lines.

I told Elle that I'd discovered her machination to steal Andrew's sword and scabbard. That her action would make the king vulnerable against Modredus in their contest over the Wizr board.

She did not deny her theft. Instead, she offered herself to me if I would teach her the secret of immortality. I refused. She offered herself again. Again, I refused. She promised me the next time she offered, I would not dare refuse her. And then she invoked a word of power that took away my breath. It could not suffocate me, but it did stop me from speaking. Her guards closed around me.

At first, I defended myself, but the Medium compelled me to surrender, so I did. When she discovered I didn't have the tome with me, I was bound in chains and taken to a grove in the wilderness surrounding Ploemeur. I discovered that she had acquired the Gradalis. Sir Owain was there, guardian of the grove, and in the grove, she used the Gradalis to conjure a storm that sent me back to the world of my nativity.

Before it sent me away, she warned me that she would come to my world and wreak vengeance on me by destroying it.

—Myrddin, Prisoner of Brythonica

CHAPTER TWELVE

The Flood

S till shrouded by the spell of invisibility, Eilean and Hoel walked hand in hand down the bridge. The noise of the surf crashing in the sloping gap was an interesting sound. The waves were relentless, battering the tiny island on all sides. A continual roar pounded against the rocky shore. No fleet of ships would have been safe crossing the gap. Even smaller vessels would have found the approach impossible, and the steep cliff leading up to the majestic castle of Tintagel would have daunted anyone but the truly reckless.

This was the bridge that Ulric had crossed with Maderos's help. She recalled so much of what she'd learned reading the tome about the birth of Andrew and his rise to King of Leoneyis. The seneschal and his lackeys had already crossed and were just on the other side. But the closer Hoel and Eilean came to the castle, the more ominous the situation felt. The king's seneschal was a murderer. That completely defied the goals of the order of knighthood Andrew had formed when he'd founded the Ring Table.

"I'm worried," she said to Hoel. "Getting in will be easy. Getting out may pose a problem."

"Under normal circumstances, I like to study a place for weaknesses. But we don't have the luxury of time. Neither of us know this place."

"At least we have the Cruciger orb," she said.

"How long can you maintain this spell?"

"I feel rested. It's hardly a strain to me now. But I have a feeling that I'll be using other words of power once we reach the king. I just want to deliver the message and then go back to Ploemeur to get the tome."

"It may not be as easy as that."

She sighed and squeezed his hand. "Let's find out, shall we?"

As they approached the gate leading inside the castle, the giant portcullis was beginning to close. The groan from the winches and chains made the ground tremble. It looked like a wall of fangs. Guards wearing the Raven badge lined both sides of the bridge, each holding a poleaxe and armed with a longsword belted to his tunic. Beyond the portcullis, she could see a huge, reinforced door that stood open, revealing a courtyard beyond. Several horses were already saddled and at the ready. Other mounts were being led to a barn door on one side, and she could smell the scent of manure from the paddock.

Hurrying to pass the barrier before the ponderous gate shut, they entered the courtyard. She saw knights milling about, wearing their full armor, bantering back and forth.

"Did you hear how much the king is paying for the man who brings back Peredur's head?" one man blustered.

"Aye. It's a king's ransom. I could rule Ceredigion with that treasure!"

"He ignored the rumors too long. Seems everyone knew about the queen's treachery but him."

"He didn't want to believe it, poor man. Just like one of us. But I'd kill the man who cuckolded me too."

They had to step carefully through the courtyard, lest they be noticed, moving past the horses and knights until they reached the rampart and doors leading to the interior of the castle. Above the door was a huge golden crest of the Raven badge. The walls of the castle were thick with ivy vines, layer upon layer of them, as well as the tint of moss, but the bare stone could be seen higher up, battered and worn with age.

As they reached the threshold where two guards were posted, she wondered how the men would react if she reached out and pulled open one of the doors before their eyes.

Her concern was abated when the doors suddenly opened from within, and another troop of knights came marching out, led by a distinguished-looking fellow in battered armor. His skin was weather-beaten, his hairline receding, and there were streaks of gray in his beard.

"Farewell, Sir Grenant," said one of the guards on duty.

The leather-faced knight looked stern and angry, and Eilean could sense his troubled thoughts as he prepared for war. She could read in his thoughts that Andrew had commanded them to overwhelm Brythonica. Sir Grenant didn't *want* to fight Sir Peredur. He didn't think he could defeat him. But he would do the high king's bidding and flood the coastal kingdom with his armies.

"Humph," snorted Sir Grenant.

After he passed, Eilean and Hoel, who had stepped aside, slunk into the castle before the doors were shut again.

The interior reminded her of an abbey in decoration and design. But it did not feel like one. A heavy, oppressive feeling hung in the air. Even with the massive stained-glass windows, it felt like it was full of shadows. She continued down the corridor, bypassing servants and then another group of knights who came marching down the hall. The marble tiles were soiled by the continual march of boots.

At the far end of the corridor lay another massive door. Her heart tugged her toward it.

"This way," she said.

"I won't let anything happen to you," Hoel promised. He lifted their entwined hands and kissed her fingers.

Her heart began to race faster, both from nerves and his show of affection.

The ornate door was embossed with gold and engraved with the symbol of the raven. Servants stood outside the doors, holding trays of food and pitchers of drink. They seemed to be waiting for permission to enter and do their duties.

Please, someone open the door, Eilean thought. When they reached the place, standing at the crack of the opening, she was surprised by how quickly her wish was fulfilled. The door opened, and a man in a servant's livery motioned for the food to be brought in.

Eilean tugged on Hoel's hand, and the two of them slipped in before the first of the servants could step forward.

The great hall was awash in the color purple. There were curtains of that color in plentitude, but the tint came from the enormous stained-glass windows fixed into pewter frames. Colonnades of pillars lined the room, and no less than thirty chandeliers hung from the vaulted ceiling, each made of glass.

The center of the hall contained the famous Ring Table, which was nearly empty of occupants. It was the width of a massive tree, the kind that grew in the mountains of Pry-Ree that would take a dozen men linking hands to surround. Some of the chairs were pulled askew.

Immediately she recognized the voice of Sir Queux and saw him standing next to another man, whom she assumed to be King Andrew because of the majesty of his garb. He wore a sweeping cape, so dark purple it was nearly black, with a decorative fringe of gold. A gem-studded velvet tunic was beneath it, strapped with two belts securing a dagger and a sword, the tongues of the belts ending in gold chapes.

His long hair, combed back, reminded her of brown bark. But it was his face that transfixed her. It was a face riddled with guilt and anger. This was a man who was ravaged by his emotions. It surprised her how young he looked. He wasn't even forty yet. Probably closer to thirty. She and Hoel followed the row of pillars slowly and silently as they approached the king and seneschal.

"My lord, you cannot allow such a trespass to go unpunished," Sir Queux was saying to the king.

"Are you sure it was Elle?" the king said in a low voice. Eilean could sense the brooding anger within him, the clash of feelings it revealed to her.

"How can anyone be sure when Wizrs are involved?" Queux replied.

"Why not come directly to Tintagel?" Andrew said. "With her power, she could have bypassed the bridge entirely."

"As I said when I arrived, I feared she did it to draw me away from you. She wanted to speak to you and you alone."

The king held up his hands. "She didn't come, though. There's been no sign of her."

"My lord, I must warn you again. If she does appear to you, in your chamber, you must call for your guards immediately. Do not allow her to speak."

Eilean could feel the seneschal's worry that Elle was coming with news of Myrddin. He was determined to prevent that from happening for reasons that were entirely unclear.

"Can I prevent it, Queux?"

"We'll have your rooms searched, of course."

"What do you think she wants? A truce?"

Queux sniffed noisily. "Of course. She knows you're about to destroy her kingdom. Even with all her vaunted power, she cannot prevent you from smashing Ploemeur into oblivion. She's harboring your enemies. She *must* be punished, my lord. It's long overdue."

"You know I value your honest advice, Queux. You've been invaluable to me from the start."

Eilean felt a prickle of pride coming from Sir Queux's thoughts. He loved it when the king praised him.

"I only want what is best for you, my lord."

Eilean felt the lie as it was spoken. No, Queux wanted what was best for himself. She gazed around the room. The servants were quietly setting up the food and drink. Some of the knights had already wandered over and were beginning to partake. She sensed discontent from many of them. She sensed fear from the servants.

Now.

The nudge from the Medium caught Eilean by surprise. The Medium wanted the warning to happen publicly, in front of the servants who'd gathered and would talk about it. The seneschal would try to prevent her speaking, of course. He'd desire to use force, but not as he did in their previous meeting. He wouldn't reveal the extent of his cruelty in front of the king.

"It's time," she whispered to Hoel and let go of his hand. She dropped the spell of illusion. Holding it for that long had tired her, but she still felt capable.

The king noticed them first. He frowned, his brow wrinkling in confusion.

Sir Queux's back was to them, but he noticed the sudden alteration of King Andrew's expression and glanced quickly over his shoulder. When he recognized her and Hoel, he gaped in surprise, his mind whirling with confusion at how they'd gotten through without raising an alarm.

"My lord, it's her!"

"Silence," Eilean said, holding up her hand. *"Ilemim,"* she whispered under her breath, invoking the word of power that would rob him of speech.

Sir Queux opened his mouth to shout, but no sound came out. Eilean lowered her hand and stepped closer to both of them. Hoel was right by her side.

The king looked confused and wary. His hand went to his sword. "You're not the Queen of Brythonica. Whom do you serve?"

"The Fountain," Eilean answered. "And I've come to warn you."

Sir Queux began gesticulating wildly to the knights, urging them to hurry. She heard swords clear scabbards.

"Defend the king!" someone shouted.

"Gheb-ool," Eilean invoked, raising a shield around the four of them. She felt impressed to add another word, the one for light. *"Le-ah-eer."*

A glow, like a circle of light, came down around them. She waited, her eyes fixed on the king. With her thoughts, she warned Hoel not to move out of the light.

When the first knight hit the boundary, he was thrown back violently and clattered on the marble tiles, cracking one in half with the impact. Another was thrown back, then another. The seneschal's eyes widened with panic. He put himself in front of the king and then drew his sword.

Hoel reluctantly drew Firebos, which began to glimmer in a sheath of blue flame.

When the king saw the blade, his eyes widened with shock.

Eilean felt the strain of holding so many spells. The last time she'd conjured so much power was in front of the High Seer, and she'd fainted from it.

"Where did you get that?" the king asked Hoel, his eyes glittering with deep emotion. He knew the weapon. He wanted it for himself.

Eilean could sense the desperation from him, the spasm of longing to have it again.

"I tried to come speak to you," Eilean said, "but your seneschal forbade it. He tried to have us killed. I come with a warning from the Fountain. You have betrayed your oaths. You are a false king. If you do not desist from the evil you've done, your kingdom, the great Leoneyis, will be drowned in the depths of the sea."

Knights had gathered around them on all sides. They had their weapons drawn. Some were shielding their faces from the brightness of the light, which seemed to be intensifying as Eilean spoke. She hadn't intended that, but she felt the power of the Medium surging within her.

"Who sent you!" the king roared at her, his face contorting with confusion and rage.

"The Fountain."

"What does that mean?" the king demanded. "The Fountain isn't a person. You came to my palace to threaten me? To threaten my people?"

"No, Your Majesty. I come to warn you. To warn your people. Turn back before it's too late."

She could sense the desperation in his mind. Sir Queux looked terrified. His lost voice made him frantic.

The king shouted, "Where do you hail from? The East Kingdoms? Occitania? *Where?*"

The king's eyes were hazel. In them, she saw the boy who had been an assistant pig keeper. She saw the deep pain of a husband betrayed. But she saw something else too. She saw a ruthlessness, an infection of jealousy, and a powerful man who no longer followed any law but his own desire.

It grieved her to see it. It made her want to weep.

"He thought so highly of you," she said, shaking her head. "He had such hopes for you."

"Who?" the king snarled.

"Your friend. Your companion for all those years. He *made* you king. He saved your life when your mother wanted you dead."

The king stared in bewilderment. "You . . . know Myrddin?"

A sob threatened her voice. "He's the one who taught me," she whispered. "It's not too late, Andrew. It's not too late to turn back."

Black crowded her vision, but she could not faint. Not now, not in front of everyone with only Hoel to defend her.

She sensed Sir Queux's intention. He was going to run her through with his longsword. The other knights and guards were surrounding them.

A word of power came to her thoughts. She uttered it without thinking.

"Hammayim."

A deluge of water came down. She revoked the shield before it hit, and the waters slammed like a waterfall into the great hall of Tintagel. Hoel wrapped one of his arms around her and pulled her to him as the torrent pummeled them. Water splashed on tiles. She heard knights shriek in terror, some of them slipping and falling because of the rush.

Her dress was soaked through. Her hair hung wetly as the rush of waters continued to flood the room. And then it ended as abruptly as it had started.

"Sahn-veh-reem," she whispered, invoking invisibility one last time to cover herself and Hoel.

The king was on his knees, his hair dripping into his face. He looked up, terror his primordial thought. Sir Queux had shuffled back onto his feet after fetching his dropped sword. Water was rushing out the door of the great hall, and the servants beyond were crying in bewilderment.

Eilean knew she was about to faint. *Help me,* she thought to Hoel. *Find us a place to hide.*

He sheathed his weapon and then lifted her off her feet and carried her into the shadows of the colonnade. She felt his mind frantic to find a door, a way out.

Unable to hold the invisibility any longer, she dropped it. She lay her head against Hoel's chest and gripped his shirt, squeezing it with all her will.

Her grip went slack as she blacked out.

My prison was Dochte Abbey. A kishion was my guard and tormenter. He tried to hurt me every way he knew. I was thrown from the upper spire in the dead of night. Blades had no effect on me. Starvation made me miss food, but it did not weaken me. He tried drowning. He even buried me alive for four days. Each time, the Medium delivered me from harm.

Still, I would not reveal where I'd hidden the tome.

The Medium delivered me from that dungeon as well. A druid, who had also been a prisoner, took pity on me. When his companions rescued him, he used his magic to kill the kishion and released me from my bondage. I went with them to the island of Moros, the last kingdom where druids were not persecuted.

And started a new life once again.

—Myrddin, Prisoner of Dochte Abbey

CHAPTER THIRTEEN

Blood

Eilean was dizzy when she regained consciousness. The smell of linens filled her nose. Uttering a little groan, she pushed herself up on her arms. Her damp dress chafed against her skin. It was dark.

"Hoel?" she whispered.

"I'm here."

A hand touched her shoulder. Then she heard him working at a leather strap, and soon a gentle glow came from the Cruciger orb, revealing their surroundings. The smooth, cold stones beneath her hands could now be seen, along with shelves that extended up to the ceiling. Cloaks, capes, and tunics were stacked and hung all around them, as well as reams of fabric of different kinds—velvet, brocade, and even silk.

Hoel was leaning against the wall of the strange wardrobe, and she saw he was wearing a tunic with the Raven standard woven into it. His rucksack, sword, and other weapons were poking out from beneath a heap of linens.

"Are we in a closet?" she asked him, brushing some of the wet tangles from her face.

His lips pursed into a smile. "Indeed we are. The door is around the corner over there." He gestured by jutting his chin. "I wasn't sure how long you'd be asleep."

She sat up the rest of the way and rubbed her arms. "I'm still damp. How long has it been?"

"A few hours? It was quite a commotion you caused."

"I'm glad I didn't faint in front of the court."

"You almost did. That waterspout you caused must have drained you. I'm glad I had a sense of what was coming from your thoughts, or we might have been separated."

"It wasn't my idea," she said. "The Medium inspired it."

He gave her a sympathetic look. "Do you want to change clothes? Even the servants' clothing is better than what most nobles wear in Pry-Ree. I think this one would fit you."

He scooted a bundle of dark blue cloth toward her.

She touched the fabric and found it to be velvet. She nodded to him.

Hoel rose and went around the corner, holding the orb to give her light. He sat back down and put his back to her while she quickly changed from one dress to the other. She sensed his firm self-control, his unwillingness to steal a glance at her, and she was grateful he was so honor bound.

The dark blue dress had some strips of lighter blue at the sleeves and hem. It fit her well, and she smoothed the fabric down her arms and stomach before coming around the corner so he could see she was finished.

"Thank you."

He looked up at her and nodded. She knelt and brushed hair from his forehead.

"Changed your mind about inviting King Andrew to invade our world?" he asked her with a teasing smile.

She snorted. "Have I ever. Whatever he once was, the man he is now is nothing but a snarl of anger, jealousy, and vengeance. Those are not the ideals that coax the Medium to you."

"Agreed. Our world has troubles enough of its own."

The words were innocuous enough, but something about his tone snagged her attention.

"What do you mean by that?"

Hoel sighed. "While you were unconscious, I had a brief vision."

"Tell me!"

He scrubbed a hand over his face. "It wasn't encouraging."

"Please. What was it about?"

"The Naestors' invasion. They've attacked Mon and Paeiz. The emperor is drawing his army back to his own lands to defend them. Hautland has been spared . . . so far, but the Naestors encroach from both sides. Villages and cities have been sacked. My vision ended with that. With suffering."

"You saw nothing of Pry-Ree?"

"The vision didn't show me our kingdom. And that worries me. I want to know that my kin are safe." He looked away, as if he didn't want her to see the extent to which that troubled him. She didn't need to see it in his eyes, though, she *knew* him.

"Thank you for telling me. I know we need to return, but we must do something to help the people here if we can. The Medium wills it."

"I know, Eilean. But this realm is on the verge of open war too, for different reasons. From what they say, the king's wife betrayed him. It would be a blow to any man."

"True. I'm not sure I could forgive that transgression. But there is more to it than just her betrayal. The seneschal has betrayed him too."

Hoel gave her a confused look. "What do you mean?"

"Sir Queux seems diligent and powerful, but he's riddled with guilt and worry. He pretends to be one thing on the outside, but he's totally different within. Maderos would have called him a *pethet*."

"So you don't think the king knows about Sir Queux?"

She shook her head.

"We need to get out of here. We have to get back to Brythonica, get the tome, and then get far away."

An unsettled feeling troubled her. A warning not to leave. "I don't think we're done here yet."

His eyes widened. "You want to go back to the great hall and tell him again? He didn't take it so well the first time."

She still felt unsettled. "I think that message was more for the servants. Think on it, Hoel. Such a display in the middle of Andrew's court. Everyone saw it. The warning will spread quickly."

"Undoubtedly. The king won't be able to stop it from happening. That will make you even more dangerous to him."

Her insides squirmed. "I still feel like I should talk to him again."

"Eilean," he said warily, shaking his head.

"It might go better if he wasn't with all his men. Especially the seneschal." She sighed, doubting herself again. She hated feeling this way, but the doubt had been with her so long it seemed woven into the fabric of her being. "But why would he listen to me? I'm a stranger to him. I'm even a stranger to myself." She looked down at their interlocked hands, her mind whirring and her heart burning with the sudden desire to know her parentage.

He stroked the edge of her face. "You doubt yourself? After all you've done?"

"I've done nothing without the Medium's help." She'd wanted to wait until they made it back home to ask him to tell her about her parents, but the urge to know was stronger now. Part of her needed it. "Tell me, Hoel. I need to know who they were."

"Your parents? Their identity needn't define yours. You are powerful in the Medium regardless of who they were," he whispered, his eyes intense.

She raised his hand to her mouth and kissed his fingers. "Tell me, Hoel. I think I'm ready now."

"Are you sure you want to know?"

She nodded, but a shiver of worry went down her spine. "Is it that dreadful?"

He gave a little half shrug. "It surprised me, but it's not dreadful."

That was a little relief. "Tell me."

"Your father's name was Asmund."

Her brow wrinkled. "That's not a Pry-rian name."

"No. He was from Naess."

Dread enveloped her heart like an icy shroud. The Naestors were a warlike people who had been attacking the maston kingdoms. They were the Blight summoned by the Medium to puncture the maston order's pride. "My father was a Naestor?"

Hoel nodded. He stroked her hand. "Your mother was Pry-rian. Her name was Siân."

She felt her throat clench with tears. "S-Siân? My mother's name was Siân?"

"She was a peasant. Probably cared for the fields of flax near Tintern."

Eilean wasn't sure how she felt about that. Truthfully, she'd wondered if her parents were learners who'd had an illicit romance, and both were too ashamed to claim her. Wouldn't that have explained Eilean's strength with the Medium, which tended to grow stronger from generation to generation of those who believed?

"Maybe I'm a little disappointed," she admitted. "I'd assumed my parents were learners."

Hoel squeezed her hand. "I thought the same," he said. "How else to explain your powers?" He slowly shook his head. "The Cruciger orb gave me their names and informed me of their deaths, and then the Medium granted me a vision. Your father was wounded. He'd been injured during a skirmish and left behind with the dead. They sent the peasants to bring the dead to the burial fires. Your mother found him, alive but barely. She had pity for him. Compassion. So she hid him and tended his wounds. And fell in love with him. And he with her."

Eilean felt tears blur her vision. She wiped them away, eager to hear more—but worried about what she might learn. "Go on."

"He was discovered eventually. He'd been watching her work in the flax fields and was too careless. He was caught and, as you can imagine, blamed for all the violence against our people." His voice was sad. "He should have been brought to the king for justice, but the villagers killed him. Your mother was devastated and learned, not long after, that she was with child. You. She didn't want to live, not without Asmund. But she kept herself alive until the very end of her time. That happens in some women. She gave birth to you and died, without revealing the name of your father. You were taken to Tintern as a wretched and given to Ardys and Loren to raise. They couldn't have children. You were precious to them."

Eilean began to choke on her tears. She hugged Hoel and wept softly on his shoulder, her heart overflowing with emotion. She missed Ardys and Loren so much. She missed Celyn too. Her life had been so simple back then. Perhaps because *she* was simple. There was no lost ancestry, no claim to some august family name. She was Eilean . . . a wretched born of tragedy. It made her heart hurt to know she could never be more than that.

Hoel stroked the back of her neck, beneath her tangled hair. She was so grateful to him for being there, for sharing this knowledge with her with such compassion and love. Not even Aldermaston Gilifil would have known the truth about her birth. Only the Medium knew, and through the Cruciger orb and his rare Gift, Hoel.

"Thank you," she said after the storm of feelings had ebbed. Her nose was dripping, which embarrassed her. She was about to wipe it on her sleeve, but Hoel shook his head and took the edge of one of the hanging cloaks in the closet and gave it to her instead. She was grateful for that mercy as well.

"How do you feel?" he asked, sliding his fingers into her hair by her ear.

"Disappointed? Grateful?" She sighed. Then she kissed his cheek. "At least I know their names. Asmund and Siân. Thank you for telling me, Hoel."

"I still think you would have made an excellent hunter," he quipped with a flash of a grin.

His words were meant as a jest, but they made her flinch. "I suppose it is in my blood," she whispered.

Hoel's brow wrinkled. "I didn't mean it like that."

"I know. But it hurts all the same." She sighed again. "The Medium is using the Naestors as a Blight against our people because of the unfaithfulness of the maston order. If people knew . . ." If they knew of her true ancestry, she could be persecuted for it.

"No one knows but you and I," he said calmingly. "No one else will know."

"The orb could just as easily tell someone else," she said. "I don't want the High Seer to find out."

Hoel nodded, his expression mirroring her own concern. It comforted her to know he was truly on her side—that he wouldn't forsake her.

A feeling came from the Medium. A strong one.

"I need to see King Andrew," she said. "Now."

Hoel frowned. "I don't think it would be wise."

"Nevertheless, I must," she said, rising.

He came to his feet too. "Let me gather my weapons."

A feeling of impending danger came when he said that. "No."

He gave her a fierce look. "I'm coming with you."

Again, there was a strong prompting against it.

"No, Hoel. I must go alone."

"You can't use the Cruciger orb in your state. How will you find him?"

"The Medium will guide me."

He gripped her shoulders. "I don't like this."

"You have to trust me, Hoel. I have to go, *now*." But she felt his worry bloom in his mind. "Wait for me here," she added. "Promise me you'll wait."

"I don't want anything to happen to you," he said with concern.

"If you come, something bad will happen. I feel it." She tried to pull away, but his grip tightened. "Hoel, please. You have to trust me."

They'd come this far together. The next part she had to do alone.

He was in mental agony, and his expression revealed it. A worried brow, a frown of concern. His teeth were slightly bared. He wanted to trust her, but worry raged in his mind like flames.

She cupped his face in her hands. "Trust is hard when you don't want to let go of something you care about. Don't trust *me*. Trust the Medium."

There was a haunted look in his eyes, but he nodded slightly, bringing the turmoil in his mind under control.

He released her shoulders. "Be careful, Eilean. By Cheshu, be careful."

Her love and regard for him deepened in that moment. And she realized, as she turned to leave, that being trusted was a greater compliment than being loved.

I tried my best to prepare Andrew and his world for the coming of Safehome in the time I was given. My hope is that he will flourish. He is surrounded by honorable men, knights who espouse the principles of Virtus. He has a devoted queen who loves him deeply and sincerely and is a wise and merciful counselor. The Harbinger's daughter said I will not be permitted to return to that world for many seasons, not until the purposes of the Knowing are fulfilled.

So I begin again, learning the ways of the druids so that I may bridge their knowledge and help them see a better way. Some within their order use the old lore in perversity. Such is always the case no matter who the people.

Integrity without knowledge is useless. Knowledge without integrity is dangerous.

—Maderos, Druid of the Isle of Moros

CHAPTER FOURTEEN

Tintagel Castle, Kingdom of Leoneyis
Thirteenth Year of the Reign of King Andrew Ursus

Andrew sat at the Ring Table, but the discussion amidst his fellow knights did not penetrate his mind. There was a dilemma that pressed on him day and night. It robbed him of sleep and soured his breakfast. He was drawing closer to thirty years old, and he still had no heir to defend Tintagel and the empire he had fashioned. The stakes of the Wizr game caused him unending anxiety. His empire felt composed of sand, like the castles children would fashion along the seashore. How long before a wave came along and melted it all away?

"My lord, Sir Owain has just arrived from Brythonica."

Andrew blinked, rousing from his dismal reverie. Sir Queux had nudged his elbow.

It was true. Sir Owain was standing in the great hall of Tintagel, equipped in armor that shone a multitude of colors in the light spilling from the multicolored glass windows. The knight's cloak was secured by the Raven badge, and he held his helmet in the crook of his arm.

Andrew waved him forward, and Owain came and took his seat at the Ring Table. The murmurs of discussion quieted. There were twelve other seats at the table, not including Andrew's. Myrddin had said there was some significance to the number twelve in the other worlds the Wizr had visited. The knights were a brotherhood. He'd chosen each man who sat at the table. Sir Queux was on his right hand. Sir Peredur, on his left, sat in the Siege Perilous, the favored chair.

"Welcome home, Sir Owain," Andrew said, inclining his head to the knight who had just seated himself.

There was a brooding look in the man's eyes. He seemed uncomfortable. Guilty, even. How Andrew missed Myrddin's ability to read other men's thoughts. The wisest at the table was undoubtedly Sir Queux. Andrew would ask him later if he'd seen any worrisome marks coming from Owain.

"It is good to be back," said Owain. "I've returned from the mission you gave me, my liege. But alas, I bring bad tidings. Myrddin is gone."

A stab of disappointment pricked Andrew's gut, although he'd guessed as much given the man's demeanor and the fact that he'd arrived alone. "Truly?"

Sir Owain held up his hands. "The Queen of Brythonica has not seen the Wizr for many, many months. I have gone as far as the Fisher King's realm, chasing shadows. Queen Essylt believes that Myrddin has departed this world. He may not be back in our lifetimes."

Andrew's stomach clenched with dread. Memories of the pig styes in Farfog Castle surfaced in his thoughts. With them came memories of Elle. How would things have turned out differently if he'd chosen the scullion over the Princess of Atabyrion? Elle's feelings for Andrew had withered over the years. But he, without a son, was tortured by the notion that he'd made the wrong choice all those years ago.

"Has any man here heard anything of the Wizr Myrddin?" Andrew asked, looking from face to face at the men assembled around the table.

Silence came in response. Andrew shook his head regretfully. "Thank you, Sir Owain, for your pains. Did you pass through Brythonica on your return?"

"I did, my lord."

"And how fares the queen?"

Sir Owain's lip twitched. He shifted in his seat.

Perhaps Owain wasn't comfortable speaking in front of the others. That was odd. Andrew had always encouraged openness among his knights. He'd chastise him later for not being more forthright.

"Why are you fidgeting, man?" Sir Queux asked Sir Owain in a challenging tone. Andrew was grateful his seneschal had noticed it too.

"There is one bit of news," Sir Owain said softly.

"Oh?" Andrew pressed. He rested his palms on the table, enjoying the feeling of the wood grain against his skin.

"I would prefer to share it privately, my lord."

"This is the king's council," Andrew reminded him. "We share one will, one oath, one rite. I see you are distressed. Speak!"

The look of anguish on Owain's face was as ripe as a cara fruit. The other knights began to fidget and exchange worried looks.

"Your loyalty is to the king," Queux reminded gravely.

Sir Owain sighed. "He made a prophecy before he left."

"Speak up, man!" Queux scolded.

Sir Owain glared at the seneschal. Then he slammed his hand on the table and rose from his chair. "I'm told Myrddin uttered a prophecy ere he left. It does not bode well for our empire. That is why I am hesitant to speak it. But I shall if my king commands it again." He looked at Andrew pleadingly. He didn't wish to speak before everyone.

Why was there guilt in his eyes? When struck by an arrow, the best thing to do was pull it out.

"Speak it," said Andrew. He waved his hands to include those gathered at the table. "We are all friends here."

Sir Owain bowed his head in defeat. He took a deep breath, then lifted his chin and swung his gaze around to those assembled at the Ring Table.

"Those who heard Myrddin speak are calling it the Dreadful Deadman prophecy. I was told it by Lord Lodovic, Queen Essylt's seneschal."

Andrew glanced at Queux, but the knight's eyes were fixed on Owain's.

"It goes thus: *When E is come and gone, take heed, for war shall never cease. After E is come and gone, then cometh Ceredigion next to destruction by seven kings. The Fountain shall cease to flood the land, and after that will come a Dreadful Deadman with a royal wife of the best blood in the world. And he shall have the hollow crown and shall set Ceredigion on the right way and put out all heretics.*"

Andrew was baffled by the pronouncement. He leaned back in his chair, feeling perplexed and uneasy.

"Ceredigion is the land you rule," said Sir Queux to Owain. "Why is the prophecy about Ceredigion's destruction? Why is its destruction 'next'?"

Sir Owain turned back to the king with pleading eyes. "Didn't you hear it?"

"Hear what?"

"The whisper of the Fountain," said Owain softly.

The king felt even more baffled. "What do you mean?" He looked from left to right.

"I did," said Sir Peredur.

Sir Owain's head jerked up. "You heard it too? Thank the Fountain I'm not alone!"

"You are both babbling nonsense," Andrew said angrily. "What whisper? I heard nothing but a prophecy of the Dreadful Deadman and another man's kingdom."

"My lord," said Sir Peredur stiffly, "the words of the prophecy are like a warhorse. They only carry the message to those who are meant to hear it."

Owain pointed at Peredur and nodded in agreement. "I'd not thought of it like that. My lord, when I heard the prophecy for the first time, I heard a different message attached to the words. Did anyone else hear it?"

He looked around the room. Sir Moriaen raised his hand and nodded.

"Three of us," said Owain. "Only three." He sighed.

"What did you hear?" asked Sir Queux with a throb of righteous anger in his voice.

"Leoneyis will be destroyed first," said Sir Owain. "There is no heir to the throne. The king's sword is lost. Myrddin is gone. The prophecy of the Dreadful Deadman is about a child who will be born to rule the next empire. To rule Kingfountain."

"What is Kingfountain?" demanded Sir Queux. "There is no country of that name."

"I don't know what it is," Sir Owain said. "I just heard it in the whispers. But it will be the *next* kingdom to rise once this one falls."

Andrew stared at his friend and felt a twitch of jealousy in his heart. He hadn't heard any such whispers himself. He regretted now not having asked Owain to explain in private. Why had Myrddin left such a prophecy? When "E" comes and goes? What could it mean? Who was E? Was it Elle? Was this a warning about her rising up?

"Sir Queux, write down the prophecy," Andrew said. "Have it saved in the archives."

"Of course," said the seneschal.

"My lord," Sir Owain said with tears choking his voice. "My lord, you are in mortal danger."

***

Night had fallen over Tintagel. The news of the Dreadful Deadman prophecy had affected everyone. How could it not? Andrew was shaken by it, and so was his wife. He had tried to comfort Genevieve, but she blamed herself for being barren. In the end, he couldn't endure her tears any longer and had fled to his solar to be alone.

That was where Sir Queux found him.

"I almost set the whole castle searching for you when you weren't in your room," said Queux with a chuckle. "I was going to search among the piglets next."

Andrew had been gazing at the fire in the hearth, watching the different colors dance in the flames. With the sun down, the panes of stained glass no longer filled the room with a whorl of colors. He picked at his beard, remembering something Myrddin had once said.

"Do you know that colors are just in your mind?" he asked Queux.

"My lord?"

"Myrddin tried to explain it to me once. Color comes from light. Like the fire in the hearth. Like the sunrise. Part of it breaks off when it strikes things. He showed it to me with a shard of glass once. All the colors danced on the wall. From reds to oranges, to greens and violet. It's all there, in the light. We only see it because of how the Fountain made our eyes. Isn't that strange?"

"Myrddin said many things that were strange. Like being 'happy as a pig in filth.' I never understood how muck could make one content. Even pigs."

Andrew chuckled. "I remember that. But it was true. It was all true."

"And you are worried this prophecy might also be true?"

Andrew turned and looked at his seneschal, his friend. "He also taught me that I can achieve whatever I set my mind and heart to."

"Now *that* I believe," said Queux with a smile.

Andrew rose from the couch and turned. "I'm going to name an heir."

Queux blinked in surprise. "What?"

"The high kings of the past did it," Andrew said. "I can do the same. If I die, at least someone I choose will rule Tintagel."

"What about the Wizr board?" asked Queux. "Do you think naming an heir will prevent the destruction of Leoneyis?"

"It has to," said Andrew. "I will make it so with my thoughts. The magic will obey me if I'm convinced it will. I am convinced."

"Why not take another wife?" Sir Queux suggested.

Andrew shook his head. "This is a test from the Fountain. I will name my heir and act as if Genevieve will conceive. I'm young still. So is she."

Sir Queux stepped forward. "And your heir? Have you decided on someone?"

Andrew nodded. "Peredur."

"Of course," Sir Queux said with a grunt. "Of course you would choose him."

"He's ruled in my absence before. He's trustworthy, faithful, and the people admire him."

"They do indeed," said Sir Queux.

"No. Tomorrow. I cannot stop the rumors about the prophecy. I don't intend to. I'm not afraid of it, Queux. Myrddin said that our greatest success often comes just after the moment of greatest alarm. When we faced Modredus, I thought we were all going to die. Instead, I more than tripled the size of my domain. This is another test from the Fountain. I will prevail."

Sir Queux smiled with enthusiasm. "If any man can, my lord, it is you. I spoke to Owain after the meeting. I'm worried about his loyalty. There was something in his eyes."

"The prophecy has gotten to him, no doubt."

Queux shook his head. "It was more than that."

"Speak your mind," Andrew pressed.

"I'm going to keep my eye on him," said Queux. "It's probably nothing. I'm eager to ensure everyone at the Ring Table stays loyal to you."

If only everyone in Tintagel were as steadfast as Sir Queux. Andrew put his hand on Queux's shoulder and squeezed. "I'm going to talk to Genevieve about Owain. I want to hear what she has to say about your suspicions."

"She's talking to Peredur. You can tell them both."

Andrew frowned. "He was with her just now?"

"I went there looking for you," said Queux. "They've always been . . . friends."

That subtle hesitation in his words sent a jolt of emotion into Andrew's heart. Yes, if he were to die, it would leave Genevieve a widow. Just as his own mother had been left a widow after her husband perished in the war. A feeling of unease gathered within him, but he squelched it. Thoughts could be so dangerous. Like weeds, the bad ones could take over a garden. Myrddin had warned him of that.

Sir Queux gave him an encouraging smile, and Andrew felt a wave of gratitude for the man's years of faithful service. He'd thought about naming Queux as his heir, but Queux was better in his role as seneschal. He was the second-most powerful man in all the realms and had juggled the numerous responsibilities with an ability and dedication that any king would admire. He could be a bit hot-headed at times, but he was fearless in battle, upright, and he could be relied on to fulfill his responsibilities with the utmost diligence.

No, if the Fountain demanded Andrew's death, then he'd want Peredur as his heir.

Peredur was one he could trust with his life.

Surely.

The mastons see druids as heretics and persecute them. Some of their beliefs and magic may be heretical. I am uncertain on that score. There are other worlds, to be sure, and they are not as they are assumed to be. Understanding is the bridge we need here, not violence or hatred, and it takes time to build bridges.

Druid lore is fascinating. They are a peculiar people, steeped in traditions that go beyond this world. They are arbiters of justice, sought out for their impartiality. They revere the Dryad trees and are the self-proclaimed guardians of them. They revere and honor life, from the smallest of beetles to the wildest of beasts. I have a little companion now—a spirit creature they call a púca. It loves to be flattered incessantly.

Druids have no innate magic of their own but harness power through agreements made with spirit creatures. That being said, this is true of most but not of all. And they think words of power in order to tame the flames. Who taught them these words?

—Maderos, Druid of the Isle of Moros

CHAPTER FIFTEEN

Words Spoken Softly

E ilean walked the corridors of Tintagel without using magic or otherwise drawing any attention to herself. The dress that Hoel had found for her helped her blend in with the myriad servants busily at work. She judged it was twilight from the darkened curtains and the torches lighting the corridors. Every time she reached an intersection, she paused and listened for the Medium to guide her path. And each time she felt a little nudge one way or another.

Until she saw another servant, a woman, carrying a silver tray and walking toward some stairs.

Follow her.

Eilean hastened up to the woman, who was only a few years older than herself, joining her on the steps winding up a tower shaft. She could hear the noise of the tray, the jostling of a bowl and spoon as the servant continued past the next level to an upper floor and then left the stairs.

Walking as quietly as she could, Eilean reached the landing.

Do not be seen.

Eilean invoked the words of invisibility and then entered the corridor. She immediately felt the strain of using her magic. Not enough time had passed for her to fully recover from the incident in the hall, but the spell was necessary. Two knights stood at the far end, guarding a door, and the servant bearing the tray walked toward them. Eilean quickened her speed so that she could slip in behind her.

"The king's supper, Maciel?" one of the knights asked.

"Aye. He asked for soup and bread tonight," replied the servant.

"The king's seneschal is meeting with him presently. Be quick and depart, lass. Unless the king *asks* you to stay. If he does—obey."

The knight gave her a meaningful look, and Eilean sensed dread in the girl's thoughts. Flustered, she bowed her head to the knight, who was now gazing at her with a wicked gleam in his eye.

The other knight opened the door, and the girl hefted the tray and walked in. Eilean saw both of them ogling her, giving each other appreciative nods.

Eilean slipped between them, following Maciel into the room, which she discovered to be the king's personal chamber. There was an enormous bed against the far wall with huge draped curtains hanging from the posts. Several doors led to various closets, a bath, and even a rotunda of sorts, veiled in gauzy curtains. It was an immaculate space, each couch and chair made of sumptuous materials, and there were pillars with statuary from a variety of places, no doubt gifts from other kings.

The king and his seneschal were sitting on couches opposite each other, deep in conversation. King Andrew saw the girl enter and motioned for her to bring the tray to the table between the couches.

The seneschal glanced at the girl, then ignored her.

"Although we leave tomorrow to humble Brythonica," the seneschal said, "I thought it prudent to mention that a madman was arrested by the port guard earlier today. He was raving that Leoneyis was about to be drowned in a flood."

Andrew's eyebrows forked in displeasure. "I thought you barred the castle doors here and at the citadel."

"I did, my lord," said Sir Queux. "No one left. But he was making his claims before that woman and her knight mysteriously appeared in the great hall. They may have set him off."

The king frowned. "Who is the man?"

"His name is Penryn. He had his granddaughter with him. From what my guards explained, he brought them across the sea from Brythonica. Clearly the queen is trying to disrupt the invasion by spreading falsehoods."

Eilean could sense the thoughts of both men. Sir Queux wanted to have Penryn silenced—permanently. His life was in danger. The king was still rattled by the display of magic from earlier. He had his own suspicions about who was behind it. *It would be just like Modredus, Occitania's king, to arrange for such a thing.*

The woman, Maciel, set the tray down in front of the king.

"Go," the seneschal told her, without looking at her. Eilean felt her relief as she hurried away. The knights shut the door.

"I want to see the madman tomorrow," King Andrew said.

Eilean sensed immediate resistance from the seneschal. He didn't like that idea at all, but when he spoke, it was in a conciliatory tone. "Of course, Your Majesty. If you wish it."

"I do. I want to see what he knows about the two who came to court today. It may have something to do with the Dreadful Deadman prophecy."

"Naturally. Although . . . my *men* are interrogating him now. I thought it beneath your station to handle such a trivial matter. But if you wish to spend your precious time, right before we launch a military campaign, then of course you may do as you think right."

Eilean would have felt the manipulation woven into the words even if she couldn't sense his thoughts.

"What happened today is important, Queux. It may be a sign from the Fountain."

"Or a rather brazen display of a Wizr's power. Does it not seem like a calculated attempt to take your focus off your main objective? That objective being, of course, to punish those who have *wronged* you."

Andrew lifted the chafing dish lid and leaned forward to smell the soup. He broke the loaf of bread and then dipped part of it into the broth.

Sir Queux was watching the king intently, trying to see if his words were being received as he hoped. His insidious motives made Eilean want to bash his head with a tray. Besides which, she was now worried about Penryn and the girl. Both were innocent of any machinations against the king. But with someone like Sir Queux pulling the strings, she feared for their safety.

"Do you think Myrddin is back after all these years?" the king asked after chewing and swallowing. "What if Penryn is *him* in disguise?"

That whimsical thought nearly sent Queux into a panic. Eilean felt the frenzy of his mind, his loathing for and abject fear of the Wizr. But he was incredibly good at dissembling. His face revealed none of his inner turmoil.

"Oh, I doubt that," he said languidly.

"But you do remember the prophecy those years ago. The one that Owain brought to us." Upon saying the knight's name, the king's mouth warped in displeasure.

"Owain is a traitor. The first to break his oath."

"But does that make the prophecy false?"

"My lord, I don't know. Let's consider the facts. Three men claimed to have heard the whispers from the Fountain that day. And now all three of those men have betrayed you and joined their loyalty to the Queen of Brythonica." He held up his hands and shrugged. "Is that a coincidence? We both know the King of Occitania would like nothing better than to annex her lands. If she allows it, if she gives him her loyalty, then they switch sides on the board. They will save their own lands at the cost of yours, and your destruction will come at no cost to them. How is that for loyalty?"

The king dabbed another hunk of bread into the soup and ate it. Eilean felt a surge of desperation. She needed to warn the king against Sir Queux. The man was totally unfaithful, yet the king was blind to it.

Patience.

"I appreciate your candor, Queux. You say what you feel."

The seneschal bowed his prickly scalp and gave the king a kindly smile. "Thank you, Your Grace. I've served you with all my heart."

The stink of his falsehood made Eilean wrinkle her nose.

"I hope I've rewarded you sufficiently for your faithfulness."

"Serving you has been the deepest reward I could ask for."

The king sighed, enjoying the flattery as much as the púca would.

"I have one more reward for you, Queux. One you deserve more than any other man."

Eilean sensed the seneschal's inner delight. "Oh?" he said complacently.

"I was wrong to name Peredur my heir. I see that now. I thought he loved me too much to betray me. To seduce . . ." The king's feelings roiled with anger, jealousy, and misery so acute that they robbed him of words. And there was another feeling behind those, tucked in deep. Guilt. Terrible guilt. He swallowed, trying to master his emotions.

"You did not deserve what they did to you," Queux said with sympathy.

"No man does," said the king hoarsely. "I am going to name you my heir, Queux. Years ago, you surrendered the kingdom to me willingly. Now it's my turn to surrender it to you."

Eilean was horrified.

JEFF WHEELER

"It was only right, my liege. You found the sword in the well." The seneschal's emotions throbbed with hopefulness. He was going to rule after all. Years and years of patience and subservience would finally be rewarded. He chided himself to be careful, to not let his glee show.

Eilean bristled in her hiding place, eager to reveal his subterfuge.

"You're too modest. I should have given it to you earlier. I will fix that error on the morrow. If something happens during this campaign, I want all to know that *you* are my legitimate heir."

Sir Queux dropped from the couch and knelt on one knee before the king. He took Andrew's hand and kissed the coronation ring.

"May the Fountain bless you, my liege, with a long and prosperous life."

And may you drown in the Deep Fathoms before we ever reach Brythonica.

Horror clutched at Eilean's throat. She'd heard the unspoken thought as clearly as if he'd spoken it aloud.

Andrew reached and gripped the other man's shoulder. "Best of friends. Loyal to the last."

Queux reached for Andrew's shoulder. "Best of friends. Loyal to the last."

"You should get some of this soup from the kitchen yourself," said Andrew after the moment had passed. "It's truly wonderful."

Sir Queux rose from the couch and brushed off his tunic front. "There is much business to do before I can retire, my liege. About that madman. Shall I . . . take care of it?"

"You're right. I shouldn't be bothered with such trivialities. I should rest. I haven't slept well in days. My thoughts are still in commotion about what happened today. About *everything* that has happened. Maybe Elle really was trying to play a trick on us."

"She thinks you've wronged her, and revenge is an act of passion."

"Wisely said, my friend. I won't keep you from your many difficult duties."

The seneschal bowed elegantly, barely hiding a smirk. He'd won. The king had eaten from his hand like a tame squirrel in the woods.

"Would you like companionship this evening, my lord? I can send someone who can make you forget your sorrows. Once we leave the palace, such . . . trifles will be much harder to acquire. The serving girl, Maciel, perhaps? She's pleasant to look at. I've seen you smile at her often enough."

The king stared down at his bowl. Eilean could feel the king's inner struggle. Part of him knew it was wrong. Part of him just didn't care anymore. Guilt flickered within him again, an old wound.

"Yes. Send her. Or anyone. As long as she's willing. I trust you."

Sir Queux flashed a smile. His thoughts were veiled from the king. Oh, they'd be willing to do as ordered. They all enjoyed their positions in Tintagel. None of them wanted to be cast out in disgrace at the seneschal's command.

"You do me great honor, my lord. Thank you."

"Good night, Queux."

"Sleep well, my liege. I suspect you will." He gave the king a knowing wink and then started for the door. His departure would provide her with an opportunity to address the king, but it would also make it more difficult for her to leave. Should she follow Queux out? Perhaps the Medium had simply wished for her to witness their conversation?

Patience.

The seneschal left the room. Andrew stared down at the bowl, taking a few more hunks of bread to sop up the remains of the broth, then rose from the couch. His thoughts were in turmoil. Memories of his wife tormented him. Eilean could sense the queen in his thoughts—the years of shared laughter, sorrow, victory, and near defeat. Emotions collided within him powerfully. He missed her. He hated her. And he was tormented by something he'd done to her.

Andrew let out a gasp of pain and dropped to one knee, squeezing the cushion of the couch until his knuckles were white and quivering. The look of anguish on his face tore at Eilean's heart.

His thoughts came as a prayer. *If the visitor today truly was a warning, give me a sign—O thou Fountain holy! I know I'm unworthy. My shame slashes me like a sword. I don't deserve your help or mercy. I know that. I plead for it anyway. Before I throw away my soul. Please!*

She felt his sincerity, his determination, and his torment. Tears trickled down his cheeks, and then he hung his head and wept.

Speak the words in your heart. Nothing more.

She felt her invisibility spell fall away. She stood by the couches.

The king's head turned slowly. When he saw her, he trembled in fear and fell onto his back, scrabbling to get away from her.

"King of Leoneyis," she said, feeling a rush of magic like the murmuring of waters come through her. As before, the words came to her mind. She knew exactly what to say. "You are deceived. Your wife was faithful to you. You put your trust in villains. I am the Fountain's warning. I speak the truth. Hearken, assistant pig keeper, before it is too late to save your people. If you perish, so will they. Your sins are theirs and theirs are now yours. Turn back from your pride. Remember what Myrddin taught you. It begins with a thought."

He cowered from her. He gaped and gasped like a fish flung from a river.

She felt nothing else to say. So she just stared at him, imploringly, sending the truth of her words into his mind with her determination.

"Who . . . who are you?" he whispered in fear.

"I am the sign you prayed for," she said softly.

He fainted. Her words had so bewildered him, as had her sudden appearance in his most private chamber, that he collapsed in a daze.

She stared down at him and then turned her gaze to the rest of the room. The chamber was suffused with so many memories. She could almost hear them, the shriek of a woman in distress. The moan of a man in despair. The echoes of old thoughts made her shudder.

Eilean walked to the door but paused. If she opened the handle and left, invisibly, the guards would find the king sprawled on the floor. It would raise a cry. But should she stay until the servant girl Maciel was brought? What should she do?

She sensed the thoughts of others coming to the door and quickly reinvoked the invisibility spell. From beyond the door, she heard the seneschal's muffled voice.

"It would please *me* if you please the king tonight."

"I-I will, my lord," stammered the girl.

The door opened, and Eilean stepped back.

As soon as Maciel entered the room, Queux quickly shut the door behind her.

Maciel didn't look frightened. In fact, she gazed around the room with a smile of appreciation and a smirk of delight. Then she saw the king sprawled on the floor.

"I can tell you're still in here," said the servant. "I felt you from outside when you spoke the word. *Ekluo.*"

The invisibility spell wrinkled and vanished. Eilean started with surprise.

The serving girl watched her, eyes twinkling, then began to metamorphose into someone else.

"Asphuxis."

Eilean's breath was sucked from her body. She couldn't inhale. It felt like her chest had been constricted. Panic filled her. Black dots began to crowd her vision.

"Let's go back to Ploemeur, shall we?" asked a woman's voice as a hand gripped Eilean's arm. It was a voice Eilean had never heard before. *"Kennesayrim."*

It felt as if the stone floor vanished, and they were both plunging down a cliff into the crashing surf below Tintagel.

The true art of memory is the art of attention. Observe the little things. The things unspoken. The things others miss. The druids have been successful in Moros because they notice when passions run high and why. Big tumults are often caused by small incidents. Repair those, and the larger matters may take care of themselves.

If I am to influence the druid order, to help them better understand the Knowing and its patterns, I must start small. Little woad tattoos might help bridge my understanding of who they are and why they are here. If you want to understand someone, understand their smallest acts.

—Maderos, Druid of the Isle of Moros

CHAPTER SIXTEEN

The Queen of Brythonica

A gasp of air, an unclenching of her chest, and the dizziness and blackness quickly faded from Eilean's consciousness. The panic she'd felt started to ebb, and she realized, with relief, that she wasn't going to die.

"Acquaint her with the situation, Kariss. Tell her I will come speak with her when I am ready."

Eilean realized she was lying on marble tiles and could hear the patter of a fountain nearby.

"She's awakening. Stun her."

"Yes, my lady," said Kariss in response to the command.

A sharp prick to the back of Eilean's neck dropped her again.

When she roused some time later, she was disoriented by the change of smell. The scent of a tallow candle, the same kind she'd used at Muirwood, flooded her senses, temporarily confusing her. But Mordaunt—Maderos—was not in the next room unable to sleep and waiting for her company. As the fog of unconsciousness faded, she rubbed the sore spot at the back of her neck—and felt a small prick of pain.

Panic.

How long had she lain unconscious on this mat? How many days had passed since she and Hoel had crossed the mirror gate? For a moment, she couldn't remember, and the thought of being trapped in King Andrew's world nearly paralyzed her with fear. Especially knowing that a flood was coming to destroy Leoneyis—a flood massive enough to bury it that would certainly drown Brythonica as well.

"You're awake at last?"

Eilean recognized Kariss's voice. Lifting her head, she saw the tallow candle sat on a table, and by its light saw the gleam of Maderos's tome, the Sefer Yetzirah. Two chairs were arranged at the short, squat table, and Kariss sat in one of them, her friendly smile belying the crafty look in her eyes.

"Tenumowet," Eilean said, invoking the word of power to make Kariss fall asleep.

When she said the word, she did not feel the tingle of magic go down her arms. Nothing happened at all.

Kariss smiled even wider. "Your words don't work in this room," she said, tilting her palms and gesturing to the chamber. "This is where she practices her magic. She invoked a word before we put you in here so that you'd understand our language."

A pit of dread opened up in Eilean's stomach. What day was it? She was still wearing the blue servant's dress. There were no windows in the room, and the metal door revealed no light, so there was no way to discern the time.

"Are we in her castle?"

Kariss nodded. "Where is Captain Hoel? Is he still at Tintagel?"

The question made the pit open wider. Hoel was indeed back at Tintagel. He would be worried sick about her, especially when she didn't return. Thankfully, he had the Cruciger orb. He'd be able to find her with it. That thought brought some measure of hope.

"What does the queen want from me?" Eilean asked, ignoring the question.

"You already know. It hardly requires imagination. The tome is before you. So are some sheafs of paper and an abundance of ink. How long is your covenant at the mirror gate?"

Eilean stared at her, not wanting to reveal anything.

Kariss sighed. "I can *make* you tell me. There is a poison that will loosen your tongue. It will put you in a trance of sorts, and you'll answer anything I ask you. If *she* commands me, I will. But I'd rather gain your cooperation. It would go better for you in the end."

Eilean felt sick to her stomach. She'd fought Kariss in the dungeon beneath Dochte Abbey, but Hoel had been with her then. Even with the brief training she'd done, she didn't feel up to the challenge of defeating this woman without the assistance of her magic.

"Why would I want to help the queen?" Eilean asked. "And why would she trouble herself with me? King Andrew is coming for her."

"I know," said Kariss. "That does make the situation a little more urgent." It would take time to translate the tome. Time Essylt didn't have.

Eilean was grateful that her gift for discerning thoughts still worked in this room.

"Again, why would I choose to help her?" Eilean asked.

"Because of the consequences if you do not. Let's begin with your druid friend. He's a prisoner in Avinion. He can make flames with his hands. How interesting. He will soon be condemned as a heretic and put through an ordeal of fire, which, as I understand, not even his magic will protect him from. How would that make sweet Holly feel?"

There was a pretend pout. "Only, her name isn't Holly, just as yours isn't Gwenllian."

The threat against Stright's life made Eilean squirm inside.

"What are you offering?" Eilean asked.

"Ah, that's better. I'm a member of the Apocrisarius. Well, that's what *they* believe. I can help your friend. Even bring him here as a sign of good faith. If you begin translating the tome out of that forgotten language, you will be rewarded. There is a certain passage my lady wants first."

Eilean wasn't sure what to do. Although her conscience forbade her from helping the woman who had betrayed her mentor, she also did not want to condemn Stright to death. She listened for thoughts from the Medium but heard nothing.

"How long is your covenant?" Kariss asked again.

"It was a fortnight when we left," Eilean answered.

Kariss looked at her closely. "You speak the truth. Do you know how I know that?"

Eilean shook her head.

"Because I've been trained as a poisoner. I know when someone lies. You will not escape this place. There is no magic that can get you out of here." Kariss clucked her tongue. She rose from the chair. "I'm going to tell my lady you're awake now. Consider obeying her, Eilean of Muirwood. You won't like her when she's angry."

With the unspoken threat lingering in the air, Kariss went to the door. She inserted a key into the lock and opened it. Beyond, Eilean saw little but shadows and darkness. Was it nighttime, or were there no windows in that chamber either?

The door shut, and there was the snick of a key. Eilean knew the word that would unlock any door. She waited, listening, then tried it as soon as she felt confident Kariss was gone.

"*Ephatha,*" she whispered.

Again, nothing happened.

Why had the Medium allowed her to be captured? Why hadn't she been warned?

Time was running out. The tome she'd sought was right in front of her, but both she and the tome were trapped in a room that voided magic. Eilean paced for a while before stopping and sitting down before the tome. She handled its aurichalcum pages carefully, studying the script. Then she turned it to the page where she had left off, after having spent an entire night reading it.

She knew what Essylt wanted—information that would lead her to the fruit that bestowed immortality.

Tears blurred her vision. She felt like a failure.

Hoel, she thought, wondering if the connection between them could bridge the sea.

Silence, her only answer.

✷✷✷

Eilean had to light another tallow candle before the original burned out because she didn't want to be plunged in darkness and unable to do anything about it. Hunger and thirst began to afflict her, but there was no food or drink in the chamber. To pass the time, she read from the tome, picking up where she'd left off. She read about King Andrew's invasion of Occitania, which had nearly gone so badly for him. She read about the knights' fruitless quests to find the Gradalis, a bowl that could transport someone between worlds. That made her chuckle because she knew where it was—hidden in a grove in Brythonica. She looked for clues, especially about the scullion girl, Elle, whom Andrew had forsaken for another bride. She read about the faithfulness of Genevieve—and how the people had come to love and respect her. It was a sad tale, for she knew where it led. And then, as Leoneyis became more and more powerful, Andrew and his knights began to show signs of pride and superiority.

It reminded her of the success of the maston order. Both groups had fallen under the same spell, having conquered so many kingdoms and claimed dominance over every land.

Power changed people.

The sound of the lock turning startled her. Eilean quickly stood from the chair. When the door opened, she saw Kariss, who smirked at finding her at the desk. The room beyond glowed with sunlight, revealing an array of brightly colored drapes and tapestries hung on the walls. No, Eilean wasn't in a dungeon. She was in a small subset of the royal chambers.

And then she saw Essylt.

The Queen of Brythonica wore an exquisite silk gown that was a turquoise color. Her hair was a mix of golds and reds that dazzled in the sunlight, accentuated by the gold necklaces draped over the opening of her low-cut gown and a golden vest of sorts that hugged her slim waist. She looked beautiful and haughty as she strolled into the cell, bringing a feeling of magic with her—the tingling of spells already invoked.

"Leave us," she said to Kariss. Eilean recognized her voice from the night before.

Eilean made a curtsy.

"Good morning, Eilean," the queen said. "You've been here for a couple of days; have you written anything for me yet?"

Eilean hadn't, but that was obvious from the blank paper next to the tome. "You ask for knowledge that isn't mine to give."

The queen's head tilted slightly, and her smooth forehead wrinkled just a little in displeasure. "He trusted *you* with the tome. That was his mistake. You're nothing but a young woman who is in over her head. And is in more danger than she knows."

"You dress like a queen," Eilean answered, "but we both know that you started as a scullion."

Resentment flashed in the queen's eyes. "And look where I am now. I'll tell you this, Eilean. I no longer want a throne or a crown. I've achieved everything I set my thoughts to. And I will achieve this," she said, coming forward and grazing her fingertips along the surface of the tome. "You have no power here. And I can make those you love suffer."

"And that is supposed to win my compliance?" Eilean said.

"Self-interest will always win in the end. I know the tome doesn't contain all the secrets I desire. But it has the one I want most. I don't want to be a queen any longer. I want to be an Unwearying One. Like *him*."

"He didn't choose it for himself. The Medium chose him."

"Your pretty religion means nothing to me. I know of the maston order. I could defeat them in a fortnight if I set my mind to it, but I don't much care about that world. Or this one. I want to walk freely between them all, and I have the means to do so. He stands in my way. And so do you."

Eilean could sense the queen's ambition. Her thoughts were powerful, well trained, and very disciplined. But she was trying to force something that could not be forced. One submitted to the Knowing; one could not compel it. And yet the queen's thoughts felt like an immovable boulder.

"You're wrong," Eilean said, shaking her head. "You know this already. The Fountain, the Medium—they are both the Knowing. It teaches you the path you must walk. Humility, diligence, patience, knowledge, long-suffering. Those are the railings. Look how Myrddin dresses compared to you. He could make himself youthful, yet he doesn't. You're proud. And pride repulses the power of the Knowing. Even if I gave you what you seek, it would turn to your destruction."

The queen's lips twisted into a sneer. "How well you play the parrot. Croaking his lessons. Mimicking what you don't understand. The emperor-maston of Hyksos built a city that could float in the sky. Was not that pride? Was not that conceit? Your own High Seer is as petty as a preening cat. I've met her, Eilean. Do not moralize with *me*."

Had she? Eilean could not tell whether Essylt was lying. Her thoughts were shielded, either by magic or an iron will. Eilean suspected the latter.

"And she's *wrong*," Eilean pressed. "None of our natural passions is so hard to subdue as pride. Beat it down—"

"Enough!" snapped Essylt, her temper flaring. She held up her palm, her long fingers spread apart.

Eilean fell silent.

"Where did you leave Captain Hoel to await you?"

"I'll not tell you," Eilean said, fearful of the queen using him against her.

"Where did you leave Captain Hoel to await you?" she asked again. This time, Eilean felt a compulsion take root inside her. Nausea stirred in her gut. Eilean put her hands on the desk, trying to steady herself, then her guts wrenched so violently that she sank to her knees and began to vomit. Sweat trickled down her ribs. Her mouth tasted terrible, but the sickness only intensified.

"Where is he?" Essylt commanded.

Eilean looked up and saw the queen's eyes were glowing silver. Darkness seemed to surround them, and chittering voices sounded in Eilean's ears. The Myriad Ones. Fear sank deep into Eilean's bones, for she realized she was cowering in front of Ereshkigal herself. The two-faced queen. The dark empress. She could sense the evil being's thoughts. Her goals were not the same as Queen Essylt's. No, the knowledge she sought from the tome was the location of the fruit that made someone mortal again. She wanted to *kill* Maderos.

The compulsion to speak grew even more powerful.

An image came into Eilean's mind: the closet where they'd hidden together.

The power washing over her vanished. Eilean started sobbing against her knuckles as she squeezed the edge of the table.

The queen turned and flung open the door. "Kariss. I know where he is. Go and bring him to me."

"He will recognize me, my lady," said the poisoner warily.

"Not when what he sees is *her*," the queen said with triumph in her voice.

King Aengus of Moros asked to speak with a druid who knew the mind of the mastons. The druids are led by a group called the Thirteen, reminiscent of the maston order of Twelve. An emissary from the Thirteen came to me and asked if I would visit the king and answer his questions. I agreed.

Aengus is a superstitious man, strong in might but not a warmonger. He has won respect by mediation as well as conquest. But like every new ruler, from the boy Andrew to the Holy Emperor of Paeiz, he knows that his life is limited and that what he has built will not endure beyond him if he does not establish a firm enough foundation. He feels threatened because he is surrounded by other kingdoms that share restrictive beliefs in the proper use of magic, which would imperil his druid friends. He asked me to help him understand the mastons' way of thinking, believing it is only a matter of time before his kingdom is invaded by his neighbors.

This is what I told the king: If your determination is fixed, do not despair. Few things are impossible for those who possess both diligence and skill. Great works are performed not by strength, but perseverance.

—Maderos, Advisor to King Aengus

CHAPTER SEVENTEEN

The Queen of Leoneyis

What would Eilean do if Hoel were captured and tortured? She remembered when Kariss had captured him before. He'd been stripped of his chaen, forced to wear a kystrel and a kishion ring, and the ignominy had nearly ruined him. As she knelt by the table, she pleaded with the Medium to help him.

When she opened her eyes again, the candle was burning low, so she opened the casket and lit another one. She stood in front of the table, staring down at the ripples of light coming from the aurichalcum pages.

If Hoel could discern Kariss's deception, there was still a chance he could come to help her escape. The Cruciger orb would inform him of her location. It would also—hopefully—help him find a way into the castle. But what then? How would he get past the queen?

Thinking of their confrontation made her shudder. It wasn't until Essylt had let her anger consume her that the dark queen's presence had manifested itself.

Was it possible that the queen didn't even know her body was act-ing as a host? As Eilean pondered what had happened, she felt certain of it—she'd felt a sudden transition in the woman's thoughts. As if two different beings inhabited the same body. Although Ereshkigal was incredibly powerful, she could not resist the power of an Aldermaston who cast her out. Eilean knew that from the legends of the maston order. Hoel's father had taught her as much. But would Eilean be able to accomplish such a thing? Was she strong enough in the Medium?

She? The daughter of a Naestor and a flax maiden?

Eilean rubbed her forehead. It made her stomach queasy just think-ing about trying such a thing. And what if she failed? What if Ereshkigal realized that Eilean knew who she was?

What if Ereshkigal determined to take over Eilean's body instead?

Hoel had had a vision of Eilean as a hetaera. His visions were of the future. Her stomach roiled at the thought.

No! She closed her hand into a fist and bumped it against the table-top. Eilean would not allow that. Her chaen would prevent it—unless they stripped it from her as they had done to Hoel . . .

Without a window, there was no way to determine the passing of time. Eilean felt caged and began to pace around the table.

Finally, with nothing else to do, she sat back down at the chair and began to read Maderos's tome again. She read about the intrigues of King Andrew's court. The rivalries that existed between the knights of the Ring Table. Maderos had tried to help them achieve a unity of purpose that would enable them to set aside petty jealousies. She read about the scheming of King Modredus of Occitania and how he had created an order called Vertus to mimic that of the Ring Table. It was his determination to make Occitania the predominant power in the world.

As she read, she lost track of time. She could tell as she turned the tome's pages, one by one, that even if she hadn't the use of Essylt's invo-cation of xenoglossia, she had read enough of the tome to decipher the cadence of the language. While her understanding wouldn't have been perfect, it evolved each time she practiced, with or without the spell.

She read about the missing sword and scabbard and how Maderos had returned to the Bearden Muir to seek council from the Dryad tree. What advice would she give to Maderos?

The lock on the door clicked and turned. Eilean felt a jolt of fear plunge into her breast. She looked up, surprised to see the replacement candle had burned down so low, and then a woman entered holding a tray. It was a slender woman, perhaps five years older than Eilean. She had a look of sadness about her face and a purple bruise on her temple. Eilean did not recognize her, yet the woman seemed familiar to her.

"Are you hungry?" asked the woman with an accent that was reminiscent of a Pry-rian one.

"Yes." It was true, she realized. Eilean wasn't even sure when she'd last eaten.

The woman's gown was green silk with a gold vest similar to Queen Essylt's, although it wasn't as fine. The woman had no jewelry either. Was she a servant?

There was a guard standing at the door, a knight, whom she *did* recognize. It was Sir Peredur. His arms were folded across his chest, and he looked at Eilean with wariness and distrust.

As the woman set the tray down on the table, Eilean looked into her eyes.

"Are you Queen Genevieve?" she asked.

Sadness exuded from the woman's thoughts. A deep, wrenching sadness. "I am no longer a queen."

The tray contained bread with little seeds baked into the crust, a small dish of fresh berries, as well as a cup of water and a small rind of cheese. Eilean thought how strange it felt to be served a meal by a queen.

"Thank you," Eilean said simply. Her eyes noticed the bruise again. It had the purple tinge of a fresh mark.

"I didn't want you to suffer with hunger," said Genevieve. There was compassion in the woman's eyes—sympathy for Eilean's plight.

"My lady," said Sir Peredur. He looked as if he feared Eilean would rush from the table and strike the queen. She could feel the Medium emanating from him again, surprising her with its strength, but this was not the knight she'd encountered at the grove in Brythonica. His voice was unfamiliar.

"I must go," the queen said. "I wasn't given permission to tarry."

Eilean was curious now. She knew about the charge of infidelity—it was said the queen had carried on an affair with Sir Peredur, yet, if so, why was the Medium so strong with him? And why did the queen seem so meek? Her thoughts were not riddled with guilt or shame. Quite the contrary. There was a feeling of steadiness about her.

Genevieve turned and started back to the door.

"The tales about you and Sir Peredur. They aren't true, are they?" Eilean asked.

She wasn't expecting Genevieve to answer. She merely wanted to sense her thoughts. The queen flinched at the question, but her mind told the tale that her lips would not. Eilean saw the furious contortions of Andrew's face as he raged at her, accusing her of betraying him. Eilean sensed the queen's despair as she tried to defend herself against his accusations. Her professed innocence had only inflamed his anger—so much so he'd stormed out of the room. She had followed and caught him by the arm, trying to stop him. He'd wrenched his arm away with enough force that she'd fallen backward, knocking into a doorframe. She'd fallen to the floor in the middle of one of the palace corridors.

Peredur, who'd heard the conflict, arrived moments later. He absorbed the scene—the queen on the floor, holding her head. The king, staring at her guiltily.

And he drew his sword to defend her from further abuse.

The charges, Eilean knew, were completely groundless. She sensed Genevieve's virtue, her steadfastness, her complete devotion to the man who had turned on her.

"Farewell," Genevieve said, her voice thick with painful memories.

Eilean's gaze turned to Sir Peredur, whose mind was laid bare to her as well. When Andrew saw the blade in Peredur's hand, he drew his own sword and shouted for the guards. He knew he would be arrested if he remained. So he'd knocked the king unconscious and then taken Genevieve, with a veil to conceal her identity, and fled Tintagel in the night. Everyone believed him to be a villain, but he, too, was innocent of the charge of adultery. This scene was still fresh in their minds.

The information flooded into Eilean's mind, so fast and complete it only took a few moments.

As soon as Genevieve reached the door, Sir Peredur began to tug it closed.

"You are innocent, Sir Peredur," Eilean said, her own voice throbbing with emotion. "And so is she. You are a true knight."

The queen paused at the threshold, turning back, her eyes still haunted with the memories that Eilean had summoned. Her hand strayed to her wrist, as if she were reliving that awful pain.

"You are not from Leoneyis, despite your garb," Sir Peredur said.

Eilean felt a prickle go down her back. Words came to her mind. "No. I came through the Deep Fathoms."

The queen's gaze shifted from Peredur to Eilean. Her brow wrinkled.

"Sir Queux will try and murder the king before they reach Brythonica," Eilean said. "They are coming."

"If he dies," Sir Peredur said flatly, "we will all perish."

Now she understood why the knight was so strong in the Medium. He'd allowed his own reputation to suffer in order to save lives. Eilean's heart went out to him. Only the bravest of men could face such injustice and not flinch from it.

"I am here to stop that, if I can," Eilean said. Would she have had such courage in the face of injustice? She thought of how she'd stood up to Aldermaston Gilifil, trusting the whispers in her heart instead of the respected man's reputation. It had been difficult. It had been agonizing.

"Only the Fountain can stop it," said Peredur. "But we no longer deserve its blessings. Modredus will win. We're doomed."

"Where will you go?" Eilean asked.

The two looked at each other. "The queen has promised to help us," said Genevieve. Again, her thoughts were laid bare to Eilean. Essylt had promised to equip them with magical rings that would conceal their identities. They would be granted sanctuary in Brythonica, unknown to those around them.

They left, and Peredur shut and locked the door behind them. Even though she could no longer see them, she could sense them standing outside. Genevieve leaned against him, weak with grief, disappointment, and the shame of a reputation that was undeservedly tarnished. Eilean sensed Peredur putting his arm around her and leading her away.

Eilean heard the muffled voice of the queen. "There is something about her."

"There is."

Soon they were beyond the reach of her thoughts, and she was left alone to ponder the strange encounter. The Medium wanted her there. She'd been meant to witness this, to learn the tragic tale of the knight and the queen. Then she remembered King Andrew's guilt. Yes, she understood him better too. He'd succumbed to a storm of savage rage, believing his wife had been unfaithful with his friend. How had that come about? Eilean didn't know. But she had a firm suspicion that Sir Queux and his lies were involved. He feared Myrddin's return because he knew the Wizr could discern men's thoughts.

Hungrily, she ate the bread, cheese, and fruit. What had Essylt told Genevieve about her prisoner? Whatever it was, she was grateful that

Genevieve had asked to bring food to her—and that Essylt hadn't been so heartless as to refuse.

When she finished the meal, she sensed someone approaching the door. It unlocked, and Queen Essylt entered once again and closed them in together.

Eilean swallowed and bowed her head. "Thank you for the food."

"Kariss has not returned yet," said the queen. "But she is faithful. I know she'll succeed."

Eilean did not sense the ire of Ereshkigal's thoughts. No, this was all Essylt.

"She's failed you before," Eilean said.

"I give others the blame. And she was clever enough to steal the tome from *you*," Essylt replied with a mocking smile.

"Putting your trust in her is a mistake," Eilean said.

"Oh? When I'm the one who commands her loyalty?"

"You may command her actions, but you do not command her loyalty. She is a poisoner."

"You know nothing of this world."

"That is true. I am a stranger here."

"Yet you imply that she serves another master?"

"She serves you and your interests. When it suits her. Just as she pretended to serve the mastons at your request."

"I don't like you," Essylt said abruptly.

"Because I speak the truth?"

"What is truth but the lies we tell ourselves to justify our desires?"

"I know Kariss deceives you because I can see into her heart," Eilean said. "Just as I know that Queen Genevieve is innocent. *Truly* innocent."

Essylt frowned. "I know she's innocent. But that false king in Tintagel will not hear of it. He'll throw his might against us out of revenge. I care not."

"You don't care for your people?"

183

"No, because I know he won't win. He's offended too many of his peers. People serve him out of fear now, not loyalty."

Eilean thought that a bold statement coming from a woman who likely wielded power the same way.

"And your people are loyal?" she asked.

Essylt brooded. "I know Andrew's ships are coming. I cannot beat him by sea. But King Modredus of Occitania is coming to aid me. And so is King Owain of Ceredigion. We're not as defenseless as he supposes."

"I've read the tome. I know about the game. You're on Andrew's side of the board. If he dies, you all perish in the flood. He doesn't have the scabbard to defend himself against treachery."

"I know. I'm the one who took it from him. I know his weakness. He'll relent. And I also know that your friend, the dear captain, has the sword Firebos. Which I will get back at long last. The high king won't risk losing face before his knights by refusing to fight, but he cannot hope to defeat Sir Peredur, especially if Peredur has the sword Firebos. I will soon have all the pieces I need to win this."

There was bravado in her words. But Eilean sensed the doubt in Essylt's mind. An invasion by Leoneyis was fraught with peril. And risk. They could all lose their lives. But the queen could escape calamity. If the world was going to be destroyed, she could flee through the Gradalis in the grove and travel to another world, and not through a mirror gate, which required covenants she might not wish to give.

"You tamper with powers you do not fully understand," Eilean said.

"Oh, I understand them," Essylt said with disdain. "I've been to the East Kingdoms. I've learned words that are not written in that tome. There are other words of power, my dear."

In the queen's thoughts, Eilean saw another book. Not a tome—but a book bound with leather or . . . human skin. Darkness shrouded the vision from her mind. She felt Ereshkigal snarl.

"You know how to take life," Eilean said. "But do you know how to give it? I've seen that happen. Someone come back from the dead. Can you create? Or can you only destroy?"

Eilean wasn't sure if she said those words to Essylt or Ereshkigal. But she felt anger and resentment. *Hatred.*

"Leave her," Eilean said, raising her hand with the maston sign. "I adjure you, Ereshkigal. By the Medium, I cast you from her."

Eilean felt a new awareness in the room.

The queen laughed. "You cannot command *me*," she said with an eerie echo in her voice. Where Essylt's thoughts had been, there was blankness, a daze. Eilean didn't think that the queen even knew when Ereshkigal took over.

Fear wriggled inside Eilean's stomach. She worried she might vomit up everything she'd eaten. She could hear the mewling noise of the Myriad Ones snuffling about the cell.

"You are the daughter of a Naestor," said the otherworldly voice. "You are nothing. I will destroy the maston order. I will destroy this world as well. And they *welcome* it, child. They welcome it." Her mouth lifted into a chilling smirk. "He was a fool to send you to stop me. Soon I will destroy him and everyone he loves."

In Ereshkigal's thoughts, Eilean saw Maderos, a desperate look on his face.

Then the queen turned and left the room, locking the door once again.

The feelings of darkness and dread faded away, replaced with fierce determination.

Eilean was determined that Maderos's faith in her would not end in ruin. He'd chosen her to reclaim his tome. He'd known she would follow the whispers of the Medium and do what was right. Hungrily, she went back to his tome and read the next passage.

And discovered the prophecy of the Dreadful Deadman.

When E is come and gone, then take heed to your-
selves, for war shall never cease. After E is come and gone,
then cometh Ceredigion next to destruction by seven
kings. The Fountain shall cease to flood the land and
after that will come a Dreadful Deadman with a royal
wife of the best blood in the world. And he shall have the
hollow crown and shall set Ceredigion on the right way
and put out all heretics.

Eilean stared at the passage over and over.

When E is come and gone.

When E is come and gone.

She blinked at the words, her heart hammering in her chest. *When*
E is come and gone.

Then she heard the Medium whisper her name.

One of the Apocrisarius infiltrated Aengus's castle in Moros. He came in disguise to tend stables. He worked hard, doing his duty with diligence, at least where shoveling horse muck was concerned. He diced and wagered with the others and was a gracious loser. Everyone appreciates a gracious loser when there are coins on the table.

This servant of Lord Nostradamus was clever. He learned the castle's byways, made friends with butchers and kitchen help. I knew his true role, of course, but I let him sneak his way closer and closer. He was looking for me, seeking a way to bring me back to Avinion in chains. I let him find me after he had a cart, a crate, a nag, and a man he'd paid to bring the crate to a certain ship at the docks of Moros at midnight.

When the box arrived in Avinion, the hunter was gagged inside wearing the heavy chains meant for me. One shouldn't play a game of Wizr with a Wizr, Lord Nostradamus.

—Maderos, Advisor to King Aengus

CHAPTER EIGHTEEN

Whispers in the Dark

You are the daughter of a Naestor. You are nothing.

Eilean sat on her sleeping mat, her back pressed to the wall, the lonely candle dripping slowly against its shrinking base. Her arms were wrapped around her knees, but she wasn't staring at the candle. She was staring inside herself, seeing herself as the helpless wretched from Muirwood. Locked in a room. Her magic rendered useless.

You are nothing.

She could sense the Myriad Ones prowling outside the door. It sparked a memory of the night she'd camped under a wagon while crossing the Bearden Muir to Muirwood. She had seen eyes glowing in the dark and had felt the sinister presence of the Myriad Ones. Her chaen would protect her from them taking over her body. But only as long as she wore it. And she feared that soon even that protection would be stripped away from her.

Hoel had been there that night in the woods. She'd sensed something was wrong, and he'd heeded her warning and sent men to search for the dark druid lurking in the shadows. Even back then, there had been something between them. His Gift of Seering had empowered him to see her potential.

You are nothing!

Eilean gazed at the door and scowled at the intruding thoughts.

You are a stranger in this world. An outsider. You don't belong here. You don't belong anywhere.

The words were barbed, yet another voice warred with them, a stronger one, pulled up from her memory. *Precious.*

She may be the daughter of a Naestor and a servant, but the Medium had chosen her. That long-ago day when she'd left the castle of Muirwood and ventured into a thicket of scraggy oak trees in the swamp, it had spoken to her for the first time, and that's what it had said.

Precious.

Tears stung her eyes. Tears of gratitude and relief. The feelings of the Medium stirred in her heart.

She heard angry hissing from the Myriad Ones, but it was drowned out by that other voice—richer and kinder and so, so wise.

No matter what they strip from you, they cannot take who you are away.

Feelings of warmth settled through her, and the power of the Medium filtered into every part of her body. She realized now what Maderos had known about her—that the Medium would choose her— long before they ever met. Her name had whispered into his mind when he had written the prophecy of the Dreadful Deadman. And when she was assigned to serve him in his own prison, he was already aware of who she would become and the role the Medium wanted her to play. She thought of the crate she'd escaped in Isen because a nail had been hammered into the wood at a strange angle—exactly what she'd needed to free her bindings.

She was the nail this time.

The memory of that crate—and Hoel, who'd shut her inside back when he thought capturing her would be his best way of helping her—made her smile as she wiped away a tear that had trickled down her cheek. She lay her forehead on her arm, relishing the feelings suffusing her being. She was the help the Medium had sent to Maderos. Her.

You are nothing!

She lifted her head, staring at the door with contempt. Her voice came out soft but forceful. "You keep repeating that as if it were true. But it isn't. I am precious to the Knowing. You refused a mortal journey because you were too afraid or too proud. I'm *not* worthless, no matter what you say. I know my worth. Now leave me alone."

As she said those final words, she issued a mental rebuke. A mewling sound followed, then a groan of pain, and she felt the presence of the Myriad Ones slink away from the door.

The quiet in her mind was a relief.

One of Maderos's first lessons to her had been that people tried to claw atop one another in a never-ending game of dominance. They established ranks and customs to impose divisions, to make some better than others, and used shame and ridicule to enforce those ranks and customs. But it was all an elaborate *lie*. The Knowing cared for everyone. It constantly tried to reveal that love through starlings sweeping across the dawn sky, through the smell of purple mint, through the tangy sweetness of a crisp apple. Eilean's heart continued to swell with confidence and courage.

She'd always feared sleeping in the dark, worried the Myriad Ones would prowl about trying to sneak up on her and invade her body. But they had no true power. They only won power if she surrendered to their thoughts and acted on them.

Eilean rose from the mat and made her way to the table. Then she blew the candle out and returned to the mat. She lay her head on her arm and closed her eyes.

And slept peacefully.

***

The click of the lock awakened her. Eilean sat up, rubbing her eyes, when the sudden light from the queen's chambers momentarily blinded her. She winced, turning her head away.

"You let the candle die?" The Queen of Brythonica's voice held a note of surprise.

Eilean stretched her arms and then slowly rose. "I wanted to sleep."

The queen was worried. Eilean sensed the troubled thoughts on the surface of her mind breaking through the iron control she normally maintained. Perhaps Kariss still had not returned. Hope strained within her. Hoel was wary, and perhaps he had not been outsmarted.

"No Kariss?" Eilean asked, her eyes adjusting to the shaft of light.

The queen was wearing a gown the shade of dark plums, with a surcoat of the same fabric adorned with gold embroidery. It was an impressive gown, though its neckline would have been considered scandalous by the maston standards. The youthful look of her face was clearly an illusion. How much of her strength was drained by maintaining that illusion?

"Were you the one who visited the grove the other night?" the queen asked. In the queen's thoughts, Eilean saw a flash of memory of the silver bowl she'd seen the night the púca had shown her the Dryad tree.

"Yes," Eilean answered. "I know you have the Gradalis."

"How did you know it was there?" the queen asked.

"The Medium told me."

"Oh? You are lucky you left when you did. Sir Owain would have slain you."

Eilean recognized the name from Maderos's tome. He was one of the knights of the Ring Table—or had been. Andrew had made him King of Ceredigion in order to check the growing threat posed by Occitania, but he had been the first to remove himself from the king's service.

"Would you have permitted him to?"

"You were an intruder. What were you seeking if not to steal what is mine?"

Only, Eilean sensed the Queen of Brythonica had stolen the bowl herself. Just as she had stolen Maderos's tome.

"Oh? Is it yours?" Eilean asked simply, grateful for the flash of insight.

The queen frowned. "I *really* don't like you, Eilean."

"Maybe because I remind you too much of yourself. Long ago."

The queen's lip curled.

"I've read the tome," Eilean pressed. "I know your story. We share many things in common."

"Things I'd sooner forget. The smell of the kitchen still makes me ill."

"I miss the kitchen, actually," Eilean said. "I miss gooseberry fool."

"Gooseberries are too tart."

"Not if you eat them with cream," Eilean said.

The queen gave her a sly look. "You are just a child, aren't you? A kitchen waif. A few words of power and you believed yourself my equal."

"I'm not your equal," Eilean said with a laugh. "But I have made oaths to the Medium. It will defend me and help me fulfill my mission."

"I captured you, Eilean," the queen said, raising an eyebrow. "*That* was the Medium's will?"

"I believe so."

The queen chuckled. "Convenient, isn't it? Whatever happens must be the Medium's will." She said it in a mocking tone.

Eilean felt a strong impression to say something. "My lady, do you remember when you left me last night?"

Instantly the queen was doubtful. More worries seeped out from her thoughts. When she'd awakened the next morning, she couldn't remember the conversation she'd had with Eilean. It was in a fog. In fact, she was worried that harm might have come to her prisoner. That's why she had come straightaway after dressing.

"Is there something you wish to say?" the queen asked, deflecting the question.

"Do you remember it?"

The queen's face showed no confusion. But her mind was trying to remember and failing.

Eilean rose and stepped forward. "You don't remember. I know you don't. That is because you were not yourself."

Suspicion flashed through the queen's mind. "What are you saying?"

"You have a brand on your shoulder. Your left shoulder."

The queen's nose wrinkled. She looked at Eilean with surprise. "How can you know that?"

Images flashed through the queen's mind. She'd used the mirror gate to travel to their world in her pursuit of more power. She'd learned about the hetaera during her sojourn, and she'd welcomed the ability to enhance herself.

Not being from their world, not fully understanding their history, she also had not comprehended the cost of the power she sought.

"It's from my world," Eilean said. "It's not one of your traditions here. It's part of the maston lore. Now, you are part of it too."

"I don't believe in such prohibitions."

"What you call it is irrelevant. The Fountain. The Medium. It matters not. You are capable of channeling it, so if you utter a word of power without making the null gesture, the power of that word is invoked. But we are not the only beings capable of power."

"Of course. There are water sprites: Sirens and Ondines."

"And there are souls too wicked to be born. In my world, they are called the Myriad Ones. You have one inside you. That's the reason you cannot remember things."

The queen narrowed her eyes. "You will not trick me with your tales."

"When did you get that brand on your shoulder? Do you remember? It was after you banished Myrddin, wasn't it?"

"Why would that make any difference?"

"Because he would have sensed it in you. And he could have driven it out. You need an Aldermaston's help."

"I need no one!" The queen's eyes flared with offense.

Eilean sighed. "Do you remember what happened just before you woke up with the brand?"

The queen blinked rapidly. She was trying to remember, but her thoughts were getting murky.

"Stop," Eilean said, holding up her hand.

The queen stared at her in confusion.

"Trying to remember is rousing her again."

"'Her'?"

"The *being* inside you. It's bound to you, my lady. I tried to adjure it last night but failed."

"What do you mean you tried to adjure it? You cannot use magic in here."

"It's not magic. What is inside you . . . it is a soul. She has been possessing your body and using it to do her will. They are stronger at night. And when she claims control, you don't remember what you did."

"You're lying."

"My lady, I speak the truth. There are tales of times past when the dark empresses ruled our world. I've seen mosaics representing this era. The Dark Empress Ereshkigal had a symbol—a woman with two faces."

Essylt stiffened, her nostrils flaring. Thoughts swirled in her mind. She had envisioned the sigil after Myrddin had gone. She'd thought it her own idea.

"It's from our history," Eilean said, "and it's emblazoned all over Ploemeur. If the mastons were to come here, they would see you as their mortal enemy. The being inside you used to rule our world. She's using you to try and win it back. After she takes your world."

From Essylt's reaction, Eilean realized she wasn't behind the return of the hetaera. She didn't even know she was one or what any of the symbols meant. She was being used by someone else. Someone who wanted the two worlds to collide.

"Try to remember when you got the brand," Eilean pleaded. "But think on it during the day, not at night. Their power is the weakest when the sun is at its highest."

The queen looked shaken.

"You are not your true self, my lady."

A knock sounded on the exterior door. Eilean saw a maid hurry to answer it and then an armored knight strode inside.

The queen turned toward him, before glancing back at Eilean, her look troubled.

"Think on what I asked," Eilean said.

"No, you think on this. Find the page I asked you to translate, and do as you're told," the queen said angrily. "I want to find that tree. It has to do with the tale of the garden with the stone faces."

"The Garden of Leerings," Eilean said, an idea blossoming in her mind.

The queen stormed out and locked the door, plunging the room into darkness again. Eilean went to it and pressed her ear against the wood. She heard a man's muffled voice, speaking in urgent tones, but she couldn't make out his words or the queen's reply.

She didn't need to. The man was close enough that she could sense his thoughts.

A boat had arrived in southern Brythonica with an old man, a young girl, and a swordsman. The beaches were being patrolled in preparation for King Andrew's invasion, and when the soldiers had demanded they come in for questioning, the swordsman had refused and drawn his weapon. The blade had glowed bright blue.

The swordsman had defended himself against the guards rushing him, and he had severed the hand or arm of every man who had lifted a weapon against him. They'd all lived, except one knight whom he had slain with the sword.

Eilean closed her eyes and leaned forward, touching the cool wood with her forehead.

Hoel, she thought, her heart surging with emotions. *Don't come at night!*

The future is purchased by the present. It sometimes comes at a bargain. Other times at a king's ransom. I counseled King Aengus that bending the knee to the High Seer now may create more advantages in the future than trying to bend a will so implacable with the sword. There will be new leaders in the future. He agreed to meet the envoy the mastons sent to him.

—Maderos, Druid of the Isle of Moros

CHAPTER NINETEEN

Hieros Castle, Kingdom of Leoneyis
Fourteenth Year of the Reign of King Andrew Ursus

The window was open, bringing in the scent of the sea with the gentle breeze. Hieros Castle was on the western edge of Leoneyis with a view of the cliffs of Legault. Andrew lay beneath the sheets of the bed, feeling Genevieve tucked up against his body, her arm draped over his chest. The room was dark, and only a sliver of moon shone between the window drapes. There was the faint noise of reveling in the town below.

"My lord, you're not sleeping," she said softly in the darkness.

"My mind is still wondering at the blessing we received from the Fountain. That storm destroyed the Legaultan ships, ending the war before it even began."

He'd come to Hieros to defend against an attack by the Legaultans, who had recently sworn allegiance to King Modredus, putting another realm under his thrall—more weight to tip the balance of the scales.

There was no letting up of Modredus's ambition. Or Andrew's, for that matter. Too much was at stake.

Andrew had sent Sir Peredur and some knights first, to reinforce the castle while he summoned ships to bring soldiers from his lands on the continent. Genevieve had insisted on coming with him, to see if she could convince the Queen of Legault to reconsider the alliance. But none of that had been needed. The Legaultan ships were wrecked, many knights drowned, and now Andrew was preparing to send Peredur to lay siege to Connaught castle. To strip away their strongest fortification as punishment for their rebellion—to lay claim to the kingdom through conquest. That would teach both Modredus and the Legaultans a lesson in humility.

"It *is* a blessing." Her hand stroked his chest. "But it's not the blessing I've been seeking."

He knew what she meant. The longing for the child that had been denied to them these many years. It was a constant grief to her.

He lifted her hand and pressed it to his lips. "We'll keep trying, Genny."

He'd spoken the words so often they were rote now. He wanted to reassure her that he wasn't concerned. They were both very young still. But the hope and ambition of former days had dwindled each month her flux came.

"I love you, Andrew," she said, scooting up closer and kissing him on the mouth. "Thank you for being patient with me. Do you like the nightdress I brought?"

He gazed at her, smiling. Enjoying the sight of her in that nightdress.

"Murder! Murder!"

The cry came rushing in through the open window, shouted from the town below.

"What was that?" Genevieve asked with a gasp.

Andrew sat up and rolled off the bed. He grabbed his tunic and hurriedly put it on, his heart pounding in his chest. He was about to strap on his sword, but she forestalled him.

"Your hauberk, Andrew. You don't have the scabbard anymore."

He paused, holding the belt in his hands, but she was right. Only a very few people knew about the scabbard and its powerful healing magic, or the sword's unique qualities. And no one knew both had been stolen from him or that Myrddin had disappeared while trying to find out who had done it. Was it Rucrius, Modredus's Wizr, or Elle? He still didn't know.

Obeying his wife's suggestion, he garbed himself in the chainmail first. She'd left the bed and helped him with the tunic since they'd dismissed his squires earlier for privacy. A heavy knock sounded at the door.

"My lord!"

While Genevieve hurriedly put on a robe to cover herself, Andrew marched to the door and removed the latch.

One of his knights stood there, holding a torch in one hand. He looked bewildered.

"What's happened?"

"My lord, I don't know. Some disturbance in town."

"Where is Sir Queux?"

"He's already down there. Some of the Legaultan knights, the ones who didn't drown, were being held for ransom. Maybe they tried to escape?"

The possibility made him angry. He'd chosen to be lenient to the survivors. "Where is Peredur?"

"He's down there as well. I know nothing save that the cry of murder was raised."

Andrew turned and looked at Genevieve's worried face. "Don't go," she said. "Let Sir Queux handle it."

"No, I'll see that justice is done. If those Legaultans tried to escape, they'll pay for it with their lives."

"Have mercy," she implored. "They're frightened."

"I did have mercy," he shot back. "Sir Pinnock, is my horse being saddled?"

"As we speak, my lord."

"Let me dress. I'll go with you." Genevieve's voice was plaintive.

But he was too angry to consider it—his victory had been marred by treachery. "No, I wish you to stay here."

"You're too angry to confront them now, Husband."

She was right, but he didn't care to admit it. "I will withhold judgment until the morning. Will that satisfy you?"

"Yes. Thank you."

She was too compassionate sometimes. He had a vast empire to rule, and a ruler had to dole out punishments at times as a warning to conniving nobles. He shut the door and followed Sir Pinnock downstairs. When they reached the courtyard, the horses were already prepared, and the knights who would accompany him had donned their armor. He mounted his steed, and then they rushed down the ramparts to the town below. The night concealed the wreckage littering the shores. He had no doubt the local fishermen would be finding bodies for days to come.

Torchlight blazed from the lower defenses, and as they ventured closer, Andrew saw knights with the Raven badge bearing arms. Soldiers were everywhere, many with weapons drawn. Some had men in chains.

Murmurs rose up. "The king! It's the king!" The voices sounded worried . . . as if the men feared being rebuked.

Andrew looked about and found Sir Queux sitting on a decorative boulder, panting.

"Sir Queux, what is the meaning of this?" he said, riding up.

Queux lifted his head and immediately looked worried. "My lord, you needn't have come in person."

"There was a cry of murder."

"Yes, that was . . . unfortunate. They thought we might need reinforcements from the castle."

"Did the Legaultan knights rise up?"

"My lord?"

"What caused the disturbance, Queux?"

"I don't know the full circumstances yet. It's only just ended."

Andrew glanced around in confusion. Then he saw Sir Peredur on his knees, panting as well. Sweat dripped from his face. Two burly knights held on to his wrists and forearms to restrain him.

Confusion washed through Andrew at the strange scene. "What happened?" he asked again.

"Someone made a jest," Queux said. "A soldier who was drunk. The men have been celebrating a little too freely, I'm afraid. Sir Peredur took offense. A brawl began." The seneschal rose to his feet and brushed off his pants.

Andrew looked at Peredur, who stared down at the ground, his jaw clenched. He looked exhausted. There were bloodstains on his tunic.

"Are you injured, Peredur?" Andrew asked, his emotions in turmoil.

"No," he said simply. That meant the blood was not his own. Peredur was frightening in battle, engaging his foes without any heed for his own safety. Not many could best him. It had probably taken a dozen men to pin him down.

What had been said that had riled Peredur up so much?

Andrew looked at Sir Queux, who was clearly uncomfortable about the situation.

"Did Peredur start the fight?" Andrew asked in a low voice.

"My lord, I cannot say. I wasn't there to see the outset."

"Yes," Peredur answered, his voice throbbing with emotion. "It was my fault."

"In the morning, go back to Tintagel, Sir Peredur," Andrew said. "We've done our work here."

The knight lifted his head, his eyes widening with shock and humiliation. Everyone knew that he'd been given the command to siege Connaught castle.

"Is this the way you thank the Fountain for delivering us from our enemies?" Andrew stated, turning around slowly, spreading his rebuke across them all. He could smell the wine in the air. Most of the men were drunk still.

There were guilty looks everywhere, but the gall of disappointment was bitter in his stomach. He'd gone to bed that night reveling in the easy victory. Soldiers could ruin even the best outcomes with their lack of discipline and diligence. But he'd expected better from his knights. To secure their position in the order, they needed to be better than Modredus's men. More disciplined.

He looked at Peredur again, feeling disappointment writhe within his breast. The other man hung his head, his expression like stone.

***

Genevieve had been relieved to hear that there was no justice to be administered to the Legaultans, and she implored Andrew to forgive the soldiers and knights for excesses brought on by their celebrations. When morning came, he donned his clothes with the help of his pages and then went to breakfast with Sir Queux. That was a tradition they'd shared for many years, a chance to speak frankly to each other and to organize the affairs of the day. There was always more to be done than could be, but that was what made Queux so helpful.

Breakfast was poached eggs, green onions, some ringed slices of cara fruit, as well as a slab of fresh salmon that was still steaming.

"What caused that row last night?" Andrew asked after using a three-pronged fork to break off a bit of salmon. He was still upset about the incident. It was so unlike Peredur to lose control and cause a scene.

"Nothing that you should worry about, my lord. It would be best to put it behind us."

His failure to explain piqued Andrew's curiosity all the more. "Peredur does not normally rampage among our own men. I thought the Legaultans had broken free of the dungeon."

"So did I at first," said Queux with a chuckle. "No, some ill-spoken words at an ill time of night. Peredur feels chagrined. I spoke to him after you left last night. He suffers the disgrace keenly."

"As he should. He never loses his temper except in battle. Once roused, he's . . . I can't even think of the right word. He's irrepressible."

"Unfortunately so," added Queux. "There were many men being tended by healers, including Sir Anselm of the Ring Table."

"Peredur hurt Anselm?"

"He did. But I'm sure he'll recover."

Andrew took a drink and then continued eating. "So what was it about?"

"You know the saying of old, 'in wine there is truth.' Men say horrible things when they're drunk. It's not worth repeating."

Worry twisted within Andrew's stomach. "Say it anyway, Queux. I want to hear the truth."

"It's not the truth, per se, my lord. And I'd rather not."

"Why not? Do I need to ply you with wine to get *you* to speak freely? You're my seneschal. My trusted friend. Tell me."

Sir Queux let out an exaggerated sigh, which he liked to do when there was something uncomfortable that needed to be said. "According to Peredur, the soldier told him they'd all be on duty that night until the cuckold crowed."

Andrew's brow narrowed. A cuckold was a man whose wife was unfaithful to him. Andrew's own father had cuckolded his enemy, using magic from Myrddin to accomplish his deception.

The implication was clear. The soldier had implied that Andrew was a cuckold, and he'd said the jest to Sir Peredur as an insult. That meant the soldier believed *Peredur* was the one betraying his king.

Andrew's appetite for salmon quickly diminished. He wiped his mouth on a napkin.

"Sir Peredur nearly killed the man with his bare hands," Sir Queux said. "A few heard the jest. Most didn't. But when the soldier's friends tried to protect their companion, everything spun out of control. I believe Sir Peredur might have killed the man. If Sir Anselm hadn't intervened, there would have been more blood. There is no honor in knights fighting soldiers. Only other knights."

Andrew let out a breath. Now he was even more angry at Peredur than he'd been the night before. Not because he'd defended his wife's honor against a salacious quip. But because the quip had been made in the first place. Although he knew Genevieve was faithful to him, the rumors infuriated him.

"There are other more important matters to discuss, my lord."

"More important than my wife's honor?"

"Surely you don't take a drunken soldier's word as truth? Of course the rabble gossip about such things, especially after you named Peredur your heir. Though I'll admit I was surprised that the queen came to Hieros with you in such dangerous circumstances."

"Why should you be surprised?" Andrew challenged. "She was hoping to negotiate peace with the Queen of Legault."

"Ah. That makes sense. I think sending her to Connaught to help finalize the peace would be very appropriate now that you're sending Peredur back to Tintagel."

"Do you think I'm wrong to send him back?"

"Absolutely not. But the Legaultans are *eejits*, as they say. What if they won't surrender the castle?"

"Then I'll send you to take it from them," Andrew declared. His emotions were running hot. He felt conflicted and confused.

"It would be my honor to serve you," said Queux. "Now, I believe the queen wished to visit the prisoners this morning. I've already been writing about our victory to those we contacted for help before we left. No need to mass an army here after all. No doubt King Modredus will feel he's been robbed of an opportunity to stir up trouble against you." He smiled wryly. "Maybe he'll start carving into Ceredigion again."

Andrew wasn't in the mood for banter. "Let's go talk to Genny. We should summon the Queen of Legault here. I'd prefer to have this discussion on our terms."

"Agreed. If you're no longer hungry, we can go now?"

The food was good, but Andrew's appetite was gone. They walked and continued to speak together as they returned to the king's suite.

As they entered, Andrew heard Genny's maid say, "Here comes my lord."

"I'll take my leave." It was Peredur's voice. Andrew arrived in time to see him lower Genevieve's hand after kissing it.

"Don't go. Stay, and I'll speak with him directly."

Peredur looked toward Andrew, his brow knotting at having been discovered in the room. "I'm not well at ease, my lady. I must obey the king's orders and return."

The knight let go of her hand. The queen turned and smiled welcomingly at Andrew.

"Hmmm," muttered Queux. "I don't like that."

To keep your secret is wisdom; to expect others to keep it is folly. People cannot help but share what they know. Even if it will hurt them.

—Maderos, Advisor to King Aengus

CHAPTER TWENTY

The Sea of War

The candle was relit for Eilean whenever food was brought to her. She had hoped to see Queen Genevieve again, but instead it was a serving girl who neither spoke nor answered any questions. The steady march of time increased Eilean's worry about the mirror gate. If she and Hoel did not cross it—both of them—then it would collapse into rubble, and they'd be stranded in the doomed world.

Certainly the palace in Ploemeur itself would be spared devastation, but the coastline of Brythonica would be brought to ruin if Andrew died. The magical game of Wizr guaranteed it.

What kind of person would have willingly accepted such a risk? Certainly one whose overconfidence could imagine no failure.

To pass the time, she continued reading Mordaunt's tome, learning about his duty as the advisor to King Aengus of Moros. She enjoyed the little bits of wisdom she gained from it, and she could hear his voice speaking the words scrawled onto the metal pages. It made her feel less alone. He had risen among the druids' ranks and earned their respect, but he was no heretic. His goal had been to learn their ways so that he could build a bridge of understanding that would connect them to the Knowing.

The only bridges the mastons built were the ones leading to Avinion.

The door was unlocked, and Eilean looked up as Queen Essylt entered once again and shut the door behind her. The queen's demeanor was subdued and thoughtful. Unsettled thoughts spilled from her mind—the renegade swordsman was still missing, and Kariss had still not returned.

"You carry heavy burdens," Eilean said to her.

"Ships from Leoneyis were seen from the lookout posts," the queen said. "I've summoned fog to make their approach more difficult. Did he teach you that command?"

"Vey-ed min ha-ay-retz," Eilean said. But nothing happened since her magic was being blocked.

Essylt nodded approvingly. "You say it well. He was always a meticulous teacher."

"Did he tease you about pronouncing things wrong?" Eilean asked.

"Of course. I've noticed your speech is very proper. What land are you from? I don't remember all the names of the lesser kingdoms."

"Pry-Ree."

"Ah, yes. What did you sound like before you met him? Say something in that tongue."

"We all spoke in the language of Moros as well," Eilean said. "It was a far larger kingdom than ours."

"The last to bend the knee to the maston superstitions. Speak in your language. I wish to hear it."

Eilean wondered at the odd request. She hadn't spoken in pure Pryrian for a while, but there were many phrases she could choose from. There was a saying about persistence she'd always liked. *"Shaw, dyfal donc a dyr y garreg."*

Essylt tilted her head. "Tapping the stone breaks it?"

"Tapping it persistently," Eilean corrected. "That's the saying."

"What does 'shaw' mean?"

"It's just a word. It doesn't really mean anything."

"I like the saying. It means if I keep tapping you, soon you will break."

"I won't break before the mirror gate does," Eilean said firmly. "I'm not even sure how much time is left before the covenant destroys it."

"All the more reason to cooperate with me."

"All the more reason for you to let me go," Eilean countered. "King Andrew is coming. He isn't who he once was. And the men who advise him now are corrupt."

"I know," said Essylt. "He's changed. We all have."

Eilean sensed the melancholy in the queen's thoughts. Yes, she reveled in her power and authority, but she missed those earlier days when things had been simpler.

"Why did you betray Myrddin?" Eilean asked softly.

The queen didn't look at her. Her gaze was settled on the tome. "He betrayed me first."

"He taught you."

"But not everything." Her gaze lifted to Eilean's face. "He kept certain parts from me."

"Maybe keeping them from you was for your own good."

"Or maybe it was for *his* own good." The queen's eyes flashed. "Every kingdom has its myths, Eilean. A higher power we must kneel to and serve. The Essaios. The Aos Sí. The Medium. The Fountain. In Chandigarl, there are other traditions—grave kingdoms ruled by the dead. But what if there is nothing beyond this life? What if after we become ashes and dust, there is nothing? Or, if not nothing, a prison? If immortality isn't such a prize, why do so few earn the precious gift? Why not share the secret? Or is the secret that death is truly irrevocable?"

Eilean sensed the queen's disturbed thoughts, the twisting of her imagination. She was feeling her own mortality as she aged, a fact she repeatedly disguised with magic.

"Death is not irrevocable," Eilean said.

"You say that because you believe in the silly traditions of the mastons. You think your ultimate destiny is to become one of the Essaios, the world makers. But does that hope not bind you to their whims?"

"It does not," Eilean answered. She looked into the queen's eyes, imploring her to believe. "I have seen someone brought back from the dead. With my own eyes."

The queen was curious. "You mentioned that before. Who was it?"

"My friend. She's more like a sister, actually. She got the sweating sickness when we came to Muirwood, and she died. Maderos brought her back to life." Eilean swallowed. "When she was gone, she saw another world. The Medium . . . the Knowing . . . is real. And I know that for myself. It's what brought me to you."

"Oh, I believe power belongs to those who claim it. To those few who master its secrets. But you are wrong. It brought *you* to *me* because *I* willed it."

Eilean heard a snickering sound at the door, accompanied by the sound of claws scratching the wood. She knew it at once—the púca.

The queen whirled around, startled.

Eilean's heart leaped in her throat, and she got to her feet, reaching down to close the tome on the desk.

The queen opened the door, and Hoel pointed the blade Firebos at her throat. Blue light glimmered along the sharp edge.

"Do not say a word, madame," he announced in a cold voice. "Or it will be your last."

The queen's eyes blazed with fear, and her thoughts skittered in a panic. She'd never come so close to dying before. The blade's power still worked, even inside the voided room. The null sigil didn't affect it at all.

Essylt stepped backward to put some distance between herself and the sharp bite of metal, but Hoel advanced, his eyes locked on the queen's.

Eilean, get behind me, he thought to her.

Eilean gathered the tome in her arms, feeling its weight and the bursting joy inside her heart, and hurried past the queen to the doorway. Seeing Hoel's face again spread a thrill through her. He'd come for her. And he'd used the púca for help, which showed his willingness to see reason. To accept that he didn't know everything about their world and its magic. As if sensing her thoughts, the púca snickered again and grinned at her.

The balcony window was open, the pale curtains fluttering with the chilly breeze, and Eilean could smell the mist in the air. The sunlight was failing. It was nearly dusk.

"You'll regret this," Essylt whispered.

"I don't doubt it," Hoel answered. Now that Eilean was behind him, he began to retreat.

To the window, he thought to her again.

He held the sword firm, still pointing it at the queen.

The púca had brought Hoel here, but could it take the two of them away? She didn't think so, not from what Stright had told her.

Then she realized it didn't need to. After the queen had captured Eilean, she'd uttered a word of power that had transported them both away from Tintagel. She'd only heard the word spoken once. But the Medium helped her remember it: *Kennesayrim.*

I can get us out of here, she thought to Hoel.

How?

Trust me.

Now that she was out in the queen's chambers, she saw the lush furnishings, the splendid bed and wardrobes, the casks of jewels on dressers. Then the main door of the bedroom opened, and Sir Peredur walked in, wearing his armor. He saw the scene before him and drew his weapon.

Púca, go! Eilean thought to the spirit creature.

She gripped Hoel's arm with one hand, clutching the tome to her chest with the other. Essylt rushed toward them, her face twisting with outrage.

"Kennesayrim," Eilean said, picturing in her mind the beach with the mirror gate.

The magic snatched them away as both Sir Peredur and Queen Essylt rushed them. They had to move quickly, for surely Essylt would know where they needed to go—and if she confronted Eilean outside of the cell, she would be able to rob her of breath again.

An echo of a shriek vanished into the noise of the thunder of the falls. The sensation of falling to their deaths ended with them both collapsing onto the sandy beach. And then a wave hit them, knocking Eilean sprawling and forcing her to drop the tome. Hoel stood quickly, still clutching the blade, and then gripped Eilean's arm while she choked on seawater.

"The tome!" she spluttered. Her dress was soaked, as were Hoel's clothes. He looked around in astonishment, still unsteady on his feet.

"Help me find it!" she said, sinking back down onto her knees and breaking his grip on her. As the water receded and another wave came to replace it, she saw the tome half buried in a wash of sand. She grabbed it and stood as the next wave collided with her.

"The mirror gate!" Hoel said, pointing. A thick mist roiled over the sea, but they could both see the shadows of ships from the coming armada.

It was Andrew's fleet, come to destroy Brythonica. And he would die. She knew that would happen, especially with so much treachery afoot. And when he did, the curse of the Wizr board would be unleashed, and it would destroy his kingdom in a flood. Her heart ached at the thought. If only there were a way to stop it.

"Come on!" Hoel said, seizing her again, this time around the waist. They trudged through the surf toward the stone arch in front of them.

A piece of driftwood floated by. At least they wouldn't need to swim far on the other side. As soon as they were back in their world, she could use the word of power to magically transport them to another place.

Eilean's heart was racing in her chest. Part of her didn't want to abandon Leoneyis to its fate. She knew that couldn't be what Maderos wanted. Despite everything, he cared about Elle and Andrew. He'd done everything in his power to help them be good and noble people. And now both of them were corrupted—the queen by the hetaera brand and the king by his seneschal—but before that had happened, both had succumbed to pride. It had happened so gradually they'd been blinded to it.

Anguish churned inside her. Another wave crashed into them, but Hoel continued to slog toward the opening. They had no boat this time. Wouldn't that make crossing the mirror gate more dangerous? The tome alone would drag her down below the waves.

As they drew near the mirror gate, she sensed the magic guarding it. She was reminded of the oaths they'd made and grateful that they'd made it back in time. What would they find awaiting them at Dochte Abbey? But that didn't matter. It couldn't. She could turn them both invisible, and they could sneak through the Apse Veil and return to Cruix Abbey with the tome.

Had Aldermaston Kalbraeth been able to summon the other leaders for the conclave? He'd been very sick before they left, and she'd had a premonition that Hoel would never see him again.

"We're almost there," Hoel said, wiping spume from his face. He'd sheathed his sword in the raven scabbard.

The waters crashed and swirled around the arch, but a closer inspection revealed the sand at the bottom of the arch was dry. Another wave crashed around the rocks, but the interior of the gate remained unaffected by it. Something was wrong with it, and that realization made her stomach tighten with dread.

They reached the border of dry sand and encountered a wall of invisible energy protecting it.

"Did you think I would leave the door unlocked?" shouted the queen over the surge of the storm.

Eilean and Hoel turned and saw Essylt coming toward them, her eyes glowing silver. As she walked, the waters parted around her so that her shoes only touched damp sand. It was still dusk, the day waning but not gone. And Ereshkigal's power was growing by the moment in the failing light.

Eilean could sense the surge of fear in Hoel's breast. He was terrified of the hetaera. And he had no idea that they were facing the Queen of the Unborn.

The mirror gate was barred to them. At least for now. And she knew that if they faced their enemy now, even together, they'd fail.

"We need to go," Eilean said to Hoel in a low voice. "We have to get out of here while we can."

He looked at her worriedly. "I saw a vision of a waterfall and a tower. We were both there."

She peered into his thoughts and saw the place he'd described. There was an enormous waterfall, surging off a cliff. But in the middle of the expanse of the river was a small, rocky island. And on that island was a tower.

"Kennesayrim," she said again, uttering the word of power that would take them to the place in Hoel's thoughts.

"Ke-ev had!" shrieked Ereshkigal in an otherworldly voice.

Once again, the magic rushed them away. But not before the invisible blades Ereshkigal had unleashed struck them.

None are happy with the anticipation of change. Change in itself is nothing. Everything in this universe is in a state of flux and change, either from a higher order to a lower or from a lower order to a higher. When change has remade us, the next fear is for it to happen again.

The emissary of the High Seer offered King Aengus a choice. He will be provided a wife of the maston order, a daughter of the Dahomeyjan king currently studying at Dochte Abbey. As a wedding gift, several abbeys would be founded within the realm, paid for by the High Seer as a token of good faith. If the offer is refused, the king was led to expect confrontation and war.

I asked Aengus what the cost of this bargain was, for no deal forged by other than the Unwearying Ones is ever truly magnanimous. He looked at me with despair and spoke not a word. But I knew his thoughts. I was the prize to be handed over.

At least it grieved him to betray me.

—Maderos, "Temporary" Advisor to King Aengus

CHAPTER
TWENTY-ONE

Kingfountain

W hen Essylt uttered the words of power to unleash the blades upon them, Hoel turned and shielded Eilean with his own body just as her magic swept them away. She felt no sting of pain, only the terrible knowledge that Hoel had taken the brunt of it. His brows lifted with pain, his eyes so wide she could see all the whites around his pupils.

They collapsed on stony ground amidst the roar of a waterfall that vibrated in the very stones. Mist from the falls rose from the edge of the island they'd landed on. Hoel groaned, and Eilean scurried to him on her knees, ignoring the tome. Her heart sank with dread. He lay on his side, eyes blinking, body quivering with pain. She'd had nightmares about the Fear Liath mauling him near the Dryad tree in the canyon where she'd found Maderos's tome. Now it had happened again.

On her knees, she studied him, taking in the slashes in his tunic and chaen and the red welts across his back, neck, and legs. His breath came in rattling sips as he fought against the torture he was bravely enduring.

The raven sigil on the scabbard was glowing fiercely. Its magic was the only thing keeping him alive.

He stared at her, his eyes full of pain, as he struggled to breathe.

She bent closer and kissed his forehead, her heart tugging in pain at what he'd endured for her sake. He had saved her.

"I'm so sorry," she murmured.

His teeth were clenched because of the pain. But his thoughts came to her soundlessly.

I did it willingly. For you.

That almost made her weep. Her clothes were still soaked, and there was a breeze buffeting the shores of the island that chilled her to her heart. They needed shelter, heat. She looked around the island and then saw the tower she'd seen in Hoel's thoughts.

The tower had a square middle with rounded turrets at three of the four corners. The turret facing them was taller than the other two, which were equal in height. The tower had a steep sloped foundation with water marks from where the river must have overflowed the island. The turret facing them had three narrow windows leading up its side and a round window at the very top, the structure crowned by crenellations of stone. The square interior portion of the building had larger windows and stone balconies halfway up the side.

There was a lower door made of oak and iron, which she noticed when it opened with a squeal and several armed men emerged.

Eilean lowered her head, overcome by weariness and emotion. If the Medium hadn't reminded her of the word of power to transport them away from the mirror gate, she felt certain the queen—be it Ereshkigal or Essylt—would have killed them both then and there.

Hoel had heard the sound. He tried twisting his neck to see who was coming up behind him, but she squeezed his arm with one hand and grabbed the tome by the rings and drew it onto her lap.

"I will deal with these men," she said. "You've done enough."

I can't fight, he thought to her.

"I know. You don't have to."

Eilean rose and stood as the men approached. One of them radiated the power of the Medium, much like Sir Peredur, and they approached warily, hands on swords. She cradled the tome in her left arm.

The man in the middle had a chain hood covering his head, but she saw the brown hair streaming out of it. He looked twice her own age and had the bearing of a man accustomed to being in command. He asked her a question, but she didn't understand it over the roar of the falls.

She shook her head in confusion.

The knight wrinkled his brow and came closer. "I said, how did you get to the island? I don't see a boat."

Now she recognized the voice. This was the knight who'd ridden out to confront her at the grove in Brythonica. Her spell hadn't worked on him.

Did he recognize her? It had been nearly dawn in the grove.

"The Fountain brought us," Eilean answered, her voice quavering despite her will to stay calm. "Is this your tower, Sir Knight?"

"Aye. As is this river and the trees on both sides. And the land as far as you can see. This is my realm. I am the King of Ceredigion."

She knew the realms of her own world. But she didn't remember Maderos ever mentioning Ceredigion specifically, though she remembered the name from the Dreadful Deadman prophecy.

"You are Sir Owain?" she asked, hoping her memory was right.

"Aye, lass. I hail from Atabyrion. Your friend looks in a bad state."

"Can you shelter us?"

"From whom?"

Eilean glanced at the other two knights. They were both loyal to their lord and looked upon her with open distrust.

"We are cold. He is injured. And both of us are weary. Is there no claim of hospitality in your realm?"

The knight pursed his lips. "You seem familiar to me, lass. Have we met before?"

She felt another pulse of worry. Was he remembering?

"You serve the Fountain," Eilean said.

"Aye. I do."

"Then in the Fountain's name, give us shelter. I serve the Fountain."

He stared at her quizzically. "I didn't know the Fountain *had* a lady in its service. But I see the truth of things, and the sun sets fast in this land," he said. Turning to his men, he nodded. "Carry him." He opened the crook of his arm to Eilean. "Come with me."

Eilean tightened her grip on the tome and heard Hoel grunt as the two men lifted him up. They all walked through the oak door leading into the tower, into a cramped inner corridor that smelled of smoke from the torches burning in iron rings hammered into the walls. They immediately went up some stairs.

"We don't have many accommodations on this ragged rock," said Sir Owain. "Will a pallet do?"

"That will be well," she answered.

They reached a small room, and Owain opened the door. It was a cramped little space with a pallet on the floor, a single window embedded higher on the wall. A few barrels had been left in there for storage purposes. The two soldiers lowered Hoel onto the pallet, then brushed their hands.

"I'll bring you some supper," Owain said. "Wait here. Oh, Mack, bring some candles. It's getting too dark."

"Yes, my lord."

In a few moments, the soldier returned with candles and set them on some of the barrels for light. Then the knight's men left, closing the door behind them. She listened to see if it would be locked, but she heard nothing.

She knelt down next to the pallet, setting the tome down by Hoel's head, then stroked his chest. "Is the pain still great?" she asked.

It lessens with time, he thought back. *The scabbard is working.*

She could again sense that it was—its glow adding to that of the candles.

"What are we to do, Hoel? She's barred the mirror gate. And she tried to kill us."

Wouldn't killing us have destroyed it?

"Yes. But it was dusk, and she wasn't in her right mind. Besides, the queen has the Gradalis, so she probably doesn't need the mirror gate. She has other ways of traveling to our world."

His eyebrows wrinkled in confusion.

"The queen has Ereshkigal trapped in her body," Eilean explained.

Hoel weakly lifted his hand and clasped hers. Although he did not appear to be surprised, worry wrinkled his brow. Worry . . . and fear. She could sense in his mind the image of the double-faced woman from the maston rites.

"I've tried warning Essylt, but I don't think she fully realizes what—or who—she is. She loses her sense of herself at night, or when she gets very, very angry. I think she blacks out and Ereshkigal takes control."

The High Seer needs to know this.

Eilean bit her lip. She had come to this other world to find the missing tome and seek Andrew's help. So far, nothing had turned out as she'd expected. But at least she had the tome.

"Do you still have the Cruciger orb?" she asked.

Yes.

"Maybe there is another way back. If not, I need to find a way to break the protections guarding the mirror gate."

She will come for you here.

Eilean sighed. "Does she have a Cruciger orb too? How will she know where I am?"

His fingers tightened against hers. *I saw you facing her. Here . . . on this island.*

Eilean's heart sank. "I don't want to face her again. She's stronger than me."

You will. You must.

Dread made her stomach clench. "She knows so much more than I do, Hoel. She knows a word of power to take someone's breath from them. That's how she subdued me in Tintagel Castle. When I left you, I invoked an invisibility spell and ventured into Andrew's chamber. He was talking to his seneschal, Sir Queux. Hoel, that man has twisted Andrew's mind for years. It's disgusting. While I was there, Essylt came in disguise. She stole my breath away and transported me to Ploemeur—to a room where I couldn't cast any spells. Nothing."

What did she want from you?

"She wanted me to translate the tome. There's knowledge in there she craves, about how to achieve immortality and take it away. I think Ereshkigal is goading her on. Something in the tome reveals the location of a tree whose fruit will make Myrddin mortal, and it's obvious Ereshkigal wants to *destroy* him. I know it's complicated, but that is what I've been able to discern."

The door handle jiggled and the door opened. Eilean turned and saw Owain enter carrying a wooden tray.

"We have a lot of fish," he said wryly. "Not much game. I hope you don't mind."

Soup had been poured into a trencher bowl of bread. There were two spoons and two mugs. Sir Owain set the tray down on the floor next to her, then leaned against the barrel, folding his arms.

"Thank you for the food," she said. It smelled amazing, and she was ravenous.

He shrugged and gave her a stern look. "Maybe you can answer a question for me, lass."

She sensed his thoughts before he spoke—*I know your name. I know who you are.* So it surprised her when he casually asked, "Your name?"

You are from the prophecy. I know it.

It was strange hearing the disparity between his thoughts and his words. He was excited but pretending to be indifferent.

She gazed up into his eyes. "I am."

He scowled. "You are what?"

"I am who you think I am. I'm not from this world, Sir Owain."

"Are you from the Deep Fathoms, then?"

In a way, she was. She had come here through the water. But he wouldn't understand such things.

"I've come to warn the people. The pride of King Andrew will destroy Leoneyis. A flood is coming."

He covered his mouth, disrupting a gasp, and choked on his emotion. She could sense his turbulent thoughts.

I knew it. I knew it! Gods help us!

"I warned him," she said. "But he will not listen. I've warned the Queen of Brythonica too. The flood will also destroy her realm."

That sent a wave of panic through Sir Owain, and he stood abruptly as if his bottom had been burned. "I must warn her."

"She *has* been warned."

The look of conflict on his face showed his inner turmoil. In his thoughts, she saw the grove she'd visited the other night—the one with the Gradalis. Sir Owain was bound to it somehow. Yes, he was the one she'd met. There was no doubt in it.

"You protect the Gradalis," she whispered.

His stared at her in shock. "How do you know my thoughts? I've told no one. Not even my king!"

"You didn't tell me. The Fountain did."

He started to pace in the cramped cell. "By the Laws, I can hardly believe it. You are her. The one from Myrddin's prophecy."

"I am," she said.

"Is that why you brought the sword? I'd know Andrew's sword anywhere. Have you brought it . . . have you brought it for *me*?"

She felt a ripple in her heart. She knew what to say.

"Yes," she answered. "But not yet." She felt the words come to her heart. "You will build a sanctuary here, on this island, to honor the Fountain. And you will build another castle from which you will rule Ceredigion."

"A castle? Here?" His eyes widened with wonder and confusion.

"You will call it Kingfountain."

She could see the ambition in his eyes and the recognition of the castle's name. It triggered a memory within him. She could feel the wonder and hope she'd unleashed within him—as well as the first spark of pride at having been chosen by the Fountain.

We are never so defenseless against suffering as when we love. Before I was given the chance to partake of the immortal fruit, I always sought to expel from my life physical pain and mental anguish. I tried to latch on to a state of continuous ease and comfort. But then I met the Harbinger and learned the truth about sorrow.

Character cannot be developed in ease and quiet. Only through trials and suffering can the soul be strengthened, ambition inspired, and success achieved. Pain and suffering are inevitable for those who seek intelligence and nurture a deep heart. The really great ones must, I think, have great sadness.

But as my friend Ovidius once taught me, "What is the good of dragging up sufferings that are over, of being unhappy now just because you were then?" The Bearden Muir isn't so awful as other cages I've been in.

—Maderos, Prisoner of Muirwood

CHAPTER TWENTY-TWO

The Queen's Revenge

E ilean could feel the thrum of the river rippling through the stone floor. The noise of the waterfall was muted by the walls of the tower, but it was loud enough to hear, and it flooded her senses as she fell asleep, cushing with Hoel on the floor pallet.

When morning came, the glow from the scabbard was gone. His wounds, miraculously, had healed. He sat up, stretching his arms, gazing at the tears in his tunic.

She lay still on the pallet, head propped on her hand, gazing up at him in wonder as he rose.

"The pain is gone?" she asked.

He nodded. "It was difficult falling asleep last night." He approached the window and looked out the smeared glass. Then he unlatched it and pushed it open, which brought in a chilly breeze and the untempered noise of the falls. The morning light bathed his face. He turned and looked down at her. "But having you near helped me endure it."

"I'm so sorry you were hurt."

"I would die to protect you," he said simply. She sensed the sincerity in his thoughts.

She rose from the pallet and embraced him, pressing her cheek against his neck. "I don't want to lose you."

His arms wrapped around her and pressed her close. Then he kissed her hair. They stood like that for a long moment, and she enjoyed the heat coming from his body and the cool breeze from the window. At least her dress had dried out during the night.

"I brought your things, but they're in the boat still," he told her.

"What boat?"

"Penryn's boat."

She pulled back and looked at him in relief. "I'm so glad that they made it safely away."

Hoel nodded, smiling. "We escaped together. They were bringing him across the bridge when I left the castle. Only two guards. It wasn't much trouble."

"What about Kariss?" Eilean asked. "Did she find you?"

His look darkened. "Aye. She did."

Eilean felt the brooding thoughts he'd prefer to keep from her.

"What happened?" she whispered, running her hand across his chest.

Still, he hesitated, but she gave him an encouraging look.

"Somehow she knew where I was hiding and came disguised as you. The Medium warned me it was a deception. She said to follow her to one of the fountains in the palace. The feeling of dread—of wrongness—was so powerful. I loathed what I had to do. I told her I would follow her, but when she turned to the door, I grabbed her from behind to subdue her. I didn't believe my eyes. I trusted my heart."

Eilean was relieved he had. She suspected the rest. "You had to kill her."

His lips frowned. In his thoughts, she could see the fight. Kariss had stabbed him with poisoned daggers in their fight. His strength waning, he'd gotten her in a chokehold before he could faint from the poison. When he revived, she was slumped against him—dead, her neck broken. Guilt twisted and swirled within him.

"I suppose. After I awoke, I used the Cruciger orb and learned that you were at Essylt's castle."

"When did you get there?"

"I left with Penryn and the girl. He'd spent the entire time telling the locals of Leoneyis to flee for their lives. In one village, when the people didn't believe him, that girl caused the well water to come leaping out of the shaft in a plume. Everyone listened then. Word got around fast, and a lot of people left. We sailed east first, then went to Penryn's village. It's on the coast by a town called Averanche. After we spread word of what was coming, we ran into the blockade. I hiked on foot to Ploemeur. Penryn is still in the cove where I left him, presumably."

"You found the púca obviously."

He smirked. "Charming creature. It came to me, actually. It knew where you were being kept. The Medium told me to trust it, so I did. It flew me up to the queen's balcony."

"You were . . . my savior," she said, cupping his cheeks between her palms. She leaned up and kissed him on the mouth.

Feelings of warmth began to well up inside her. He was kissing her back, hard, pressing her closer to him. The noise of the falls diminished against the throbbing of her heart. How she loved him. How grateful she was to him.

He sighed and broke away, his eyes blinking with surprise.

She licked her own lips, still tasting him. "That was fairly done," she said.

Hoel was breathing fast. "We'd better not do it again," he said. "I'm afraid I'd get too used to it."

"That may not be a problem," she grinned at him.

He lifted her hand and kissed her knuckles. "I'm a man, Eilean. I only trust myself so far."

And she loved him all the more for his self-restraint. "I won't tempt you, then. Well, maybe a little." She backed away from him and noticed the half-eaten trencher bowl where she'd left it last night. She'd ladled mouthfuls of soup for him and torn hunks of the bread until he was satisfied. There was still some bread left, which she picked up and split between them. The salty taste of the cold, creamy soup lingered in the fluffy middle, and they each sat to devour their share.

"I wish I had a change of clothes," she said. "This gown still smells of the ocean."

"I have my old tunic, though," he said. He was still wearing the one they'd found in the closet at Tintagel Castle. He riffled through his pack and produced it. "We could put the tome in here now?" he suggested.

She nodded in agreement, and Hoel stuffed it in the bottom of his rucksack. Then he stood and began to shrug off his tattered tunic. Before her cheeks started to burn, she rose and walked to the window. Down below, she saw a man standing at the end of the island, right at the edge of the falls. It looked like Sir Owain.

She was tempted to peek as she heard Hoel put on his old shirt and tunic again, but with their thoughts so entangled, he would surely know. Besides, he was someone she loved, and she respected that love and didn't want to treat it as rubbish. Seeing Hoel differently from other men had given her a patient hunger that was entirely unfamiliar. She realized she must be learning a secret of human tenderness *and* long-suffering. One day, though. She would learn about each of his scars, each mark that made him the man she so esteemed.

When she looked back, Hoel was finished. The sword and scabbard were strapped to his waist, the rucksack hung from one shoulder. He had his bow and arrows still. And he held the Cruciger orb in his hand.

"Tell me about the vision you saw," she asked him. "The one of us out here, by the falls."

He sighed. "You faced the queen here. Not in this tower specifically, but out there, where the peak of the stone splits the river in half."

"What did you see?"

"I saw the two of you in a duel of sorts."

Eilean shuddered. "But she can steal my breath, and if I cannot breathe, I cannot speak. I cannot say the words of power."

"The Medium protected you all the same," Hoel said.

"Did you see how it ended?"

He shook his head. "No. It was just a glimpse. I don't know why the Medium has brought us here, Eilean." He joined her at the window and looked down at the man standing at the edge of the falls. "It has something to do with him."

"We're supposed to give him the sword," Eilean said.

Hoel frowned, and she sensed resistance in his thoughts. He craved the weapon—the power it gave him made him feel invincible, and being without its protection scared him.

"Eilean," he murmured hesitantly.

"The sword doesn't belong to us," she said. "You are equally dangerous without it, my love."

He snorted. His hand gripped the hilt and squeezed. The resistance within him was powerful.

"Why did Maderos have it in the first place?" he asked.

"It was stolen from King Andrew. Essylt took it and hid it in her castle in Ploemeur, then used her magic to forge another blade, a deception. Maderos wrote the story in the tome."

"Why? Did she want the king dead?"

"I don't know. Maybe she was jealous because he didn't choose her to be his queen? This trouble in Leoneyis all stems from their falling out. And now, these kingdoms will both be destroyed. All because of stubbornness, pride, and ambition."

"There is treachery involved too. How did Ereshkigal get to this world?"

"I think Essylt brought her here, wittingly or not. Now Ereshkigal is reclaiming power through the queen. I can only imagine how devastated Maderos would be to learn that his old friends are about to destroy one another."

Hoel looked at her. "Maybe we're here to stop that?"

"We can't. The warning came, and it was ignored. The Blight is on its way. They've gone too far."

"Are you sure?"

Eilean looked at him. "Don't you see the same pride in High Seer Tatyana's eyes? Both of our worlds are on the verge of ruin, and I fear there's nothing we can do to save either of them. Haven't we tried?"

He brushed his thumb across her cheek. "I don't know. But I feel we're here for a reason. That *you* are here for a reason greater than just getting the tome back. Right now, I think we need to talk to him." He nodded toward the man outside.

Eilean's fear multiplied. "She's coming, isn't she?"

"I think so."

"Hoel, I'm not strong enough!"

"You're stronger than you know," he said, lifting a hand to caress her cheek. "I hunted you across half the world and still you beat me. Because the Medium was on your side. You could not fail then. You cannot fail now."

It was a comforting thought, but she still felt the terror of the coming confrontation. Essylt knew words of power Eilean did not. And, if that weren't bad enough, the Queen of the Unborn was bound to her body and could influence Eilean's feelings. Fear, despair, helplessness would all be thrust at her mind.

"Hoel," she whimpered, her throat thickening with panic.

He pulled her close, lending her his strength. "You can." Then he gripped her shoulders and put her back from him so he could look into her eyes.

"One of the tests of the Apocrisarius, one that we all must face, is the leap. We have to jump from a cliff into the sea. We practice jumping off one of the many bridges in Avinion first and then swim against the current of the waterfall. That's a fun one. But the cliff jump is terrifying. People have died from it. Or been severely injured."

"This isn't helping." She smiled ruefully.

He squeezed her shoulders. "Sometimes what we're asked to do feels impossible. Our minds shrink from the task. There is no other way than to conquer the fear of the unknown and take the leap. When your magic whisked us away from the beach, that's what it felt like we were doing—jumping off that cliff." His eyes were so full of confidence, his expression one of tenderness and determination. "By Cheshu, you can do this, Eilean!"

She felt a subtle jab from the Medium telling her that he was right. All she needed to do was master her fear. She didn't know all that Essylt knew. But she knew enough. Maderos had given her all the knowledge she needed from his tome.

"*Shaw*, you don't have to look so smug about it," she choked out. Then she kissed him on the cheek and nodded that she was ready.

They left the cramped room and went to the stairs with their gear. It was early enough that few were about, although the smell of sizzling sausages meant that breakfast was on the way. Finding the lower level and the main door was easy enough, and they both exited the tower and began to walk down the length of the island toward the man who was still standing at the edge of the falls, the noise of which grew louder and louder.

Eilean's stomach felt unsettled, and she wrung her hands to try to quell her nerves. Hoel walked at her side, confident and compassionate.

Sir Owain turned as they approached. She'd felt his special connection to the Medium again as they came near. He looked distressed and was fiddling with his hands as well. He wore a tunic and cloak, a longsword belted at his waist. Mist from the falls had snagged in his beard.

The cacophony of the waterfall was impressive and frightening. Standing at the edge, they could look down at the seething water running both ways toward the cliff.

"You look hale," Owain said to Hoel. Then his gaze shifted to Eilean. "Your power of healing is impressive."

"The Fountain has blessed me," Hoel answered.

The feeling of so much water rushing by them made her worry that a sudden excess might burst over the banks and throw them all off the cliff. She had the urge to back away from the edge, but she stayed put.

"I've been struggling all night with my thoughts," Owain said. "'Restless' doesn't begin to describe it. You both serve the Fountain. I can sense that. I feel I can speak freely to you."

"You can," Eilean answered.

The Medium churned around them, within them.

"I'm a conflicted man," Owain said. "I rule Ceredigion because my king and friend gave it to me. But you're right, lass. Andrew has lost his way. He's done something very wrong. I'm also bound to the Queen of Brythonica. She . . . she put me under her obligation when she made me guardian of the grove. I swore I would tell no man about the Gradalis, but you already knew about it. A ring allows her to summon me to defend the grove." He had to speak loudly to be heard over the thunder of the falls. "And now that Andrew has come to wreak vengeance on Brythonica, she will summon me to fight him." He shook his head. "I cannot fight the man Andrew has become without betraying the king to whom I pledged my loyalty. And I cannot refuse the summons without taking off the ring and betraying her. There are no good choices for me, my lady."

She could feel his internal struggle. His thoughts matched his words, and she pitied his dilemma.

"You are strong with the Fountain, my lady," he said next, gazing at her imploringly. "What shall I do? Either path leads to betrayal. And the queen . . . she's not been herself either. Sometimes she comes here at night. In the moonlight. She tries to tempt me. But I'm immune to her charms. The Fountain gives me strength, but I can barely endure it. I fear . . . I fear her wrath."

Eilean could tell Owain didn't understand all the magic involved. He was being protected somehow.

She knew what he must do. "Andrew is now a false king. You have no duty to obey him or fight for him. And your allegiance to the queen is against the Fountain's will. Remove the ring, Sir Owain. Cast it into the river."

He gasped with shock. "My lady . . . dare I? I have stood here for hours, feeling that very thought but too frozen with fear to accomplish it." He clutched his chest and squeezed his tunic. "I should cast it away? The ring does not want to go."

"It is but a piece of metal. Of no value to you. Cast it into the river, Sir Owain. Trust the Fountain."

As she said the words, she felt she needed to hearken to her own counsel. Calmness encompassed her like the embrace of a warm blanket.

He wriggled with something on his hand, something she couldn't see. Then a ring appeared. She sensed the spell of invisibility that took effect when it was being worn. Owain stared at the ring in his palm, and a look of tranquility crossed his expression.

"You're right. You truly are a lady of the Fountain."

He turned and hurled the ring over the falls.

Sunlight peeked over the hilltop to the east, shrouded in trees. In that flicker of light, she fancied she saw a castle there.

Eilean turned her head and realized she was seeing Hoel's thoughts. He was gazing at the hill, at the castle that would be built in the future. In that vision, two bridges connected the island to the land on either side. And there, before them, instead of a tower there existed a shrine. A vaulted structure like the abbeys from their world.

Hoel stood in the middle of a vision, his heart swollen with the power of the Medium.

A shiver of magic announced the arrival of the queen.

"You fool!" Essylt shrieked, her face twisted with the rage of betrayal. She had sensed the ring plummeting over the falls, and she'd come immediately.

"I'm sorry, my lady," said the knight, the king at heart. "But I cannot serve you. You are no better than Andrew. Nor is Modredus. I'll stand alone now, whatever the cost."

Essylt's nostrils flared. "Then perish in the Deep Fathoms." Her voice rose to a piercing scream. *"Kozkah gheb-ool!"*

The Medium's influence in this universe always takes the form of persuasion and patience and long-suffering, never coercion and stark confrontation. It acts by gentle solicitation and sweet enticement. It always acts with unfailing respect for the freedom and independence that we possess and for what we willingly choose. Until the banquet of consequences comes. They may be delayed, forestalled, circumvented for a season or two or three. Inexorably they come, the sum of our thoughts, our wishes, our secret desires. In the end, we must accept the consequences of what we want.

—Maderos

A Castle in the Bearden Muir

CHAPTER
TWENTY-THREE

The Fountain

The words were familiar. They were the first words of power that Mordaunt had taught Eilean after she arrived at Muirwood. With the uttered command, she felt the tingle of magic, and she dreaded the unleashed force that would shove all three of them off the edge of the cliff and down into the thrashing water at the bottom of the falls.

Only nothing happened.

The words had been spoken properly. Their power had been invoked. She felt the force rush against her and the two men. But it did not affect them.

Essylt's eyes glittered with anger.

"Stop," Eilean said, shaking her head. "Please."

"Be-ray-keem!" Essylt commanded, raising her hand to the sky and then thrusting it down, pointing her fingers at them.

It was the command that summoned lightning. Eilean knew, for she had used it in front of the High Seer.

There were no clouds in the sky, but a crackling sheath of white energy slammed down around them. It blinded Eilean, but she felt no pain. The only effect it had on her was that the hair on the back of her neck and arms rose to attention. The explosion ended.

Eilean turned her head and saw that Hoel and Owain stood firm too. Hoel was fearful but safe. Owain stood resolute. In fact, he seemed unsurprised by the queen's failure.

Magic did not affect him as it did others. He had a Gifting of sorts, an immunity to magical abstractions. He could not be coerced by manipulation of his feelings or by words of power. A kystrel could not impact him either. That insight didn't come from Owain, it came as a whisper from the Medium.

Eilean turned back to Essylt, who stared at them in shock.

"This isn't possible!" the queen roared. "You are nothing compared to me! Your power is insignificant. *Thas!*"

The command summoned a pillar of fire that came down and smothered the rock on which they stood. Yet it parted, a sheath of protection defending them from the searing heat and engulfing flames. When it ended, the rocks surrounding them were glowing red and scorched black from the onslaught. But the power could touch none of them, so long as they were standing near Owain.

Essylt didn't know Owain's secret. He had never revealed his immunity to her.

Summoning so much power had weakened the queen. She was panting, the strain showing in her wrinkled brow, the slight hunch of her body.

"I will destroy you . . . one way . . . or another." Essylt pointed her arms at them, palms facing each other. "*Hamabul mayim!*"

Eilean didn't recognize the command at first, but then the meaning came to her. A flood of waters. The river swelled and splashed over the embankment, crashing around the tower. Essylt was protected from her own spell by virtue of having summoned it, but so were Eilean, Hoel, and Owain. The waters divided as they charged toward them, and Eilean was momentarily blinded by the massive force that bucked and kicked against the protective dome surrounding them. The power of the river had been unleashed against them, but the Fountain was stronger.

When the deluge subsided, Eilean saw Essylt on her knees, panting, gasping, her hair blowing in the breeze. Her arms trembled. She looked at Eilean with hatred and fear.

Then she pointed at her. *"Asphuxis."*

The taking of breath.

And still, it did not work. Eilean could sense the desperation, the confusion, the mounting terror of the Queen of Brythonica. At first, the queen assumed a null sigil must be carved nearby, so she stormed to and fro, searching for it, throwing rocks asunder and uprooting plants. Desperation drove her hard. But she found no evidence of one. Confronted with the evidence that another power was somehow deflecting hers, she lowered her head and sank to her knees. Her hands grasped at the raw stone, clutching it until her tendons blanched. She looked up again, her eyes beginning to glow silver.

"Depart," Eilean said, making the maston sign.

"Depart," Hoel echoed, now standing next to her, also making the maston sign.

The Medium swelled through and around them.

"No! No! *Nooo!*" shrieked the otherworldly voice. Essylt swore at them. She hissed. A mewling sound sent chills down Eilean's back.

"Depart," Eilean commanded.

"Depart," Hoel added.

Essylt's mouth began to utter words in a language Eilean had never heard. The earlier invocation of xenoglossia allowed her to understand the vitriol, though in her soul, she didn't *want* to know what the Queen of the Unborn was saying, the vileness of her threats, the mocking hate that spewed from her.

Blackness gathered around Essylt's body, which stiffened and began to convulse. Her fingers were like talons, raking the air in front of her. More foul words were spoken, and the ground began to shake beneath them. Thunder rumbled in the cloudless sky. Ereshkigal was uttering a foul curse, and then she pointed it at them.

"Depart!" Eilean said impassively, her tone a rebuke.

"Leave her," Hoel said, his voice throbbing with conviction.

Essylt's back arched, and she shrieked in pain before slumping onto the wet ground.

The ripples of thunder faded. The noise of the falls became a soothing sound once more. The queen's body looked slumped and lifeless.

"Is she dead?" Owain asked, his voice full of fear.

Eilean turned and looked at him. He'd saved them unwittingly. No—she corrected herself. The Medium had saved them all. It had brought the three of them together at this precise moment for a reason. Its Gift to Owain had been exactly what was needed in the moment. The wisdom of Maderos's tome had been proven once again. The Medium wasn't in the storm, the earthquake, or the fire. Its power was as subtle as a whisper.

She gave Owain a smile of gratitude, and then she and Hoel approached the queen's prone body while Owain stood farther back. Her swelling and contracting back showed she was breathing. The power she'd used had exhausted her into unconsciousness, the same thing that had happened to Eilean so many times.

"*Anthisstemi,*" Eilean whispered, putting her hand on Essylt's shoulder. The word of rejuvenation.

"*Nnnnghh,*" moaned the queen, reviving instantly. She lifted her head, her hair spilling over her face.

"Help her sit up," Eilean said to Hoel, who promptly obeyed.

The queen clung to Hoel for support as she sat, too weak to do otherwise. She looked at Eilean in wonderment. Thoughts spilled from her mind: confusion, defeat, and the recognition that she'd plumbed her powers to the limits. She had nothing else within her to summon, even the simplest command. Her stores were completely empty.

"Sir Owain, can you get some food?" Eilean asked, looking over her shoulder.

"Aye." He walked past them toward the tower and disappeared inside.

Eilean smoothed some hair from Essylt's shoulder.

"How did you best me?" Essylt asked.

"I didn't."

The queen's brow wrinkled. "What spell did you use? I didn't sense any defense. Do you have a magic ring?"

"No," Eilean answered simply. "You understand now that I spoke the truth? You have a being trapped inside you. She is gone now. But I suspect she'll be back."

The queen's shoulders slumped. Yes, she knew. She'd seen the brand on her arm—and concealed it every day with her magic. She also concealed the shadowstain that had formed on her breastbone from using a kystrel. In fact, Eilean could see the smudges as the queen lifted her head.

"I am . . . I am nothing now. I've lost it all." Eilean could sense the woman's thoughts—her desire to leap off the island and perish.

Eilean gripped Essylt's shoulder. "It is not too late."

"It *is* too late!" She looked at Eilean helplessly. "I have no power left. Nothing! The flood you promised. I've known about it. I wanted Andrew to fail." Eilean could sense the spite in her thoughts. The jealousy. The queen hung her head again and started to weep.

Eilean's heart ached for her. She pulled Essylt closer and hugged her, stroking her hair as the sobs came spilling out.

"Without my protection, my people . . . my kingdom . . . they'll all *die*. Because of me! Because of what I've done. I cannot bear it. I cannot bear it! Let me go! Let me end it!"

Eilean did not loosen her grip. Hoel looked on worriedly, crouching nearby.

"Please," Essylt lamented. "I want to die. I cannot bear it."

"You must bear it," Eilean said. "I will help you if I can."

The queen wiped her nose, looking at Eilean with bewilderment. "After what I've done to you? What I did to *him*?"

Her thoughts were naked to Eilean now. She was talking about her attempt to seduce knowledge from Maderos. Knowledge that she had not earned and with which she could not be trusted.

As they looked into each other's eyes, Eilean discerned the truth of the scullion who had risen to queen. She'd heeded Myrddin's lessons, been an apt pupil. When life had buffeted her with disappointment, she'd turned her ambition in a different direction, determined to conquer death itself. She hated what she'd done to achieve those ends. The way she'd treated Maderos, the pact she'd made with Ereshkigal. The control she'd ceded. And Ereshkigal had encouraged her to turn that hatred toward Maderos, to not only discover the secret to extending her own life but to ending his.

"It is not too late to come back from the brink," Eilean said. "What good will destroying yourself do?"

"It will end my pain," Essylt moaned.

"Will it? Can you be sure? Might there not be, as you mentioned before, grave kingdoms ruled by the dead? I ask you again, what good will destroying yourself do?"

"What good can *I* do? My people will be drowned—because I was too proud to stop! How can I ever overcome such evil? Let me face my punishment. I deserve it." She spoke with dread.

Eilean sighed and shook her head. "There is much good you can do. You used the words of power Maderos taught you to serve yourself.

Use them instead to serve others. The throne hasn't brought you the happiness you convinced yourself it would. Serving your people might."

"I cannot stop what will come to pass," Essylt said, her tone softening. "If Andrew dies, no one can stop the flooding. Not even the Fountain."

"Then *I* will stop your kingdom from being flooded," Eilean said.

It was too late to save Leoneyis, but at least Penryn had spread his message far and wide. They'd done what they could. But Brythonica and the lands that lay beyond it could yet be saved.

"How can you stop that?" Essylt demanded.

Hoel shot Eilean a questioning look.

A whisper of thought came to her mind. *Make Leerings along the coast. Empower them to hold the floods at bay.*

Leerings would stand a long time. As long as the boulders would last.

"I believe I can," Eilean said. "You must trust me to do so. If you will turn to the light, the Fountain will bless you."

The queen's lip trembled. "Isn't it too late for me? I cannot rid myself of her. I've tried."

Eilean looked at Hoel, then back at Essylt. "You need an Aldermaston."

"She needs Maderos," Hoel said.

Essylt shuddered and closed her eyes. "I cannot face him."

"Please heed me," Eilean said, taking Essylt's hands in hers. "Your ill deeds cannot be undone. But know this. The Fountain is kind. It is generous. Patient. It forgives. And so does *he*. I know him, Elle. I know he'll forgive you too."

Tears began to spill from the queen's eyes again. She sobbed like a child. Eilean hugged her once more, her own heart melting with compassion.

The tower door opened, and Sir Owain came, holding a small tray with food and drink.

"Will he?" the queen whispered. "D-do you truly believe it?"

"I do," Eilean said, stroking her face. She'd felt a change come over the queen. It was small, but it was promising. A spark of hope had lit inside her. "And it's the only way to get that demon out of you."

Essylt nodded. She turned, hearing the man's approach.

Eilean straightened and turned to Hoel.

Give him the sword and scabbard.

This time Hoel had heard the whisper too. She could tell by the way his eyes widened. He resisted the command, though. He wanted to keep it. The attachment to it was powerful.

"Hoel," Eilean said, nodding to Owain.

Hoel's eyes narrowed.

"Please," she asked, touching his fingers.

There was a stubborn set to his jaw. She feared he would resist the call . . . that he'd resent it. She feared . . .

Hoel pulled his hand away and then unbuckled the sword belt. He gave it to Eilean. "I trust you," he said, his brow furrowed.

She could sense Hoel's thoughts from that gesture. Owain's choices had shown he was worthy of the sword now. She agreed with him. Eilean, holding the strap of the belt, turned and faced Owain. "I give this to you, commanded by the Fountain. Use it to rule Ceredigion wisely. You are the custodian of the kingdom and the sword until the Dreadful Deadman comes."

She'd felt inspired to use the language of the prophecy.

Sir Owain staggered to one knee and set down the tray he still held. Eyes full of awe, he held open his palms. As she lay the scabbard and blade on them, she sensed the fire of ambition in his thoughts. He wanted her to give it to him. He coveted the blade.

"And I leave this warning from the Fountain," she added. "If you are not true to this charge, the blade will be taken from you by another more worthy."

"I accept your charge willingly, my lady," Owain murmured. His fingers closed about the scabbard. Then he stood and belted it on.

"How do we get through the mirror gate?" Eilean asked the queen. "If we do not return before the time of our covenant, it will be destroyed. Once I have ensured the safety of Brythonica, our time will most likely be nearing its end."

The queen bowed her head. "There is a password to get through it. A name."

"Tell us," Eilean pleaded.

She sensed the queen's discomfort, and then the image of a little boy flickered through her mind. The child was no more than eight years old, living in an abbey run by mastons.

"The password is Toussan," said the queen.

And Eilean knew, through the queen's thoughts, that it was the name of her illegitimate son. A secret that no one knew. She'd hidden her pregnancy from everyone. And she'd abandoned the child at an abbey in another world. Guilt and torment struggled within the queen's breast. She both loved and despised the boy.

She'd never acknowledged him or his father to anyone.

"When you regain your strength, come back to your kingdom," Eilean said. Then she reached for Hoel's hand and invoked the word of power that would take them back to Ploemeur.

I hid my tome where it cannot be found—not even by a Cruciger orb. I put it in a stone box carved by my own hands and then used a word of power to shove a boulder to seal it off. Both the sword Firebos and the raven scabbard are in there. I hid it by the Dryad tree to keep them safe from those who would steal the knowledge in the tome—the tome cared for by Ilyas and then handed down until it fell into my hands. It contains many of the Harbinger's prophecies and speaks of the coming of another seer.

For now, I must abide in a castle in the Bearden Muir until she comes. My heart is heavy with the sins of this world. I am blind to what is happening at Leoneyis and Brythonica, although perhaps that blindness is a blessing. I asked the Medium if there was any way I could assist my friends in that world, and the answer I received was to be patient. A warning is always sent before destruction comes.

—Maderos, the Druid of Muirwood

CHAPTER
TWENTY-FOUR

Ploemeur, Kingdom of Brythonica
Eighteenth Year of the Reign of King Andrew Ursus
—present day—

The harbor at Ploemeur had been abandoned, and much of the populace had either fled or taken refuge at Essylt's castle. Sir Queux had taken over the Hall of Justice, a small stone building that the kings and queens of Brythonica used to listen to pleas from the citizens of the kingdom. As Andrew arrived on his charger, he noticed the symbolism of the two-faced woman emblazoned on the pennants overhanging the walls.

Several knights were guarding the entrance, and one came to take his horse after he dismounted.

"Where is Sir Queux?" Andrew asked gruffly, gazing at the image of the double face. Something about it made him uneasy.

"He's awaiting you within, my lord. The city is abandoned."

"What of the farms?" Andrew asked.

"The farmers have fled as well. No doubt they feared your justice, my lord."

Andrew looked up beyond the stone building with its pillars and sloped roof. He saw the castle looming in the distance on the cleft of rock, a difficult trail of switchbacks leading up to it. It would be a difficult siege. But he would break Essylt's power once and for all. A feeling of guilt surged inside him upon thinking of her, but he shoved it aside.

There were times when a king had to be ruthless.

He nodded to the knights as he entered the building and then walked to the great hall. A single throne sat on the dais. The queen's throne. Her husband's had been removed following his death. There were knights assembled, all gathered around a table and talking in low voices over a map. He looked about the room for Sir Queux but did not find him.

"My lord!" one of the knights said. "Are you feeling better now that we're on land?"

Andrew had never been prone to seasickness before, but the journey from Tintagel had not been agreeable. He'd spent much of the short voyage vomiting. Even now, he was a little light-headed.

"I'm much improved, thank you," he said, lying through his teeth. "Where is Sir Queux?"

"He's in the private chamber." The knight pointed to a door behind the dais.

Another gurgle in his stomach sounded, and the knight raised his eyebrows.

"Thank you," Andrew said, walking stiffly to the room. He hoped there was a garderobe there. He was only thirty years old, but the weight of ruling such a vast domain had aged him. He felt closer to fifty than his own age. He even had some tufts of gray forming in the hair over his ears in addition to the white patch that had always resided above one of them. Maybe he'd be completely white-haired by the time he reached fifty.

If he reached fifty.

He opened the door and found Queux sitting at another table with a chalice in his hand, staring down at the box that held the magic Wizr set. It sat open on the table. Queux turned as the door opened. He'd been perusing the pieces.

"Ah, my lord. Welcome. I've been expecting your arrival."

There were three couches in the room, which was decorated with little statuary from various other realms. Elle liked to flaunt her wealth too. Decorative metal bowls were set on small tables, some filled with fruit, others with grain. There was a small, windowed door that appeared to lead to a garden behind the Hall of Justice.

Andrew slumped down on one of the sofas, clutching his stomach.

"You're still unwell?" Queux asked.

"The thought of eating makes my gorge rise," Andrew said miserably. "I haven't eaten all day."

"You need something to drink, then," said Queux. He went to another table where an open bottle of wine sat, along with several other chalices. He filled one partway and then brought it to Andrew. "The raspberry wine is especially good. It'll calm your stomach."

Andrew sniffed it, wondering if he'd have the same nauseous reaction, but it smelled pleasant, and he drank it down quickly after enjoying its delicious taste. He set the cup down on a nearby table.

"It's sweet," he said.

"Of course, my lord. As to the news. I've given orders for the blockade to be set. No ships can come in or out until you command it. The Genevese were the first to flee, and it seems the queen sent away her fleet so they wouldn't be trapped in the harbor. We command the sea."

"Good work," Andrew said, shifting on the couch to get more comfortable. "Any word from the castle?"

"I expect she'll be sending an emissary now that we're here. I will let you know when one arrives."

"She may come herself," Andrew said, rubbing his lower lip. He frowned. "She's sheltering my enemies. I don't think she'll surrender Peredur so easily. Or Genny." As he said his wife's nickname, he felt his stomach clench with revulsion. The betrayal still stung. He'd been blind to it. Willingly so. But now everyone knew of their unfaithfulness. And yet . . .

The lady who'd visited him the other night had said that he was deceived. That his wife was innocent. Her words had wrung his heart savagely, but he'd assured himself it was a deception. Queux had convinced him it had been a trick from his enemies meant to weaken him.

Once a king showed weakness, then the rebellions began.

"Justice will be done, my lord. Peredur killed twelve knights when he fled with her. Such a deed cannot go unpunished. They were valiant men all, including Sir Bannon from the Ring Table. Peredur and Genevieve are both here at Ploemeur. The Wizr set cannot lie."

Andrew did not like thinking about that night. Sometimes the echo of Genevieve's screams woke him from a fitful sleep. The mental anguish throbbed in his skull.

"I want Peredur's head, Queux."

"I shall bring it to you on a silver dish," his seneschal promised.

Andrew's stomach was getting worse. He rose from the couch and began to pace. "Who has come to ally with Brythonica? What pieces are arrayed against us?"

"Occitania, of course. King Modredus's army is at the edge of the woods in an encampment. It's a sizable host."

"What about Ceredigion? Is Owain in the fight?"

Sir Queux looked petulant. "No word either way from Owain, and his piece is still far away. His castle in the Marches is only a few days ride from here, but he's further east, at the tower in the river. I don't see why he hasn't sent word yet on his intentions. None of his pieces have moved."

"Do you think he's staying neutral?"

"Not neutral. Essylt is with him right now. I see her Wizr piece, and my spies have said he's often seen in Ploemeur. They've suggested he and the queen have an . . . intimacy of sorts."

"Oh?" Andrew asked, bristling at the notion. Elle had rebuffed him enough that he didn't want her to have anyone else.

"I can only speculate, my lord, based on what the Wizr set reveals and what my trusted men tell me. It's whispered that they're lovers."

Andrew squeezed his hand into a fist. First Peredur and Genevieve. Now Owain. Betrayal stacked on betrayal.

"And to think I gave him Ceredigion," the king said with malice.

"I sense another reckoning when this one is over. His tower will be difficult to siege, but it can be done from upriver."

A spasm of pain tore into Andrew's gut. He groaned and nearly went down to his knees.

"You're still unwell, my lord. You should rest."

His insides were on fire. This was worse than seasickness. That berry flavor was still on his tongue, but it tasted awful now. "Get me some more of that wine," he asked, hobbling back over to the couch.

"As you wish," Queux said. He fetched the goblet, then returned with more wine.

Andrew eased himself down on the couch. Another spasm took his breath away. "Here, give it to me." He took the goblet and slurped it down. The sweet taste assuaged his nausea and made him feel a little better. He set the goblet down again.

Rubbing the bridge of his nose, he lay back against the couch and lifted each leg to stretch out on it. "Sir Queux, while I want justice, I don't want it public. *Nnnghh.* I don't think I could b-bear it if Peredur begged for forgiveness."

"You think he will, my lord?"

251

"Of course he would. He knows . . . I loved him. He might use that . . . he might use it against me. *Unnghh*, I feel . . . I feel terrible."

"Let me get you some more wine, my lord."

"No . . . I've had enough. My head is swimming. It's powerful wine."

"Indeed, it is."

There was something in his voice that troubled Andrew. He turned his head and found Queux standing near the couch. The look in his eyes was almost predatory.

As soon as their eyes met, Queux smiled again. "I'm sorry you're not well, my lord. Get some rest. I'll make sure you're not troubled unless it's important."

The latch on the glass door clicked open.

Sir Queux's brow knotted with concern.

"Who's here?" Andrew asked, wincing again. His insides were still on fire. The wine hadn't helped at all.

"The wind must have opened it. There's no one there."

Andrew sat up and looked toward the windowed door. And that's when she appeared again, like a shade sent to torment him repeatedly. It was the *lady* who'd come to Tintagel.

"Her!" Andrew gasped. A man appeared next to her wearing hunter garb. The same one who'd been with her in the throne room that first day.

Sir Queux drew his sword. "Guards!" he shouted. "To the king!"

Andrew's chest constricted. He heard the woman utter a word. She walked toward them with confidence.

"Stand back!" Sir Queux threatened as he stepped in front of Andrew. "I'll not let you harm him!"

Andrew was dumbfounded. Terrified. This very woman had come to his chambers and told him that she was the sign he'd prayed for. But it was all trickery, wasn't it? All Elle's doing, using her magic to deceive him.

"My lord, I did not deceive you," she said, coming closer. The man followed her, his eyes steely and dangerous.

The door rocked as the knights and soldiers rushed to obey Sir Queux's command. But they couldn't open it. Thumps sounded and cries of alarm. "My lord! My lord!"

Sir Queux brandished his blade, threatening the pair. "Come no closer!"

"King of Leoneyis, your seneschal is the one who has betrayed you," the woman said. "Your wife committed no wrong. He has lied about her, and he has lied about Sir Peredur. They are both innocent. It is Sir Queux who is working for your downfall. He wants your throne for himself."

Andrew's fear increased.

"She lies," Sir Queux said. "I am loyal to you, heart and soul!"

The woman turned on Sir Queux, glaring at him with anger in her eyes. "You, sir, are a *pethet*."

Andrew hadn't heard that term since Myrddin had left. It was one of his sayings, a derogatory phrase he used for someone who was not trustworthy.

"My lord, I can prove my words," she said. "He poisoned you before you left Tintagel. And the wine he gave you is also poisoned. It is his intention to kill you and take your throne."

Sir Queux blanched, staring at her in shock.

"He's been twisting your mind these many years, my lord. Ever since Myrddin left. He's jealous of Sir Peredur. Jealous you chose him. He concocted a scheme to make you distrust your wife and friend, all so he could put himself in power. The poison runs through you even now to hasten your death."

A body slammed into the door. The knights were trying to force their way in. The door splintered and cracked, but it held. As if some invisible force were keeping it shut.

Sir Queux looked as pale as cheese. Andrew blinked. There was guilt in the man's eyes. He stared at the intruders, not denying their words. Then his lips suddenly contorted with hatred, and he plunged his sword down into Andrew's breast.

Pain.

He felt the blade pierce his hauberk and then plunge through muscle and bone. He saw the look on Queux's face, the hate and jealousy he had masked for so long. The wine! The wine he'd drunk at Tintagel had been poisoned too! It wasn't seasickness he'd felt.

Sir Queux pressed down harder on the blade, his mouth warped with hatred. The woman's companion tackled Sir Queux, wrenching him away. There was a skirmish between the men, but Andrew sagged down on the couch, the pain of the blade superseding the anguish of the poison.

It was a mortal blow. He knew it, could feel his insides quivering around the sharp edge. He wanted it gone. He couldn't breathe.

Genny. Genny. Genny.

He thought her name over and over, horrified by what he'd done. He'd confronted her about her adultery that dark night. He'd accused her of being unfaithful when it was *he* who had been unfaithful to her, through Queux's suggestions and help. And his jealousy had become so powerful, so inflamed by Sir Queux's words, that he'd wanted to shun and humiliate her while she'd pleaded her innocence. He'd recoiled from her so forcefully he'd knocked her down in the castle corridor, in front of their servants and his men. What would his anger have led to if Sir Peredur hadn't intervened?

All because of the poisoned lies of Sir Queux.

Genny, Genny, Genny! Forgive me! Forgive me!

She'd been faithful all along. Faithful. She was faithful. He wanted to shout it from a tower. He could hardly breathe. He was dying.

"Hoel, what do I do about the blade? Will it kill him if I pull it out?"

His vision blurred. The woman was kneeling by the couch, her face crinkled with compassion for him. Her hand gently took his and squeezed.

Sir Queux slumped to the floor. The other man approached the couch, looking down at him gravely. His look said it well enough. Andrew was a dead man. Killed by a traitor.

Queux was no true heir. Andrew understood that now, with the kind of preternatural knowledge that possibly only came with death. He had deceived himself into thinking that naming another man would end the curse, but it had to be a true heir, flesh of his flesh.

Too late.

Still, the man slid the sword from Andrew's breast. As it came free, Andrew could breathe again. He gasped, quivering in pain. Another thud struck the door, then another. Chunks began to fall away. Someone was hacking at it with a battle-axe.

"Hoel?"

"A Gifting," said the hunter. "That's the only thing that can save him now."

What was a Gifting? Andrew's vision was blurring. His life was ebbing from him. Darkness began to shroud his gaze.

"The game," he croaked. Ruin was coming. Nothing could stop it now. His people hadn't been given enough opportunity to flee. To escape the doom he'd ushered in. Had he heeded the woman, things might have been different, but he'd ignored the chance he was given.

He'd been so blind. So wrong. He was a false king, and the guilt of that was unbearable. He deserved this death. He deserved to drown in the depths of the Deep Fathoms for all eternity. Anguish, despair, torment—they were hounds barking and snapping at him.

He felt pressure on his brow. A hand touched his forehead.

He heard a woman's voice. "King Andrew, through the Medium I Gift you with . . . I Gift you with . . ." Light began to shine. He opened his eyes, experiencing a strange feeling of euphoria. Light was everywhere. She began to weep, her voice trailing off.

And then he died.

The world is seldom what it seems. If we knew the thoughts of those immediately around us, we would forever scoff at the idea that it is possible to know what will come to pass. What lies in the secret heart is revealed by the Medium's Gift. Selfishness, anger, contempt.

The girl arrives today from Tintern Abbey. I made a mess of my room so that I might have more occasion to speak to her. She will see me as an enemy. A druid. An apostate. But still, I cannot wait to meet her. I may be jaded by most human emotions and predilections, but I admit that one of them never grows old. We all love to expect, and when our expectations are either disappointed or gratified, we choose a new expectation.

—Maderos

The Founding of Muirwood Abbey

CHAPTER TWENTY-FIVE

The Flooding of Leoneyis

Eilean listened as the final breath left the high king's body. Although his face captured the moment of rapture, it began to fade as his mortal husk was left behind and his inner soul departed. Her heart grieved to see him murdered, his own supposed friend having delivered the death blow. Turning away from the couch, she stared at Sir Queux, who lay unconscious on the floor. Hoel had strangled him into submission.

She was weary from using so much magic. From the preparations she'd undergone to protect Brythonica from the coming flood. They'd gone to the beaches straightaway after returning to Ploemeur, driven there by the Medium, and she had spent a couple of days using magic to construct the protective Leerings.

"He's gone," Hoel said sadly.

Eilean's heart was injured, knowing that Maderos would also grieve. The immortal had saved Andrew as a baby. He'd been raised from an assistant pig keeper to a high king. But at the end of his life, he had proven to be a false king, lured by the lying words of a man he'd trusted and believed in.

Another cracking sound came from the door. The soldiers would be able to destroy the wood, but her spell would prevent them from entering. Still, holding the shield was draining her limited strength. It was time to go.

Eilean took Andrew's limp hand and squeezed it. If she could have prevented his destruction, she would have.

"I wish I knew the word of power that would bring his life back," Eilean said. Maderos had used it to revive Celyn, but he had never taught it to her. What cost would it require of the speaker?

Sir Queux groaned. The bloodied sword lay next to him on the floor.

"We should go," Hoel suggested.

The Medium gave her a warning not to. She felt compelled to remove the shield spell and turn them invisible again.

Releasing Andrew's hand, she rose and reached for Hoel, uttering the command after their fingers were entwined. *"Sahn-veh-reem."*

Then she removed the barrier spell on the door, and the next blow from the battle-axe sent splinters flying inward. Knights rushed inside.

Eilean tugged Hoel with her, away from the couch, so they had a better view of the room.

Sir Queux sat up, shaking his head.

"What happened?" asked one of the knights, who then gaped when he saw the king on the couch, his bloodstained tunic evidence of his murder.

"The king was attacked," Sir Queux said, climbing to his feet unsteadily.

One of the knights pointed to the bloody sword on the ground.

The soldiers turned and looked at Sir Queux. His scabbard was empty.

"Did you stab the king?" another asked in accusation. "That's your sword!"

Sir Queux looked about the room in a daze. "The murderers have fled," he said. "They went out the glass door. After them!"

Eilean saw the distrusting looks on many faces. The evidence of murder was too compelling.

"Lord Seneschal, you have blood on your tunic. On your *hands*!"

"Are you accusing me?" snarled Sir Queux. But he had a guilty look, and the words stuttered out of him in a matching cadence. "I t-tell you, they came through that d-door! I struggled against them. My sword was wrenched away from me."

"Your countenance belies you," said one of the knights. He was the one with the battle-axe. "Murder!" he shouted. "The king has been murdered!"

And that was when the earthquake struck.

The bowls atop the tables began to rattle. Some of the pedestals wobbled. Timber groaned. Then a sudden jolt slammed them, toppling a shelf. Fruit spilled and began to roll about the floor, and some of the men went down to one knee to bolster themselves. One man stood in the broken doorway, pressing his hands against the jambs. Shouts of terror began to wail throughout the Hall of Justice.

Another jolt, an even stronger one, came next, driving everyone to the floor. Cracks in the ceiling plaster set out plumes of dust.

Hoel put himself atop Eilean to protect her with his own body. Creaking noises came, followed by the noise of splintering wood.

Then the trembling ended, although Eilean still felt the world was spinning. She had never been in an earthquake before. And she never wished to experience one again.

Out of the chalky dust, a stranger's voice rose. "The Fountain has judged us, just as the lady prophesied. The flood is coming!"

"Damn the Fountain!" shouted Sir Queux. "To the ships! While we still can!"

The knights and soldiers beat a hasty escape, fleeing from the crumbling building. Hoel sat up and pulled Eilean close.

"The floods are coming now," he murmured. "We'd better flee through the mirror gate. Come."

Bits of plaster and glass clung to Eilean's dress and hair, and she brushed some crumbs from Hoel too. Once more, she looked at the high king's body as they both rose to their feet.

"He wouldn't listen," she lamented. "Now it's too late for those at Leoneyis." She felt certain that the earthquake had struck the island kingdom. That meant a wall of water was coming at Ploemeur. The Leerings she had made would hold it back.

Or so she hoped.

Grasping his hands, she bowed her head. *"Kennesayrim."*

The magic rushed them away from the stone fortress and back to the beach by the mirror gate. She fell to her knees again, dizzied by the magic that had brought them there and feeling the exhaustion down to her bones. Lifting her head, she saw the tide had gone out. No—it wasn't just a falling tide. The beach had been swept clear of water.

"It comes."

It was Queen Essylt's voice. She stood by the mirror gate, gaping in horror at the wall of surging white crests heading toward them.

Hoel was the first to his feet, and he hoisted Eilean by the arm to help her stand. She brushed the sand from her palms as she stared at the massive wave heading toward the cove. It was a line of white that filled the entire horizon. Essylt's strength was also at the failing point. She'd recovered enough at the tower to return to Brythonica, but Eilean sensed that the queen's cup of energy was nearly empty again. As was her own.

Essylt looked at the two of them. "No word of power can stop *that*," she confessed. "No one is that strong."

Eilean looked at her. "You're wrong. I have set Leerings to guard your shores. Brythonica will be protected." As she said the words, she felt the conviction of their truth whisper to her from the Medium.

Essylt turned and looked at the coming flood. As the waves drew closer, they all could see the crashing surf, the ripples that built on one another. The violence of the surge would destroy everything in its path.

Fear. Eilean could sense it festering in the queen's mind. But she stood still, watching the coming doom with all the courage she could muster.

"Go through the mirror gate," Essylt said. "Do not risk yourselves."

Eilean clenched Hoel's hand. "No, we stand with you. We will see this through."

Hoel clutched the strap of his rucksack over his shoulder, gazing at the oncoming death with a worried brow.

"Are your Leerings truly so powerful?" the queen asked.

"The same magic that built this world powers them." She remembered something she'd read in the Sefer Yetzirah, and as the waves thundered toward them with awful majesty, she recited the words.

"And the Essaios placed boundaries on the sea. And set a bolt and doors. And they said, 'Thus far you shall come, but no farther; here shall your proud waves stop.'"

A tingle went down her arms. *Here shall your proud waves stop.*

Every beach in Brythonica was protected by a Leering hidden within the caves—just like the waymarkers that surrounded Muirwood Abbey and had driven the waters away.

Essylt's breath quickened. Eilean sensed it took all of her courage to stand there when she wanted to flee through the mirror gate herself.

"Is Andrew . . . dead, then?" the queen whispered. She began to tremble, her thoughts flooding with pain. This was the outcome she'd thought she wanted, but it had been another mistake.

"Yes," Eilean replied. "Poisoned and stabbed by Sir Queux."

A ship appeared at the edge of the cove, the wind in its sails. Yes, of course Andrew's ships would try to flee. But the wind was no match for the speed of the waves.

"It's not going to make it," Hoel said. They watched the thrashing waves flip the ship upside down effortlessly. The crashing roar of the sea concealed the sound of the timbers cracking to pieces. Essylt sidled up closer and reached for Eilean's other hand. The three stood on the barren beach, watching as the surf came at them.

Eilean held her breath as the wave swooped forward to claim them. Then she felt the power of the Medium sing in her ears as the tidal wave struck an invisible barrier. She felt the power of the Leerings, chained together with the same purpose, as they defied the waters and shoved them back. The wave slammed against the shell of magic with violence and froth, skeins of seaweed and battering rams of driftwood. Even the broken ship smashed against the barrier.

The chorus of magic sang in harmony.

Waves began to slide back down the bubble of protection, which was struck again by another wave, then another. But each new surge grew weaker and weaker. The Leerings' power diminished, the song fading slowly as the threat subsided.

Then, when the final swells had ended, the Leerings' magic extinguished. It was like a sigh—a final breath.

"I'm overcome," Essylt said, squeezing Eilean's hand. "I never would have had the faith to make it happen."

"I read the tome, so I knew it was possible," Eilean answered. "The words in that book can lift mountains too."

Essylt turned and faced them. "What must I do to have this wicked spirit rooted from my heart and body? I would give up my kingdom to be free of her. I'm . . . I'm willing to face Myrddin. To admit my wrong."

Eilean turned to Hoel. "Use the orb. Tell her where he is." She bit her lip. "If he's in prison in Avinion, we must free him."

Hoel unfastened his pouch and removed the Cruciger orb. Essylt looked at it inquiringly but did not press them for details.

Hoel studied the device too, summoning the question in his mind. *Where is Maderos? Where can Essylt find him?*

The orb whirred softly. Writing appeared in Pry-rian on the surface. *Muirwood Abbey.*

"He's still there," Eilean sighed in relief. "Then that is where we will go."

"I have not the strength now," Essylt said. "And my people will need me. Those who survived will be frightened. But tell him I'm coming. I promise you that I will."

Eilean felt a nudge in her mind. "When you do, bring Andrew's body," she said. "Maybe he will be revived, just as my friend was."

Essylt nodded. "I owe you a debt I cannot repay. Should you ever need my aid, I will send it."

"Which abbey was your son taken to?" Eilean asked the queen. "Was he born here or in our world?"

The queen's anguish grew, and she bowed her head. "How did you know my shame?"

"From the Fountain. Who is the father?"

Essylt shuddered. "The high king. He . . . he never knew what I'd done."

Eilean discerned from the queen's thoughts that she had disguised herself. She'd tempted him in the guise of a peasant, and he'd succumbed. That explained his guilt over his own hypocrisy, and why accusing his wife of infidelity had tormented him so.

"He was born between the worlds," Essylt said. "In one of the in-between places. And I left him at Dochte Abbey. A wretched—like you. But he was taken somewhere else. I know not where."

"You have not seen him?"

Essylt shook her head. "I have no way of knowing where he is. Or if he's even alive."

Eilean looked at Hoel. The Cruciger orb would allow them to find the missing son.

"We must go now," Eilean said. "It will be almost dawn in our world. The time must nearly be up."

Essylt stood aside. "I will see you at Muirwood, then. Thank you, Lady of the Fountain."

"I am but her servant," Eilean demurred. Her fatigue was growing ever worse. She'd used more magic that day than ever before. Her strength had nearly failed multiple times, but she'd persisted, pushing herself beyond her natural endurance.

She clutched Hoel's arm as they approached the mirror gate. The surf was now its normal size, the threat of flooding ended. How many other kingdoms had been affected by it? Leoneyis, she knew, was destroyed.

"I'm so tired," she said with a sigh. "Can we rest a while when we reach Dahomey?"

"Of course," Hoel answered. He adjusted his rucksack, cinching it around his shoulders. The tome at the bottom would make it difficult to swim, but he had more strength than her.

"Then we can talk about what to do next," she said. "I don't need the Apse Veil to travel between abbeys now. I know the word of power that can do the same thing. We can go to Muirwood directly."

"Let's decide tomorrow," he said, his eyes focused on the mirror gate. They trod into the waters leading up to it.

"There could be trouble waiting for us on the other side," Eilean said.

Hoel had his gaze fixed on the mirror gate. "It'll be night when we cross. That will help."

When they reached the barrier, she said the name of the boy. "Toussan."

A ripple of magic revealed that they could pass. She felt the Leerings carved into the rock, unseen, above them.

Still arm in arm, they walked through the waist-high water, and the magic sent them plummeting again.

Darkness. It was night. The smothering waters of the sea disoriented her. She spluttered, trying to swim, but her dress felt cumbersome. She sucked in water as she tried to breathe and began to choke. Panic seized her chest. A wave shoved her against a rock, and she tried to grab it, still unable to breathe. She cut her hands against the sharp protuberances.

A hand grabbed her wrist. Then a strong arm went around her waist.

"I got her," said a man's voice.

It wasn't Hoel.

Aldermaston Gilifil wants to know where I hid my tome, but I would not reveal the truth to him. I will only share its location with the young woman the Medium told me I could trust. One who will not yield or bend or be broken.

—Maderos

Muirwood Abbey

CHAPTER TWENTY-SIX

Betrayed

The gentle rocking motion and the creaking of timbers revealed that she was on a boat. Eilean opened her eyes, surprised to find sunlight streaming through a bolted window. A gag was tied around her mouth, her hands bound in front of her with leather thongs. She was in a net of sorts, with interwoven skeins of ropes fixed to the wall of the cramped room at her head and feet, the slack in the line causing her body to sway with the rhythm of the ship.

She tried lifting her head, but her skull ached. There was another hammock, empty, on the other side of the room. Her feet pointed in the direction of a closed door, light streaming in beneath it. Her legs were unbound. When she tried to sit up, the net swayed and made her dizzy. She tried to lift her bound hands to remove the gag, only to discover her bonds were secured to the net itself. She could not lift her hands to her face.

Her heart began to pound with dread. Captured. Again. Where was Hoel? She strained against the bonds, trying to wriggle one of her hands free. Through the throbbing in her head, she pieced together the path that had brought her here. They'd crossed the mirror gate together, and she'd begun sinking in the sea, swallowing water. Opening her hands, she saw the little scrapes on one of her palms. The dress she wore was completely dry, so she knew she'd lost some time.

Where was Hoel? She reached out to him with her mind, calling for him.

No answer came.

A sickening feeling began to churn in her stomach. Hoel had put the tome in his rucksack.

Struggling against her bonds proved fruitless. Rather than wear herself out, she decided to rely on her other senses. The echo of boots against planking. The smell of the sea. The rough fibers of the netting against her hair.

Was it possible that he had betrayed her?

Could he have deceived her all along?

No, she knew his thoughts. She would have sensed his desire to forsake her. Except . . . what if he'd been tempted, upon capture, to say things that would exonerate him? He had willingly helped a known apostate.

But hadn't Maderos worked alongside Sir Queux for many years? Was it possible for a man to disguise his thoughts so thoroughly?

The sound of steps approached the door, and she sensed the worried thoughts of a stranger—someone who was afraid of her. The handle twisted, and a man wearing the leathers of the Apocrisarius entered. One of his hands gripped the hilt of his gladius. He didn't want to be there.

The man approached her hammock and gazed down at her. There was enough light streaming in through the window that she could see his face, although she didn't recognize him.

"You've slept a long while," he said.

She couldn't answer through the gag.

"I have orders not to remove your gag for any reason until we reach Avinion. I'm sorry, but I cannot even give you a drink. You must be thirsty."

Fear joined the turmoil. Avinion—they were sailing to the High Seer's island. She had so many questions, but she could not ask them.

"Do you need to use the privy? There's a chamber pot here. I'm ordered to help you."

Under no circumstance, except a truly desperate one, would she have agreed to that. She shook her head no, which made her ears ring.

The man was in his forties, she assumed. She could sense his skill, his strength. If she tried the fighting techniques Hoel had taught her on the beach, she would fail. His skills were beyond hers.

"Very well. We'll be there before nightfall. I cannot offer you any food until you're bound by a Leering. I'm sorry. But I have my orders."

She wanted to know who had given those orders.

"Are you cold? I can bring you a blanket. That is permitted."

She thought about it and decided she wasn't. The fabric of the now-dry dress was stiff with salt and uncomfortable, but she couldn't communicate that, nor would she want his help to change clothes. She shook her head again.

"When we near the island, I'll come get you so you can stretch your legs. Rest until then."

She wondered about his name, but she had no way of asking. His thoughts, while superficial, were all about his mission to bring her to the High Seer.

When he was gone, she wondered again what had happened to Hoel and why she couldn't sense him on the ship. If he'd been captured too, wouldn't they have put him with her?

After those first scrambling, fearful thoughts, she refused to believe that he'd betrayed her. No, he would come to help her unless he absolutely couldn't.

Had the Apocrisarius been waiting at the other side of the mirror gate? It had been very dark. Maybe Hoel had seen the danger and chosen to hide himself to better his chances of saving her later? He was good at that.

Only . . . what if she, like Andrew, was wrong?

***

The sunset was beautiful as they approached the isle of Avinion. True to his word, the Apocrisarius had returned for her and helped her out of the hammock. After untying the strands binding her to the net, he'd secured her wrists behind her back. If she could have spoken a word of power, the knots would have dropped off her like water. But speaking was impossible with the gag.

The Apocrisarius had taken her up on deck where other hunters had gathered. Her eyes went from face to face. None of them were Hoel. That bolstered her belief that he wasn't even aboard the ship.

Sunlight painted the waters orange. The sea was calm and the shrieks of gulls sounded overhead. Several of the seabirds were flying in time with the ship as it approached the isle. None of the birds had a tail or ears, unfortunately—there was no sign of the púca. She saw no harbor, but she did see glowing buildings shining in the distance and a bridge with square towers jutting up from the waters.

Since she'd had so much time to rest, she felt restless now. Moreover, her body had adjusted to the alternate sun-moon setting of the other world.

They sailed through one of the arches beneath the bridge, and she looked up at the interlaced stone. Avinion had been one of the pleasure palaces of the ancient emperors long ago. The stone looked to be at least a few centuries old.

After they passed, they followed an inland river, and the salty sea air became lighter and fresher. Some of the Apocrisarius were working at the ropes, and a few had brought gear up to the main deck. They were all armed with longbows and had quivers of arrows. Her guardian kept a hand on her upper arm, as if he feared she'd leap over the edge to escape him. His mind was constantly alert, noticing the movements of his men. He wondered if any of them were kishion.

That was a telling thought.

He didn't trust everyone on board, nor should he.

After a bend in the river, she could see the gleaming city of Avinion and the enormous waterfall below it. Unlike the waterfall beneath Sir Owain's tower, this one was long and not very steep—in fact, it appeared to have two levels of falling water. She noticed a dead tree stuck between the levels, jutting out of the crashing water. Another bridge with towers connected the lower river to the upper part of the city.

Beyond the upper falls was the city of Avinion and its majestic abbey. The abbey had a giant dome and cupola, with Leerings for light illuminating its various levels. Two smaller domes, miniatures really, sat beside the larger one, each with a pointed cupola. Ancient buildings lined the main thoroughfare. And she saw massive trees on a hill to the west of the abbey with thin trunks and sparse lower branches but huge mushroom-shaped canopies on top.

The ship docked, and her guardian escorted her to the gangway and helped her down to a carriage with bright lights fixed to the four posts. Well-groomed servants were diligently preparing for their arrival, shoveling up the horse droppings from the team of four.

Her guardian gave a command and two Apocrisarius climbed to the top of the carriage and readied their bows. Another stowed himself in the rear seat of the carriage and several others were brought horses to mount. Her guardian helped her to a plush seat inside and then sat next to her. Once she was confined, he let go of her arm and put his hands on his lap. She could sense the tension curling up from his mind. Even though they were close to the High Seer's palace, he was still nervous about being intercepted. Someone rapped at the window and asked him a question in another language—Paeizian, she thought—and he nodded. Then the horses began to clop up the road.

The curtains of the carriage were closed, so she couldn't see their passage through the city. Her mouth chafed from the gag. Her wrists were sore and swollen from the bonds.

After a bumpy ride, the wagon stopped at a palace next to the impressively domed abbey. The door opened and her escort disembarked and helped her come down so she wouldn't fall. Everyone was staring at her. It was dark now, but there were so many Leerings for light in the courtyard and beyond that it didn't feel like night. Everything had an orange hue to it. She saw decorative pillars, marbled urns full of vegetation, and then the hand gripping her arm was firmly directing her toward the manor.

Awaiting them inside was the High Seer herself, Tatyana Dagenais.

Eilean's stomach lurched at seeing the other woman's victorious smile.

"It *is* her," said the High Seer with triumph. Her thoughts were full of glee. "Bring her upstairs. I'll have one of the Aldermastons bind her to the Leering."

Eilean was ushered past her, feeling the woman's thick pride—her sense of victory. She had the tome and she had someone who could translate it. That meant she had Hoel, or he'd come to her.

Once again, Eilean's stomach sank. The conviction in the High Seer's heart was absolute. She didn't doubt what she had won.

Hoel, you didn't . . .

She couldn't finish the aching thought. Her trust in him had been absolute. Now she knew, just a little, how Maderos must have felt when Essylt betrayed him. But he couldn't have . . .

They reached the upper floor, which was immaculately decorated, and Eilean was brought to a room with a bed, a brazier, and some books on the shelves. She immediately sensed the presence of the Leering in the room. An Aldermaston stood by the Leering, which had been carved with a bearded face and balding head.

"This is the girl, Captain Grimwell?" he asked. He had a sniveling expression, the kind you see in a man who was servile and proud of it. His accent sounded Dahomeyjan.

"Yes."

"Put her hand on the Leering," instructed the other.

Her heart shivered in anticipation as the captain undid the bindings behind her back and then the ropes at her wrists. Was this how it had been for Maderos, bound to stay in his room in Muirwood Castle? He was one of the Twelve, and he hadn't been strong enough to escape the binding. How could she?

Captain Grimwell took her aching wrist and brought her to the Leering. She could have resisted, but she knew he would force her to obey him. So she didn't struggle. She put her hand atop the Leering. Then the Aldermaston put his atop hers.

"Through the Medium, I bind you—the heretic Eilean—to this Leering and this room under the authority of the High Seer of Avinion. Make it thus so."

"Make it thus so," murmured Captain Grimwell.

He released his grip on her. Eilean felt the stirring of the Medium's power as the command was spoken. She sensed a connection binding her to the Leering.

A voice came from beyond the door. "Is it finished?" asked Lady Dagenais.

"Yes," said the Aldermaston. "It is done. She cannot leave."

"So be it. You may both go. Captain Grimwell, I want this corridor guarded at all times. Inspect the room. Make sure she stays here. I understand she can turn herself invisible, like the heretic Mordaunt. Do not fall for her deceptions."

"Yes, my lady," said Grimwell, bowing to her.

The Apocrisarius and the Aldermaston both departed, leaving Eilean alone with her enemy.

"Where is Captain Hoel?" Eilean asked after tugging the gag loose.

The High Seer smirked. "He crossed the Apse Veil at Dochte Abbey and beat you here, bringing me the tome. It was written in Glagolitic?" She tutted. "An ancient language for an ancient man."

Eilean felt her soul shrivel. Was there any conclusion other than that Hoel had deceived her? Or did she only *want* to believe that he cared for her, that he was loyal to her? She closed her eyes, her heart wrenching with pain. No, his feelings hadn't felt counterfeit. So why had he forsaken her?

"You must know, my dear, that the Apocrisarius are well trained. There was a time when the captain thought that *you* might have made a welcome addition to their order. I've been learning about your adventures in another world. How exciting for you."

Eilean closed her eyes. She didn't want to hear another word. *"Kennesayrim,"* she whispered, imagining herself back at Muirwood.

She felt a wrenching from the Medium, a collision of wills that made it feel as if she were being torn apart. The pain dropped her to her knees in agony. She was still in the chamber.

The High Seer clucked. "You cannot go, Eilean. Not unless I allow it. You cannot force the Medium to work against itself."

Still feeling the tingles of agony inside, Eilean looked up at the High Seer. "Can I see him? Captain Hoel, that is." She didn't trust the High Seer. She would only believe Hoel had betrayed her when she could discern it from his own thoughts.

"Of course," said the High Seer. "His father is dead, and he will be returning to Pry-Ree as its rightful king."

"What?" Eilean gasped.

The High Seer gave a sly smile. "Yes. The noble family was wiped out by the Naestors a fortnight ago. He only just learned about it. Aldermaston Kalbraeth and his son only survived because they were not there. Now that Kalbraeth is dead, Hoel Evnissyen is the only remaining heir to the throne. He's accepted his duty. With my blessing and promise to assist his people in this dark hour." The triumph inside the woman was beyond enduring.

"No," Eilean said, shaking her head in disbelief.

"Oh, it's true, Eilean. It's all true. His childhood friend was also murdered by the Naestors. The one who was married to a woman the young captain once rejected. Lady Rhiannon will make a suitable queen, I should think. One beloved by the people." Her eyes showed she enjoyed making Eilean suffer.

Eilean's heart was about to burst. If Hoel had remained a hunter, there was a possibility they could have been together. But there was no way a king would marry a wretched. Or a scullion. And Rhiannon . . . how would the High Seer have known any of that unless Hoel himself told her?

It hurt to breathe. It hurt to think.

"Shall I send him in now? Or do you need time to compose yourself first?"

Eilean massaged her swollen wrists. She glared at the High Seer.

"Now," she said flatly.

When I feel as though I would despair, I remember that all through history the way of truth and love prevails. There have been tyrants and murderers, there have been false kings and cruel priesthoods, and for a time, they can seem invincible. But in the end, they always fall. Think of it—always. Those who only destroy hope can never build it. We were born to build. To create.

—Maderos

Muirwood Abbey

CHAPTER TWENTY-SEVEN

Folly of the Wise

Waiting was its own form of anguish. Eilean paced within the small room, her nerves raw, her stomach twisted and bent until it ached. What would she say when she saw Hoel again? Part of her was simply relieved he was alive. But if he had deceived her, betrayed her, she worried that she might never trust another person ever again.

Not that it mattered. Her life would last as long as it took to translate the tome. Or refuse the task given her.

The Leering seemed to be staring at her mockingly each time she glanced at it. She'd never thought of Maderos suffering under the gaze of the one in his tower. A man who had been free to wander between worlds, participating in the follies and wisdom of the greatest men and women, suddenly deprived of his right to leave a simple castle by a block of sculpted stone. She used her thoughts to try to annul the Leering, to banish its control on her. But it was fixed and resolute, unyielding to her mental pressure.

The torture grew worse, so she went to the window and stared from the heights of her new prison.

The small window overlooked a cobbled street leading to the steps of the domed abbey. Although it was night, the street was well illuminated, with puddles reflecting the glow of the Leerings. Stone pillars topped with light Leerings were evenly spaced along the promenade. Looking down, she saw it was a long way to the ground. Next to each pillar was a huge terra-cotta pot with a stunted tree growing inside, each tree perfectly pruned. She could hear the low rush of the waterfall to her right, but it was not visible from her vantage point.

She thought about trying to summon the púca with her thoughts, but that would likely fail. First, she knew that the creatures detested towns and cities built by men. They were woodland creatures. Second, even if it did come, the Leering bound her to the room. It was unlikely that its flying magic would work with her. But then, spirit creatures had powerful magic in their own right. Perhaps she should try . . .

The door opened, and Eilean turned to face Hoel. Only it wasn't him.

It was Celyn. She had a bruise on her cheek, her dress was torn and dirty, and there were sores around her wrists and ankles. The guard who had brought her, Captain Grimwell, shut her inside.

The shock of seeing her friend in such a state drove words from Eilean's mind.

Celyn stood still at first, watching Eilean warily as she cradled her forearm. A cut in the sleeve showed a red gash beneath it.

Eilean rushed to her friend. "What have they done to you?"

Celyn trembled, still looking distrustful. "How do I know who you are?"

Eilean could sense her friend's thoughts. She was worried her eyes were deceiving her. That someone was trying to trick her. Probably because it had been done before.

Eilean felt like sobbing, unable to endure the sight of her friend in pain. She'd been imprisoned and almost certainly beaten. Anger flashed hotly inside her.

"You are Celyn, my companion and friend," Eilean said with a choking voice.

Celyn sniffled. "I can't trust myself right now. Say something only Eilean would know."

Eilean thought for a moment before the memory came to her. "When we were children at Tintern, on Whitsunday, I climbed a barrel in the kitchen. A barrel of treacle, I think. I thought . . . I fancied I could fly. I jumped from the barrel and cracked my head on the stone floor. And spent the rest of Whitsunday in bed with the healer who was upset at me for ruining the holiday for her."

Celyn stifled a laugh. "I remember that day."

Eilean took Celyn's hands. "*You* stayed with me the whole time and missed Whitsunday too."

Celyn's face crumpled with tears, and the two embraced as sisters, all doubt gone. They clutched each other, grieving and loving and relishing that they had been reunited, even under such dire circumstances.

When Celyn pulled away, she brushed the tear streaks from her face. "You were caught?" she said disappointedly. "What about the tome?"

"Lost again," Eilean admitted, feeling like an utter failure. The High Seer had it. "How long have you been here?"

"A week maybe? We made it to Prince Derik's castle in Isen. But the emperor's soldiers overwhelmed it after abducting the prince. Then some Apocrisarius slipped into the castle and opened the gate. Utheros barely escaped. I was captured before I could flee, and they brought me here."

Eilean hadn't thought she could feel worse, but this news made her spirit plunge. "Was he captured?"

"I don't know. They knew we were close—someone had told them. So they brought me to the High Seer." She looked distraught. "To use against you."

"Stright is here too, I've heard," Eilean said.

Celyn blanched. "No . . . no, don't tell me that!"

"Hoel said he was captured in the woods outside the castle."

Celyn squeezed Eilean's arms. "They'll kill him!"

If they hadn't already.

"So you didn't know?"

"No! They asked me where you were, and when I wouldn't speak, they . . . they made me touch a Leering that compelled me to speak the truth. I . . . I told them you were at Cruix Abbey but that you were going to Dochte Abbey next. Is that where they caught you? Did I . . . did I betray you?" She began to cry again.

Eilean rubbed her back. "No, you didn't," she said, because it was true. "The Apocrisarius followed us. They knew where we had gone."

"It . . . it doesn't matter. I feel so awful."

"Shhh. We're together now." She kissed Celyn's hair.

The door opened again, and this time Hoel opened it. The relief she felt was quickly quelled by fear when she saw that the High Seer was with him, smiling in satisfaction at seeing the two young women in custody. The High Seer was convinced that Hoel was obedient to her. She relished the idea of him speaking out against Eilean and revealing his duplicity.

Hoel's eyes met hers. They were impassive, almost a stranger's. Her fear increased as she stared into his eyes and saw nothing.

Hoel, what have you done? she thought to him.

He didn't answer her thought. She could sense that his mind was locked and barred from hers—a fortress of determination. Could he have been masking his true thoughts from her all along, giving her only what he wanted her to know and think?

She didn't believe so, but she'd been wrong before. Maderos, an Unwearying One, had been wrong before.

"I shall leave you to talk privately," the High Seer said. "I don't want you to be under the illusion that I control him or speak for him. But hopefully you will become convinced that rebellion has its consequences. Know also that I reward *loyalty.*"

The High Seer flashed another smile before leaving the room and shutting the door behind her. Eilean knew that some Leerings could be used to watch others without their knowledge. She suspected that the High Seer, while absent physically, was very much present in the room.

"Hello, Eilean," Hoel said.

"You gave her the tome?" she asked, the words nearly choking her.

"I did. My mission was always to bring you and the tome back to Avinion."

"I thought you were loyal to the Medium," she said, her voice throbbing with anger.

"I am and always have been. You let yourself believe what you wanted to believe, Eilean." As he said it, she felt a strain in his thoughts. Something fighting within him.

She looked to his hands but saw no ring. Still, some rings made themselves invisible. She'd seen Owain's ring only after it was removed.

Was a kishion ring on his hand again? Was he being compelled to say these words?

Eilean needed to find out. Striding up to him, she tried to smack him across the face.

He deftly caught her wrist. Gripped it and gave her a warning look.

"So you lied to me?" she panted. She reached up with her other hand to pry his fingers from her wrist. In doing so, she felt his fingers, trying to determine if there was a ring on his finger. She felt nothing but skin. The last time he wore one, she could still hear his thoughts, feel him pleading. Had that been a ruse?

No, it couldn't have been!

He let her go. "You let yourself believe I was on your side," he answered. "You needed help to get the tome back. You needed *my* help."

She wanted to pound her fists against his chest. To hurt him. The pain in her chest was almost unbearable.

He stepped toward her, his breath dusting her cheek. "You cannot escape Avinion. The High Seer knows what you can do. I've told her. Do you want your friends to endure an ordeal of fire for heresy? The druid magic will not save either of them from the Leerings."

He opened his mind to her, and she saw the billowing flames of an ordeal that he had witnessed before. He shut his mind again.

Eilean's heart cringed at the thought of her friends meeting such a fate.

"What does she want from me?" she asked, her voice dull to her own ears.

"Admit that you were deceived into believing Mordaunt was one of the Twelve. That you acted as his pawn. For that, you deserve to die. But the High Seer may be merciful if you help her translate the tome. Reveal the secrets of the Sefer Yetzirah, Eilean. They belong to the maston order. To *us*."

"What would your father tell me to do?" Eilean challenged.

He winced, but his strength didn't falter. "My father is dead."

"And you are to be the new king of Pry-Ree? How convenient for you."

He didn't reveal pain or hurt. She wished he had. In that moment, that's what she wanted from him.

"The Naestors have murdered our people, Eilean," he said. "We were hit harder than any other kingdom so far. They need me. It's a desperate situation."

Indeed. And one that would allow him to fulfill the pride and ambition she'd sensed within him every time he lifted Firebos. He would gain a crown and the woman he'd loved. What a hardship for him.

She did not say it with her lips. She said it with her thoughts, hoping he could hear them.

His eyes narrowed. "If you want to save yourself and your friends, you'd better make a deal now. Help us."

"I won't," Eilean said in a strangled voice.

His eyes were fierce. "By Cheshu, don't make her destroy you."

Eilean stared at him, disappointed, hurt, and betrayed.

"I will do the Medium's will," she proclaimed, her voice trembling.

"Good," said Hoel in a clipped tone. "You will see that this is part of the Medium's plan for you. I've asked that Celyn be with you to help. You will start translating the tome in the morning. Do it, Eilean. For their sakes. For everyone."

Again she had the urge to smack him. She wanted to make his face sting as much as her heart. But she knew he was faster than her, stronger than her. And he had no heart.

He turned toward the door again and paused, his hand on the handle. "I'm sorry it had to be this way, Eilean. But I did warn you."

He turned his neck to look at her, implacably stern, and then he opened his thoughts as if taking the lid off a barrel.

The Naestors are coming to Avinion soon. I saw a vision of all this before we returned. I'll get you out of here. I love you.

A little smile quirked on his mouth.

Relief gushed inside her heart, so strong she nearly fell to her knees.

Careful. You'll ruin the ruse if you don't pretend to hate me.

I love you, Hoel. I'm sorry for what I said.

He twisted the handle and left the room. *I know.*

Eilean started to weep, burying her face in her hands. She was relieved beyond words that she hadn't been wrong about him. She realized now that he'd been playing his part, making the High Seer believe exactly what she wanted to believe.

Celyn comforted her, tears coming to her eyes as well. "I'm so sorry, Eilean. I'm so sorry."

But Eilean wasn't sorry anymore.

The High Seer would be.

The Naestors have attacked Pry-Ree, Moros, Hautland, and Mon. They have claimed slaves, stolen treasures, and plundered tomes that they will undoubtedly melt down to form torcs to boast of their success. Greed is an insatiable appetite. They will fix their eyes on Avinion next. Only the new harbinger can save the maston order.

The conclave held at Muirwood has come to an end. There will be a schism in the order, for not all who were invited chose to come. Dahomey, Paeiz, Mon, and Avinion will stand against the verdict condemning the High Seer and revoking her position. Pry-Ree, Hautland, and Moros will stand in favor of it. While we are attacked on all sides, the maston order divides itself in half from within.

Elle came to Muirwood today. And she told me everything that has happened. The reunion was made more fraught by the fact that Ereshkigal was shackled inside her body. It took three Aldermastons and myself to contend with her. She railed and screeched threats to destroy the maston order and decimate every living thing. I rendered her mute for a time while Gilifil fashioned a Leering to contain her. She nearly burst free from our commands in her desperation to escape, but we sealed her inside the stone through use of the proper glyphs. If someone touches it, they will be able to commune with her. It is crucially important that no one does.

When Elle recovered from the trauma, she and I spoke at length. She confessed all that she'd done. There is something powerful about the act of confession that releases the chains of guilt forged in our own hearts. We spoke. We wept. And she is determined to make amends. She brought with her Andrew's

corpse and begged me to revive him. I told her that if I did,
he would be bound to Muirwood Abbey, unable to return to
the other world. She remained adamant that we restore him
to life, and so I taught her the word of power that would do so.

It is my last lesson to the prodigal student. My newer
student has formed a deeper understanding of the Knowing,
it appears.

—Maderos

Muirwood Abbey

CHAPTER TWENTY-EIGHT

The Siege of Avinion

A bove the pillars to the entrance of Avinion Abbey, carved into the stone facade beneath a triangular roofline, was a saying written in ancient Calvrian in large, sculpted letters:

HUMILITAS EST FUNDAMENTUM OMNIUM ALIARUM VIRTUTUM.

While Eilean did not know Calvrian, the Morosian alphabet was the same, and when she read it aloud, with the power of xenoglossia, she learned the meaning.

Humility is the foundation of all other virtues.

The hypocrisy of seeing that saying out her window every day was not lost on her. Day after day, she translated Maderos's tome into the language of Moros, which she was the most comfortable doing. While she could use the words of power once her strength returned, she could not use them to leave the room without the High Seer's permission. So she poured herself into the translation. She learned new words of power as she went, words that she kept to herself and pondered. Day after day, she wondered when Hoel would return. She trusted he would. Knowing he was out there, helping her, she was patient in her confinement. And she was submissive to the High Seer during her infrequent visits to monitor the progress of translation.

For her cooperation, she had been promised Stright would not be put to death. Still, the High Seer had refused to release him from the dungeon cell beneath the palace. He would spend the rest of his life confined there. At least Celyn had been allowed to visit him, to prove that he was still alive. The two had touched hands and spoken briefly to one another. It was all they were permitted. An Apocrisarius had overseen the interaction, so Celyn hadn't dared reveal that help might be coming.

The other druids who had been captured and brought to Avinion had been put to death unless they immediately denounced their order.

Eilean shared her adventures with Celyn, telling her about the high king, Andrew, Queen Essylt, and how the two had risen from Farfog Castle to become monarchs who were both respected and feared. And how, in the end, Leoneyis's pride had led to its undoing and destruction, while Brythonica had been protected by a shield of Leerings.

From the window she could see green leaves of differing shades, the potted trees along the promenade a bright olive. Their upper room, which had been almost unbearably hot, began to cool down at night. They were adequately fed and treated with civil disdain by their keepers,

JEFF WHEELER

led by the new leader of the Apocrisarius, a native of Avinion named Stilicho. Hoel had given up the post.

It was perhaps a fortnight after arriving in Avinion, while Eilean and Celyn were eating a breakfast of eggs and sausages, that they heard shouts coming from the street below. The friends exchanged a look, and both experienced an immediate jolt of awareness from the Medium. Eilean knew, for she heard the thought echo in Celyn's mind *and* hers.

It is time.

They stood up from the table and hurried to different windows, looking down at the street. Cries of terror rose, and people were rushing to the steps of the abbey—men, women, and children. Eilean looked at her friend, her heart throbbing with concern.

So many innocents were about to suffer for the decisions of their rulers.

Just like what had happened in Leoneyis.

"The time has come," Celyn whispered fearfully. The mob in the street was growing larger by the moment as the abbey doors had not opened. From the window, they could hear fists beating on the door and people screaming to be let in.

Their door was unlocked, and Captain Stilicho entered. He was bald but had a thick beard along his jaw and scars across the dome of his head. There was fear in his mind.

"What's happening? There's a panic in the streets." Eilean already knew, though.

"The Naestors have come," he said gruffly. "They attacked the ships guarding the river's entrance. Only a few have escaped."

"How many are there?"

He shook his head. "Hundreds of boats. We received no warning."

She read in his mind an awful truth. The Apse Veils were no longer working, and no one knew why. But she did. The Medium had ceased to work for them. That meant there was no way to escape the coming danger.

288

"Pack a change of clothes. We're leaving," he ordered. He threw a rucksack on the bed and then pulled another from his own back and opened it wide, tucking Maderos's tome inside along with the sheaf of papers she had been translating. She could feel the urgency of his thoughts. The pressure in his mind to escape.

Celyn sprang into action and began gathering their clothes. Screams sounded from the window.

"Where are you taking us?" Eilean asked worriedly. She thought about Stright trapped in the dungeon. Would the Naestors hurt him?

"The High Seer has a villa in the mountains south of here. We're taking refuge there for now."

"I can't leave," Eilean said, gesturing to the Leering.

"The High Seer herself has given me permission to release you. But I have orders to gag you first lest you try and escape." He finished stuffing in the papers and then cinched the pack closed and slung it around his shoulder. From his pocket, he produced a strip of cloth.

"Come here," he said, holding up the strip. She let him tie it firmly around her mouth. Then he took her to the Leering and put her hand atop it, placing his palm over hers.

"By authority of the High Seer of Avinion, I revoke the binding."

Eilean felt the connection sever, and relief flooded her heart as it snapped. Shouts from the street below intensified. She heard bows twang. An awful fear gripped her heart.

Death was coming. It would be a slaughter.

The door butted open, and two greyfriars entered the room.

Captain Stilicho lifted his eyes and frowned. "What are you doing here?" he barked.

One of the greyfriars lifted his hands, which were suddenly wreathed in dancing blue flames that illuminated his face.

Stright.

She yanked her hand away from the Leering and backed away, tugging the gag down.

The captain drew a gladius, his eyes frantic. The other greyfriar had entered as well, holding a gladius himself.

"Kozkah gheb-ool!" Eilean said as soon as she could speak. Captain Stilicho was violently tossed into the stone wall separating the rooms and then collapsed in a heap on the floor. The flames in the druid's hands extinguished, and Stright and Hoel both lowered their cowls.

There was a look of anguish on Hoel's face. He had trained in Avinion. Like her, he knew what was coming, and he grieved it. He knew that not all the people in Avinion were devious or dishonorable. They did not deserve what was coming to them.

Celyn rushed to Stright and hugged him. "I couldn't tell you," she sobbed. "I couldn't tell you!"

"It's all right," Stright answered, hugging her back. Then they started kissing with so much desperation it made Eilean's cheeks burn.

Hoel approached her, reaching for her hand, and then surprised her by tugging her to him for a kiss. "Thank Idumea, you're all right," he said in an undertone as he pulled away. "I arrived yesterday through the Apse Veil but disguised myself as a greyfriar to avoid notice."

"The Apse Veils aren't working now. Did you disable them?"

He frowned and then nodded firmly. "The Medium commanded me to. I warned the High Seer before I left to be on her guard against the Naestors coming. I knew she wouldn't heed me. She was warned and did nothing to prevent this, believing they'd strike another kingdom."

She squeezed his hand. "This isn't your fault, Hoel. The Blight has come. You didn't bring it."

She could tell his heart was aching. But he looked somber and gentle as he brushed his thumb across her cheek. "We need to go."

"Where?"

"The faithful Aldermastons are gathered at Muirwood. They finished the conclave yesterday by choosing a new High Seer. Utheros. That should please you. When he was chosen, there was a burst of light—a literal manifestation of the Medium. I know how much you respect him. I feel the same way now that I've gotten to know him. I do not doubt it's the Medium's will. Maderos is there with them."

She gaped at him. "You said his name!"

He gave her a wry smile and then patted the pouch belted to his waist. "The Cruciger orb led me to the tome with the binding sigil. It was being kept here at the palace. I removed it." He paused, gazing into her eyes, then said, "I've seen part of what will happen, Eilean. There will be two High Seers now. Two branches of authority that will be disputed between the kingdoms. It will not end soon, but it will eventually."

"How did you get the orb?"

"I never gave it back."

"How are we going to leave Avinion?" Celyn asked worriedly. She was still embracing Stright, but her alarm was evident.

Hoel gave her a reassuring smile. "Eilean will bring us to Muirwood. She's the only one who has that power."

"We're not leaving without the tome," she said.

Hoel went over and crouched by Stilicho's unconscious body. He stripped the pack from him and then handed it to Eilean. "The tome is your responsibility."

She took the strap and slid her arm through it. The sound of fighting and shrieking rose from below, sickening her. She wished the High Seer had not succumbed to her own selfish pride.

The image of the inscription in front of the abbey came to her mind.

Humility is the foundation of all other virtues.

Once the foundation of a building was impaired, the rest of the structure would come down. It grieved her. But she had done all she could.

She extended her palms to her friends.

"Join hands. It will feel like we are falling."

Celyn and Hoel took her hands, and Stright completed the circle. Stilicho began to moan.

In Eilean's mind, she pictured Muirwood Abbey. It was almost a year since she and Celyn had left it. Her heart ached to see Ardys and Loren again. And what of Aldermaston Gilifil? She'd heard that he had changed too, that he'd defied Lady Tatyana.

She squeezed their hands and bowed her head. *"Kennesayrim."*

And they were gone as the slaughter of Avinion began in earnest.

***

When they arrived at Muirwood, dawn hadn't come yet, although the brightening sky revealed it was soon to happen. Eilean had summoned them outside the boundaries of the abbey, in the wild marshland of the Bearden Muir. The starlings were already in flight, a swarm of birds that came and went in a mass.

Muirwood Abbey glowed in the distance, the Leerings lighting up its walls. She wanted to see it from afar, to give her emotions time to settle before they reached it. But seeing the abbey made her start crying as the memories dug into her.

The two couples held hands as they approached the abbey. Eilean tried to master her tears, but they wouldn't stop flowing. Hoel put a comforting hand on her shoulder. Being with him, back at the place where they'd first gotten to know each other, startled her. It moved her more than she would have thought. She held him in her arms, squeezing him. The feelings inside of her were almost too strong for her to contain. Too strong for her to bear.

The susurration of the birds was a calming sound, and soon she felt her heart beating more slowly. She released Hoel and dried her eyes. She had been imprisoned only a couple of weeks. Not nearly as long as

Maderos had been. She wanted to see him . . . and yet she was nervous about their reunion. The feelings in her heart swirled one way and then another, just like the starlings.

It was bright enough to see their surroundings now, and she and Hoel noticed it at the same time—a new hill existed before them. It had not been there before.

The two exchanged a look of astonishment.

"There must be a story behind it," Hoel said wonderingly.

They crossed the waymarker Leering, and once inside the boundary, Eilean felt . . . safe. The grass softened each step. There were other buildings now, and the wall separating the abbey grounds from the village was complete.

The inner grounds were sculpted, and she could see the abbey reflected in the waters of the fishpond. The small grove of apple trees had grown markedly since she'd been gone. And the kitchen—her heart ached to go to the kitchen. But they continued toward the castle. Light glowed from an upper window—*the* upper window—and she bit her lip, her emotions throbbing again.

Standing at the window was her mentor. He was watching for her.

The rear door of the castle opened, and Aldermaston Gilifil came down the steps. He looked just as she remembered, but this time she could feel the power of the Medium vibrating within him. His eyes were full of compassion and tenderness as he approached.

"Aldermaston," she whispered thickly.

He dropped to his knee before her, looking up at her with respect and admiration. "I thought I had something of value to teach you, Eilean, but I should have been learning from *you*. I wronged you, and I am very, very sorry."

She wiped away fresh tears and then knelt in front of him. "There is nothing to forgive, Aldermaston. It is so good to see you again. To be back home."

She could hear Celyn snuffling behind her, and then the two friends hugged the Aldermaston. The feeling in Eilean's heart was powerful. There was magic in forgiveness. Perhaps the strongest magic of all.

After the tender moment passed, the three of them rose. The Aldermaston sighed, then brushed tears from his eyes. He looked at Hoel with respect and nodded. "Welcome back, Your Majesty."

Hoel made a subtle gesture with his hand, indicating that such acknowledgments of rank were unnecessary.

"You are my king nonetheless," the Aldermaston said. "I respected your father a great deal. Pry-Ree needs you."

Eilean felt Hoel's conflicted thoughts. He *wanted* to be king, and that very compulsion concerned him. Like her, he'd seen firsthand what ambition had done to Andrew and Elle. And yet, surely that very hesitation was what would make him a fine king. She wanted that for him. She wanted it for their people. Still, she couldn't help but twinge at the thought of her own station. Surely a wretched, even one so empowered by the Medium, would not be seen as a suitable wife for the King of Pry-Ree. "We have other pressing matters at hand. Are the other Aldermastons still here? The attack on Avinion has started."

The Aldermaston looked crestfallen. At one time *he* had coveted the role of High Seer. No longer. Eilean could sense that he was more than content to remain where he was.

"They are. An unexpected visitor arrived recently." The Aldermaston looked from Hoel to Eilean. "Another seeking forgiveness. The one you sent from the other world. A queen unlike any other. Within her was trapped the Queen of the Unborn, as you already know. She brought a dead man."

Eilean nodded. "Where is she now?"

"Back within the protection of the abbey. She's been with us for a while but needs to return to her people soon. She was hoping to see you before she did. It took our united strength to subdue Ereshkigal. Maderos"—he paused as if savoring the name—"has fashioned a

Leering to bind her. Now we will need to determine which abbey should guard it."

A snickering sound could be heard. The púca flew down from the castle and landed on Maderos's shoulder as he emerged, leaning on a crooked staff. So it *had* returned.

Celyn beamed at him. Stright bowed reverently.

Hoel's look was more abashed. When he started to take a knee, the old Wizr shook his head.

"We're fellow servants, lad. If anyone should be kneeling, it is I. Kneeling before the new harbinger."

Aldermaston Gilifil's eyes widened with shock. "Eilean?" he asked in confusion.

"No. It was never meant to be her. It's him. The new king of Pry-Ree. I never liked that language. Never cared to learn it. Maybe I never will." He turned to her with a welcoming smile. "Welcome back, little sister."

She felt like she'd choke on her joy. She rushed and hugged him, grateful for all he'd taught her. The púca crept around the other side, offering his head and long ears for her to scratch, which she did. It snickered again.

"You are the most amazing creature," she crooned. It purred and snickered in pleasure.

Maderos laughed. "Oh, you've learned to flatter it, have you? Was it helpful or simply a nuisance?"

The púca lifted its head and gave a little hiss.

"It saved us more than once," Eilean said sincerely. She hugged Maderos again. "As have you. More than once. Thank you. Thank you for everything."

He tousled her hair. "No, lass. Thank *you*. Thank you for saving them for me."

She noticed that there were two more standing at the castle door. Andrew, wearing a simple tunic and hunter leathers. And Elle, dressed in a simple kirtle made of flax.

The chains of habit are too weak to be felt until they are too strong to be broken without help. That was a precept often taught by the Harbinger in the early days of the Twelve. As I spoke to Andrew and Elle here at Muirwood, I felt, once again, the truth of that notion. The habit of pride forged a chain, link by link, that eventually bound them both and turned them from each other and from their feelings of duty.

Because Andrew was dead when he came to Muirwood, he cannot return to his world. The mirror gate would repulse him or be destroyed. Elle cannot stay any longer, for she is bound by its covenant too. He is alive, though. And he knows about their son now. There is much grief and pain they share and which they caused each other and many, many others. If Andrew had only hearkened to Eilean's warning, the son might have been revealed in time for the disaster at Leoneyis to be averted. A way had been prepared. The Medium is merciful.

Because of Eilean's example and diligence, they have both turned back to the light. They will endeavor to do the will of the Knowing from now on. It will not be easy. There will be much restitution before they can find peace. They will try to forgive each other and make amends to those they wronged. Queen Genevieve believes her husband is truly dead. I fear history will blame her for wrongs not her own. In life, there is injustice. But those who know the truth will remember her and Sir Peredur with honor.

Gwragith Annon told me, ere the wretched came to Muirwood, that Eilean's future would be known for genera-tions. But no one would remember her name. They would only remember her as the Lady of the Fountain who saved part of their world from being drowned by the Deep Fathoms. And that one of her posterity would bind Ereshkigal forevermore.

I was charged by the Dryad to write Eilean's story and the story of her family in the rest of the tome that Ilyas gave me. But I cannot tell her of her future or the futures of her coming daughters. It would be too much burden for one mortal to know. My work will not be finished, for I will remain to tell the tale.

—Maderos, Wayfarer of Muirwood Abbey

CHAPTER
TWENTY-NINE

A True King

The púca swiped the bit of cheese from Utheros's hand and began to nibble on it greedily. The wizened Aldermaston, now the High Seer, smiled and gave the spirit creature a doting look.

"He's always hungry," Utheros said, catching Eilean's eye. "A bit of a scamp, though."

The púca let out a small hiss.

"But a scamp with such a luscious pelt. Not even the finest beavers or foxes have a pelt so soft and well groomed. Don't you think so, Eilean? A magnificent creature."

The púca snuggled up to Utheros and let out a snickering sound of contentment. They were sitting together in the Aldermaston's study at the castle at Muirwood. Aldermaston Gilifil smiled in acknowledgment and pushed aside a tome that sat in the middle of his desk.

"You return to Hautland today, my friend?" Gilifil asked Utheros.

"Yes, there is much to be done to defend against the Naestor attacks. King Hoel has foreseen that they intend to strike the town of Fenton on the way back from sacking Avinion. I will stop at the abbey to warn them."

All of the Aldermastons had asked Hoel for help in identifying the forthcoming danger. Those who heeded the warnings to flee would be spared. Other kingdoms, like Dahomey and Mon, would continue to face the Naestors blindly. It saddened Eilean. But there was no avoiding it. The maston order was now in a state of schism. Their abbeys were separated, passable only by those who had the proper passwords to bypass the interdicts the new High Seer had laid on the Apse Veils.

The púca hopped down on Utheros's lap and then crossed over and jumped up on Eilean's. She stroked its ears and was careful not to stroke its back. The window was open after all.

"Give my best to Prince Derik," she said to Utheros. "And to Ruhe and Johanns and Tombert and . . . anyone else I missed."

Utheros looked at her and gave her a sidelong look. "I think he was hoping I could persuade you to return with me." His thoughts were evident to her. Prince Derik was in charge of defending Hautland after the Holy Emperor's armies had left. He still wished for her guidance.

Aldermaston Gilifil said nothing, but she could see in his eyes and his heart that he hoped she would stay at Muirwood. He hadn't asked her to. She doubted he would.

A soft rap sounded on the door, and Maderos opened it. She smiled at the sight of him. They'd had many chances to talk since her return to the abbey, and she'd told him everything that had happened to her after leaving Muirwood. He'd listened raptly, but he hadn't seemed that surprised by her revelations.

He looked at her and said softly, "Elle is returning to her kingdom. She wanted to say good-bye to you."

"Will she return to this world?" Aldermaston Gilifil asked.

Maderos pursed his lips. "I don't know. We shall see." He nodded to Eilean to come with him, and she rose from the couch, patted the púca once more on its head, and then bid farewell to the other two men.

She'd lost track of Hoel over the last few hours but knew he was somewhere on the grounds. *He* hadn't asked her to come with him either.

Maybe they were all letting her make the decision herself. Truthfully, her heart was torn. She was from Pry-Ree, but Muirwood had become a home to her. So had Hautland. She felt anxious about the fates of all three realms.

As she and Maderos walked down the corridor together, she asked, "Are you still leaving for Naess?"

His eyebrows quirked. His staff thumped on the floor as he walked. "It might be for the best."

"Are they as depraved as Hyksos was?" she asked.

"We'll see."

"Do you know about my father? Do you know who he was?"

His eyes crinkled with understanding. The knowledge had come from the Cruciger orb to Hoel. Was there a chance Maderos knew it too?

"You had a look about you when we met," he said. "The Medium whispers to those who will listen. And I listen, little sister. I listen."

They reached the door and she stopped. "Are you lonely, Maderos? You're the last of the original Twelve."

He tilted his head and gazed at her. "How can I be lonely, when I have so many friends?" She felt the warmth in his heart. His gratitude toward her for what she'd done to save Andrew and Elle. He considered her a friend as well.

He pulled the handle, and they left the rear of the castle together and started toward the Aldermaston's kitchen. Inside, the smell of pumpkin bread was evident, a delicious smell that she'd forgotten. A few fat pumpkins were stacked by some barrels of flour. It warmed her heart to see Ardys and Loren again, having been reunited with them earlier, and she cushed them both in greeting. Celyn and Stright were also gathered in the kitchen, talking to Elle, who now wore a cloak. A knapsack of provisions sat near her on the cutting table. Andrew sat at a bench with a mug in front of him.

Elle turned, saw Eilean, and came and embraced her. Feelings of guilt still plagued her. But they had softened. She looked more peaceful than she had at the mirror gate.

"It's sunset again, and I still feel *free* of her," Elle said to Eilean, then looked at Maderos. "I used to dread sunset. Sometimes, she didn't even hide herself from me. I could feel her looking from my eyes, and it felt like part of me was being shoved aside. But I was too frightened to think much on it."

Eilean turned to Maderos. "Does she still have the brand on her shoulder?"

"Yes," he answered. He patted Elle's shoulder. "Other Myriad Ones will try and tempt you. Be wary. But they cannot force their way in if you wear the medallion I gave you."

"I like how it feels here at the abbey," Elle said. "We need spaces like this in my world. Sanctuaries to protect. Places to worship the Fountain. I will build them in Brythonica to set an example for the other kingdoms." She sighed. "Speaking of other kingdoms, the King of Occitania is refusing to leave my land. I must frighten him off. I feel stronger now. My magic is returning."

Eilean had previously asked about the Wizr board, the one that she'd learned about in the tome. Sir Queux had fled Brythonica by ship with a handful of knights who were more loyal to him than the king, taking advantage of the tumult on the docks. He'd taken the board with him.

Most of the ships that had been blockading Brythonica had been destroyed in the flood. The wreckage of the vessels was washing up on the shores on the coasts surrounding Ploemeur. There was detritus from Leoneyis as well. People combed the beaches each day for relics and pieces of treasure. They would be doing so for years, Eilean imagined, thinking of Penryn and his boat and the little water sprite who took care of him.

Elle hugged her again. "You saved my people, Eilean. I cannot repay you for it. The Leerings you fashioned will protect us in the future as well."

"So long as you activate them every season," Eilean reminded her. "That duty must be performed. If it is, however, Leerings will endure for centuries."

"I will keep them secret and be true to the charge," she said. Then Elle turned to Maderos. "I do not deserve your forgiveness, but I am grateful for it nonetheless."

Maderos smiled at her and cupped her chin, lifting her eyes to meet his. "It's freely given, lass. We'll find your son. He will need to return someday to claim his birthright."

Elle wiped tears from her eyes. "Tell him I'm sorry. I've thought of him every day."

"I will. Farewell."

Elle turned and started to approach the bench where Andrew sat. He had been silently listening to their conversation. As she approached, he rose and hugged her. Then their foreheads touched, and Eilean felt the bittersweet feelings pass between them. Regret still lingered in his heart because he hadn't chosen her to be his queen. It was a delicate moment. It panged Eilean's heart.

They clasped hands, both grieving for the pain they'd caused others, and each other. There was forgiveness there as well. But the memories—those could not be so easily forgotten. Then Elle turned and faced everyone. She bowed in farewell and uttered a word of power.

"Kennesayrim."

Then she was gone, the prickle of magic lingering in the air. It struck Eilean that Elle had done to Andrew exactly what his father had done to his mother. The cup of fate had bitter dregs.

Andrew turned back to the table and picked up his mug. "Can I have more cider, please?"

Ardys, who was happily bustling around, said she'd fetch more for him. Others began to talk as well, providing a low murmur of voices that encouraged some privacy.

"Where will Andrew go, since he cannot return to his world?" Eilean whispered to Maderos.

"He'll stay at Muirwood. And defend it. When he gets old, he will tend the apple orchard."

"Will he ever return to his world?"

Maderos's expression was vague. "No. He will find love again here."

"Was that in one of Hoel's visions?" she asked him.

"No," he shook his head. "Some Dryads also have the mantic gifts." A smile crossed his lips. "There will be another Dryad tree here in the Bearden Muir. Close to the abbey. The Aldermaston gave me a piece of land here. I'll build a garden there when I get back from Naess."

She looked into his eyes. "Do you want me to come with you, Maderos? To Naess?"

Why she said it, she wasn't totally sure. She felt sorry for him, always going from one hardship to another. Part of her was also eager to give back. She wanted to serve, to be useful. If stopping the Naestors would save lives, she was willing to do it, even if it meant leaving her people for a while.

Even if it meant leaving Hoel.

That thought caused a stab of pain in her heart, but she tried her best to conceal it, to open herself to doing whatever the Medium asked of her.

Maderos took her hand. His voice was husky with emotion. "That you asked means more than you can know. Naess is a dark land, where the sun sets early and rises late. It has harsh, frigid winters. They are survivors. Warriors. But there's use for you elsewhere, Eilean. Because you have the knowledge from Ilyas's tome, you can help here while I am away. *That* is your future. You must use your own wisdom to determine whom to help and when. You are a Wizr now." He beamed at her and then released her hand and winked at her.

"One of the advantages of being a Wizr, I suppose, is that I can travel to all the lands I want to. I can help Prince Derik. I can help Aldermaston Gilifil. I can help . . . Hoel."

"The two of you are stronger together than apart," he said. "Remember that. Remember what your experience has taught you. Your future is just starting."

"Are you leaving soon?" she asked, feeling he was giving her a farewell.

"I come and go as the Medium directs me, lass. I am a wayfarer. A wanderer. Maybe our paths will cross again. But before I go, I must bring a loaf of that pumpkin bread with me!" He winked at her again.

"Thank you for believing in me," she whispered thickly.

"There is one more word of power I must teach you. I think you will need it. I also taught it to Elle. It is a sacred word. And a secret one. With it, you can bring the dead back to life." He lifted his hand and made the null sigil. "*Nesh-ama*. It is the breath of life."

She was honored by his trust in her. "I will safeguard it."

"I know you will. Good-bye, Eilean. Until we meet again."

"Will we meet again?"

"I'm sure of it."

***

The sun was gone, but there were still a few fireflies left, and the abbey glowed with the Medium's power. Eilean walked the grounds, searching for Hoel. Her heart was heavy with so many partings. She felt a little melancholy but also strangely peaceful.

Where was he? Surely he wouldn't have left without seeing her. Only one functioning abbey remained in Pry-Ree—Tintern, carefully nestled near the mountains and away from the coast and the marauding boats of the Naestors.

After walking around the castle and the abbey, she checked the fishpond, the laundry, and then decided to head toward the growing cider orchard. As she approached the young trees, she sensed Hoel's thoughts. He could see her.

She found him seated in the grass, his back against one of the young tree trunks. The branches were thick with clusters of apples, and like the one she'd tasted earlier that day, they were the sweetest yet.

She settled down on the grass in front of him. "I was afraid you'd left without telling me," she said in an accusing tone.

"I do need to go," he answered softly, tugging at some grass. "After the Naestors attack Fenton, they'll go back to Naess. But another group will come to hit York, right on the border of Pry-Ree." He chuffed. "The visions won't stop, Eilean. By Cheshu, they get worse every day."

They were burdening him. She could tell. Reaching out, she laid her hand atop his. She felt conflict within him—one that went deeper than the schism in the maston order and the Naestors' onslaught.

And then Eilean saw an image flash into his mind—a lovely woman with braids in her hair.

Eilean felt her heart sink. He was thinking of Rhiannon, his first love. Sometimes she wished the Gift she had from the Medium would cease. Knowing people's thoughts could be a burden.

"I have to see her," Hoel said.

Pain bloomed in Eilean's heart. Hoel was the new king of Pry-Ree. He had duties and obligations to his people—and they, in turn, had expectations of him. Especially about whom he married. She withdrew her hand. After all they'd been through together, it hurt to think she might yet lose him.

"I imagine she's still grieving for her husband?" she asked, trying to think of something to say. Trying to overcome the burn in her heart.

"I'm grieving for him too. He was my closest friend." He sighed. "Until you."

His hand reached out and lowered on hers. His thumb caressed the skin between her thumb and forefinger.

"I have to see her, Eilean, and tell her that I love another. That my heart is bound with knots that won't yield. I wouldn't want them to, you see, so I tied them fast."

Her heartbeat began to quicken. She glanced at him, his eyes shining in the starlight, and hope fluttered in her breast. Along with a warmer feeling.

"I want you at my side, Eilean. As my queen. As my partner. As my lover. If the people won't have you, they can't have me. I trust you with everything I am. With all I have."

She swallowed, her throat tightening. "Are you asking me to marry you, Hoel Evnissyen?"

His fingers entwined with hers. "If you'll have me. Say you'll bind yourself to me by irrevocare sigil, and I'll beg Aldermaston Gilifil to perform it this very night. I can't live without you, Eilean. And I don't want to wait until morning."

The relief she felt was only outmatched by her love for him. The irrevocare sigil was part of the marriage rite in the maston order, where a husband and wife could be bound together beyond the limits of mortality. She leaned forward and kissed him, raking her fingers through his hair and kissing him again and again until her heart felt like it would burst through her chest.

"Yes, you clumsy fool," she teased, pulling back. She felt the moistness on her lips and savored it. "I'll have you. *Shaw*, it took you long enough to ask!"

He grinned at her. "I had a vision of this orchard. With flower petals falling in the spring. The trees were much larger. I feared I'd have to wait until then before you'd say yes." He tilted his head. "But I don't think that vision was of us. I think it was a daughter or a granddaughter or a great-granddaughter. I don't know. But our family is bound to this abbey somehow. I don't fully understand it."

"Someday we will, Hoel Evnissyen. Someday we will."

And she kissed him again.

Happy is the man who finds a true friend, and far happier is he who finds that true friend in his wife.

—Maderos, Wayfarer of Muirwood Abbey

EPILOGUE

Whispers from the Future

T intern Abbey had a beautiful view of the Myniths, a range of
mountains that formed a natural border between the kingdoms of Pry-Ree and Moros. And after the Naestors' destruction of the other two abbeys, which had still not been rebuilt, it was the
only one left in Pry-Ree.

Eilean and Hoel walked together, hand in hand, through an enormous pasture of flowering flax with a view of Tintern ahead of them
and the mountains behind it. She held out her other hand and grazed
the tips of the blue flowers adorning the thin green stalks. The smell of
the pasture brought back so many memories of her childhood. It was
early enough in the day that a few bees were their only companions and
a little morning mist blurred the southern border.

"Do you remember the fields ever being this blue, my love?" she
asked Hoel.

They paused in the middle of the field, waist-deep in young flax.
It was springtime, and the harvest seemed to be a promising one. A

needed one. The kingdom was in a precarious position. Soldiers had to patrol the different farms to protect them from the ravaging hosts of Naestors that were still a lurking threat. There had also been some conflict with the sheriff of Mendenhall's men near Bridgestow. Their lack of provisions had emboldened them to abduct and kill some sheep in the borderlands during the winter months to feed the starving and provide wool for blankets. Yet another problem the King and Queen of Pry-Ree had to overcome.

"I've never forgotten these fields," Hoel said, his gaze far off. He lifted her hand and kissed it. "When I was sent to help move people to Muirwood, it was after harvest. I wished to see the fields ripe again. I never tire of the beauty of this land." He smiled at her.

"I remember that day you came," she said. She sidled closer to him and put her hand on his chest. He wasn't wearing hunter leathers anymore, because in his new role he needed to look like a king as well as act like one. "You were in the shadows outside the Aldermaston's lodgings."

"I remember it well."

"You feared I'd come to poison the High Seer."

"By Cheshu, no. You were a pretty lass. I stopped you to get a better look at you."

"I was a wretched. You didn't look twice at me."

He stroked her nose with the knuckle of his forefinger. "I looked more than twice. Aren't you glad I did?"

She leaned her head against his neck, savoring the smell of the field, the beautiful view of the abbey. "I am glad. I never would have imagined, back then, what was going to happen to us."

"Or what *will* happen," he said with a sigh.

She pulled back and looked into his face with concern. "Another vision?"

He nodded, saying nothing.

"Will the Naestors attack again?"

He kissed her hand again. "They will, but that wasn't the vision."

She could sense his brooding thoughts. His discouragement. She reached up and stroked his face. "You don't have to carry it alone."

"My Gift can be more of a burden at times, Eilean. I've seen so much of the future. Not just yours and mine, but our children's, and our children's children's."

"You mentioned one with curly hair who becomes the hunter at Muirwood Abbey. Was your vision before then or after it?"

"Before her. Lia . . . that's what they'll call her. The vision I saw was of her father. Someone who won't be born for years to come."

"Does he have a name?"

"Alluwyn Lleu-Iselin. He will have the same Gift I do. It's like we saw each other, Eilean. We were standing in the dreamworld of our visions, talking as clearly as you and I are now. He told me what had happened to Pry-Ree in his day, and my heart hurts for what he'll face. For what our people will face."

Hoel's visions were a strange thing to her. With them, he had helped Hautland and Moros defend themselves from the Naestor attacks. She and Hoel had traveled from Isen to Moros and back again multiple times, and their warnings had saved lives. In that way, his knowledge of the future was a blessing. But sometimes it truly was a curse.

"What did he tell you?" she prodded, seeing him lost in thought again.

"Moros will become our rival someday. Then our enemy. One day, we'll be defeated by them, and our combined land will be called Comoros. Alluwyn will be slain, his daughter spirited away to Muirwood as a wretched. He saw and knew his own future death as surely as if it had already happened."

"Is there nothing to be done?" she asked, her own heart panging for something that would not happen for many, many years.

"No. He's accepted his fate. But my heart aches for him."

"If Pry-Ree falls, what about the hetaera Leering? Will it be safe?" Her heart surged with fear.

"No," Hoel sighed. "It will be stolen and brought to Dahomey."

That troubled Eilean even more. "The protections we've put in place won't keep it safe?"

They had told the other Aldermastons that the Leering entrapping Ereshkigal would be concealed at Tintern Abbey. Only the new Aldermaston, Rhys, knew the truth. It wasn't at the abbey at all but in a cave at the base of the Mynith Mountains. Waymarkers guarded it with powerful magic to keep out intruders. Those who sought to free Ereshkigal from her prison would be drawn to the abbey, but they would not find it there. Hoel and Eilean had reasoned that the fewer who knew the truth, the better.

"The problem is time, Eilean. Given enough time, memories fail. Precautions are neglected. Warnings are unheeded. There is nothing we can say or do now that will be of sufficient power to endure that many years."

She gripped his arm. "But what of Maderos? Cannot he help protect it?"

Hoel shook his head. "I've seen what will happen, Eilean. He will continue to watch over our family for generations, and he'll help Lia in her quest to fulfill the Medium's will. But he cannot prevent what is coming. Nor should he, for in Lia's day, the maston order will leave these shores and establish a new homeland across the sea." He sighed again. "The Naestors will take over these lands. When the mastons return, Tintern will become like Avinion. And so the cycle of pride will begin anew. I know the future. I saw one of our posterity unwittingly *become* a hetaera. A vision I'd glimpsed before and assumed was about you. I cannot stop these events from happening."

She took his hands in hers and then pulled him down into the meadow, crushing some of the stalks of flax. The wind blew in a cool breeze that made the blue flowers ripple across the pasture.

She held his hands, forcing him to look into her eyes. "You carry an unfair burden, Hoel Evnissyen. But you are the harbinger the Medium chose to carry it." She stroked his hands with her thumbs. "Whatever happens will be dealt with in their time. Others will be lifted up to carry the burden then. You must carry it now."

"I don't know how I could bear it, being the last king of Pry-Ree. The one who saw it all come tumbling down." He screwed up his face. "I'd fight to the end."

"You'd bear it as Andrew has born his defeat," she said. "He focuses on the moment. The work to be done for the day. Yes, he regrets what happened to Leoneyis. He's haunted by what he did to Genevieve and Peredur. But he cannot undo the past any more than you can prevent the future. There is a purpose to all this, to the warp and weft of the Medium. Trust in that, Hoel."

His eyes filled with love for her. He had a certain look about him, the one that meant she'd said exactly what he'd needed to hear.

"Kiss me, Hoel. I'm not a Dryad, but I think I can help you forget for a while."

His lips began to nuzzle her neck. She wrapped her arms around him and pulled him down on her, smashing more of the tender stalks of flax. He held himself up on his arms, a protective smile on his mouth.

"I chose you, Eilean. And I choose you every day."

She looked up at his face, feeling a rush of tenderness. The delight he gave her was worth more than the kingdom. "And I chose *you*, Hoel. When you were near death, I chose to save you. When you hunted me, I chose to forgive you. Even when I thought you betrayed me . . . *You* were the one I wanted to go through this life with. And the next one too when we reach Idumea."

"I apologized for that already," he reminded her with a wink, stroking her hair away from her throat.

"*Shaw*, Hoel. A man can never apologize too often."

"Then let me show you how sorry I am," he said with a grin, nuzzling her neck again.

Soon she forgot everything but the smell of the flax field and the contentment of knowing that he was truly hers in every way. And that they would spend every day of the rest of their lives building the future he had seen—the heartbreak and the laughter, the challenges and successes, the men and women who would be full of heart and perseverance. The men and women who would define Muirwood Abbey for centuries to come.

Hoel and Eilean had been there at the dawning, and their offspring would be there until the Medium's purposes for the abbey—and for them—were all fulfilled.

AUTHOR'S NOTE

I like to wait until the final book before revealing the rest of my secrets. Mwahaha! So obviously this series has been a love letter to Arthurian legends of old. I think my first memorable exposure was the Disney movie *The Sword in the Stone*, which tells the story of Wart and Merlin and introduced Sir Kay (who, by the way, has many derivatives throughout the different versions of the story, including Sir Queux—thanks Wikipedia!). Then I read *The Once and Future King*, learned about the Welsh versions, saw *Excalibur* in high school with my friend Jeremy, and even more recently, binged an entire college course on Arthurian myths narrated by Professor Dorsey Armstrong online.

Many readers have asked over the years if I was ever going to write about King Andrew. How to do it in an original way, though? How to weave together some of the different legends and tilt some of them on their head? That's when I got the idea of mashing up several different elements. Before I start writing a new series, I go through a process inspired by my career at Intel. It comes from a quote from Andy Grove, who was an earlier CEO of the company—let chaos reign, then rein in chaos.

Notice the subtle spelling differences? I let my imagination run rampant, go crazy. I binge movies, read a ton of books, go down rabbit holes. This process fertilizes my imagination. Then, after that creative period is done, I pull in on the reins, like a horse, and force myself to outline the series and settle on a story arc.

For this series, I did a mash-up of Shakespeare's *Othello* and the legend of Pygmalion. Shakespeare's play was inspired by an Italian short story, "Un Capitano Moro" by Cinthio, published almost forty years before the Bard wrote his play. And Pygmalion, the Greek myth, is about a proud sculptor who creates the perfect woman and the gods make her come to life. I was more inspired by the George Bernard Shaw play of the same title and then watched every movie I could find based on the theme . . . and there are lots, including *My Fair Lady*, *Educating Rita*, the MGM black-and-white version of *Pygmalion*, and another oldie, *Kitty*. You probably noticed the Pry-rian slang *"shaw"* that the wretcheds kept saying. A subtle nod to Mr. Shaw.

One of the tropes that all the Pygmalion stories have in common is the pauper-to-princess typically falls for her mentor. That was my intention at first, but the more I wrote Eilean's character, and Hoel's, the more I began to ship the two of *them*. And, with all the examples in the news of people in power taking advantage of the less fortunate, the worse it sounded. So even though in earlier Kingfountain books, I suggested that Myrddin had a relationship with someone he mentored (either Eilean or Essylt)—which is what happened in the Arthurian legends—I opted to change it and much prefer how it ended.

The *Othello* angle was super fun to write as well. My favorite version of the play ended up being an audio recording from a production in England with Chiwetel Ejiofor, Tom Hiddleston, Ewan McGregor, and Kelly Reilly—it's superb! In fact, it was because of this play that Kenneth Branagh chose Hiddleston to play Loki in the first Thor movie. Iago has always been a fascinating character to me, and Ewan McGregor does an amazing job performing him. I saw some similarities between Sir Kay/Queux and him. Everyone knows the legend of how Guinevere and Lancelot had an affair. What if it was just a false accusation, as Iago told of Othello?

It was while I was writing Ransom's story that the idea came to invent the origin of the Lady of the Fountain, who is another common character in the Arthurian myths. In previous books I'd hinted that there was a connection between Muirwood and Kingfountain. The Dawning of Muirwood gave me the perfect opportunity to do both. You see, while I was writing the original Legends of Muirwood, I learned that Glastonbury Abbey—which is what I based Muirwood Abbey on originally—is rumored to be the final resting place of King Arthur. It is Avalon, a land that floods and creates an island in a marsh. So the Arthurian tie-in has been there all along. Eilean's journey provided the birth of the legend of the sanctuaries of Our Lady. She wasn't in that world for very long, but she had a huge impact on its history and culture.

Thanks for tagging along on this journey. What I have in store for you next will be completely different. It will be a series of novels set in our world, based on real history and modern technology.

Stay tuned for *The Dresden Codex*.

ACKNOWLEDGMENTS

This series has been exceedingly complicated and fraught with possible and likely things that would naturally cause continuity problems with my other books. I admit I did not have all the events of this book figured out back when I wrote *The Wretched of Muirwood* over a decade ago. Thankfully, I have such an amazing team who assists me in ferreting out the problems and coming up with creative solutions. Props to Wanda, especially, who remembered a detail from *The King's Traitor* that she suggested could fit in this book, a detail I'd long forgotten. I don't know how she does it. Angela, of course, has been a pleasure to work with for years and helped me tone down some of the scenes when I wanted to go full Shakespeare on you all. Adrienne, of course, is a fantastic editor and has been a huge champion for me. My early readers, also, provide critique and compliment, which helps refine the story and make it better.

I'd also like to thank Kate Rudd, my amazing narrator, for her work bringing my stories to life. By the time I'm done writing and editing these books, I'm pretty sick of them and never want to see them up close again, but after several months, I like to queue up the audiobook version while I exercise or go for drives. And then I listen to Kate tell my stories and get lost in wonder all over again. She's amazing.

Last but not least, one more story to share. I used to be an assistant scoutmaster to a brilliant young man named Travis. A few years ago, he died in a tragic farming accident. He and my son were friends and born two days apart, so the news hit us hard. Travis was a huge fan of my books and for Christmas one year, spent his own money to purchase my entire collection in paperback so he could give copies to all his family. He was a neat kid. During one of our conversations, he told me that he hoped he'd make it into one of my books someday. But he wanted to be the villain. It was an interesting request. And I had an idea, but never shared it with him.

I based Aldermaston Sivart Gilifil on my friend Travis (you'll notice Sivart is his name in reverse). When Covid struck and school was canceled, I promised him that we'd play a game of chess for his birthday after it was safe. That summer, he came over and we had our match. Before Thanksgiving, he was gone. I'm proud to have featured him in this series and for the impact he had on me and my family.

You got your wish, Travis.

ABOUT THE AUTHOR

Photo © 2021 Kortnee Carlile

Jeff Wheeler is the *Wall Street Journal* bestselling author of the First Argentines series (*Knight's Ransom, Warrior's Ransom, Lady's Ransom,* and *Fate's Ransom*); the Grave Kingdom series; the Harbinger and Kingfountain series; the Legends and Covenant of Muirwood trilogies; the Whispers from Mirrowen trilogy; the Dawning of Muirwood trilogy; and the Landmoor novels. Jeff is a husband, father of five, and devout member of his church. He lives in the Rocky Mountains. Learn more about Jeff's publishing journey in *Your First Million Words*, and visit his many worlds at www.jeff-wheeler.com.